WRINKLES, WIT, & WISDOM

MYSTICAL MIDLIFE IN MAINE BOOK ~~IX~~ 15!

MIDLIFE MAGIC & MYSTERIES BOOK 47

BRENDA TRIM

Copyright © October 2024 by Brenda Trim
Editor: Chris Cain
Cover Art by Fiona Jayde

* * *

❀ Created with Vellum

"Aging is not 'lost youth' but a new stage of opportunity and strength." ~Betty Friedan

CHAPTER 1

*N*ana raised an eyebrow and looked over at us. "Decorating a nursery isn't rocket science, Phoebe. Keep it simple," she remarked as she reached for a plate of cookies with a mischievous glint in her eye.

The soft glow of late afternoon bathed the kitchen in a warm embrace, casting a golden hue on the island where we gathered. Nana was a force of nature with her no-nonsense attitude. And she was usually right. She'd been quiet until now as we excitedly discussed crib designs and nursery themes for the impending arrival of the triplets.

Stella and I chuckled, appreciating Nana's timeless wisdom. "The pressure to create the perfect room for the babies of a god is real, Nana. I just want it to be right. Otherwise, I'm sure Aidon's mom will try to redo it when she visits. What do you think, Mom?" Mom and Mythia turned away from the stove where they were baking me scones. I'd gone from craving the cookies Nana was eating to wanting some of Mom's cinnamon chip scones.

Leaning on the island, Mom looked over the catalog we'd been perusing on the tablet. "Nana is right. That's incredibly fussy for a baby. Is it really necessary for it to look like an actual carriage? That one reminds me of those round tufted settees with a crown on top. And I don't even understand that one. It's modern, I'll give you that, and it costs as much as a nice used car. And that pod? Just no. Whatever happened to the classic wood ones?"

I sighed as I clicked on the other page we had open. "I love simple and classic."

"What does Aidon think?" Mythia asked as she hovered over my shoulder.

I lifted a shoulder at the tiny pixie and was startled when Nana wagged a finger at me and said, "He said he was fine with whatever you wanted. Stop doubting yourself, Phoebe. You aren't with that jackass ex of yours anymore. You don't have to allow Persephone to do anything to your nursery. She's welcome to create whatever she'd like in her own home. This is yours. If you want that pod, get it. Even if I think it's ridiculous."

"I never imagined being a mom again in my mid-forties," I confessed. "Let alone to three."

Nana snorted and waved her hand vaguely in my direction. "But the god part was?"

We all started laughing at that. She was right. The god part would never have been on my radar before. And, I needed to stop trying to please other people. I needed to find what I liked and show Aidon. He didn't care about stuff like that. I clicked on the link to one of the major stores when Stella's phone buzzed, interrupting the joyful discussion. Her expression shifted from amusement to sudden concern as she answered the call. "This is Stella."

Stella's eyes widened as she listened, her fingers gripping the edge of the island. The news she received wasn't anything mundane like what was for dinner. It was something serious, something that turned the air chilly with worry.

Hanging up the phone, Stella took a deep breath, her eyes meeting mine with a gravity that sent a shiver down my spine. "Phoebe, it's my mom. She's disappeared from her apartment in the assisted living complex."

An uneasy hush settled over the kitchen, the mirth replaced by a palpable sense of urgency. The lively discussions about nursery decorations were eclipsed by Stella's mother, Rosemary's mysterious disappearance. My mind raced, trying to comprehend the sudden shift from joyful anticipation to the harsh reality of a loved one gone missing.

"Disappeared?" I echoed, the word hanging in the air like an ominous cloud. "Did she wander off? Is she starting to forget things? Maybe she's confused and headed to her old house." She was still relatively young, but it was early onset Alzheimer's.

Nana's snarky demeanor faded into a concerned frown. Mom exchanged a worried glance with me. Mythia had no idea what we were talking about but could read the mood and had settled her tiny pixie body on Stella's shoulder to offer her support.

Stella clasped her hands together, likely to hide the tremor. She was always bubbly and cheerful, so seeing her so worried made my stomach knot. "That was the head nurse. They can't find her anywhere. I'm going to call her." Stella put her phone on speaker, and it rang and rang.

I didn't have the heart to say the nurse had probably already tried to reach out to Rosemary. We all remained silent as Stella tried calling again several more times. Next, she called her mother's friends, asking if they'd seen or heard from her. My stomach twisted into a bigger knot as she called a fifth person with no result.

Stella lifted tear-filled eyes to us. "Something is wrong. I need to go and look for her. Maybe someone in the complex saw something."

3

Nana climbed off of her stool and scanned Stella with a piercing intensity. "Well, what are we waiting for? Let's get to the bottom of this. Rosemary's a tough cookie. She didn't just vanish into thin air." That was a little too close to home for us, given our last case. Things had been quiet for the past week since we'd dealt with Aidon's crazy ex.

Mythia flew off of Stella's shoulder and said, "Let me know if I can help. I'll make your favorite for lunch. I'll even have whoopie pie for you."

Mom nodded in agreement. "I'll stay and help. We will have extra lobster mac and cheese to take to your mom, as well." Ever since Mom was changed by that vile witch, Lyra, she had mostly stuck to the house. She'd gone down to North Carolina to see the kids but preferred being at home. She was mostly in control of her vampire urges, but she still struggled at times with her shifter half, especially when she was stressed.

Stella embraced Mom. "Thank you, Mollie."

We went out the side door where I'd left my small SUV. After helping Nana in the passenger side, I drove as fast as possible across town. Stella leaned her head between the seats. "Tainted witches aren't involved in this, right?" she asked. I swallowed hard when I heard the hitch in her voice.

Nana turned in the seat and scowled at Stella. "Now, why would you think such a thing? Trust me when I say it's far more likely that she got confused and is heading to her old house. It's hell getting old, and she lived there for over fifty years." Nana reached over and squeezed her hand.

A few minutes later, I pulled into the lot. The assisted living's sterile halls echoed our footsteps as we entered. I shivered at the feeling of desolation and hopelessness that permeated the atmosphere. I had to remind myself that we were there to delve into the mystery surrounding Rosemary's disappearance, not move Mom or Nana in. I wasn't around when Stella's mom moved here, and I hadn't given it much thought before. I was just glad that Mom and Nana had one another and had never ended up in a place like this.

Stella approached the desk where a young woman sat. "Hello. I'm Rosemary Stone's daughter, Stella. Emily called and informed me my mother was missing. Has she been found? What even happened?"

The young woman gave Stella platitudes and assured her they would locate Rosemary. I tuned them out and wandered over to a large room on the left. People were gathered there and engaged in various activities.

Nana grimaced as she watched the room. "Thank God that isn't my life. I have spent ninety years avoiding an STD. I'd like to keep it that way."

I choked on my laugh and gaped at her. "Nana!"

She scowled at me. "What? Sex in a place like this is like passing around a tray of cookies at bingo night, except instead of sweet treats, it's a buffet of surprises nobody asked for. It spreads like dandelion seeds on the wind."

My hand flew to my throat, where I tried to hold down the bile. "I did not need to know that."

Stella sighed as she joined us. "They don't know shit, and none of the staff saw anything. I asked Todd to see if she went to her old house. I guess we could check here."

In the foyer, under the unforgiving glare of fluorescent lights, Nana took charge with an authoritative air. "We start in here. Spread out. Gather any piece of information you can about Rosemary's activities over the past few days."

Stella's normally bright eyes darted around, absorbing every detail like a hawk surveying its territory. "Thank you both for helping." She shot us a grateful smile before delving into the fray.

Nana adjusted her green purse on her shoulder and entered after her. I took the far-right side and approached a group of women sitting on some couches and knitting. They paused when I stopped beside them. A woman wearing a neon pink blouse looked from me to Stella and then back. "Are you here about Rosemary?"

Nodding, I smiled at her. "Yeah. We just got the call about her being missing. I'm Phoebe, by the way."

The woman in neon tapped her chest with one of her knitting needles. "I'm Margaret and the one making a gawd awful green scarf is Krista. Holly is making a blanket for her new granddaughter. What did they tell you happened to Rosemary?"

I sat on the edge of the coffee table in front of them, needing to get off my feet. "It's good to meet you all. They didn't say much, just that she was missing. Did anyone notice Rosemary leaving?"

Margaret laughed, a bitter sound. "Typical. Covering their asses. She didn't walk away. Rosemary was here in the common area, as usual. And then, poof, she was gone. No one saw her leave. It's like she vanished into thin air."

Her comment made my blood freeze. That sounded like magic. Before I let myself get too far down that path of thought, I needed more information. "Did anyone mention seeing someone or anything out of the ordinary? Or did Rosemary mention wanting to go see a friend?"

The three of them thought for a moment, and Krista said, "There was a delivery earlier.

Holly nodded. "It was those flowers." Holly pointed to a large bouquet sitting on a side table.

"It caught our attention because it's not a regular occurrence here," Margaret said. "Maybe she went to see whoever sent them to her."

It was a distraction for the rest of the residents. I could easily see someone using the ploy to divert attention, allowing someone to spirit Rosemary away unnoticed. Stella walked over and joined the conversation. Her brow furrowed as she listened to Margaret explain about the delivery.

"Flowers? That seems odd," Stella said.

Nana overheard our discussion and gestured us to the side out of the range of noisy people. "It doesn't sound like Rosemary wandered off. We need to find out who sent those flowers."

Our makeshift investigation led us to the reception desk, where Sarah, the nurse on duty, nervously recounted the events. "It was a tall man. He was wearing a weird hat. He handed me the flowers, said they were for Rosemary, and then left."

The vague description provided little to work with. Still, it was a starting point. The smile Stella gave Sarah was strained. "Thank you. I will return my mother as soon as we find her."

We followed as Stella turned to leave. I hurried to keep up with Stella's furious stride. "We're going to the flower shop, right?" I asked her.

As we emerged from the assisted living complex, the three of us were engulfed in a cloud of uncertainty. Nana's furrowed brow mirrored our collective concern, while Stella's grip on her purse tightened with each step.

"That was my thought. I bet Lyra is behind this and she enchanted that arrangement to whisk my mom away like she did us when we got our tattoos. That means Petals & Posies is our best lead right now," Stella said with a sigh.

"I had similar thoughts, but we shouldn't assume anything. Your mom could have walked out. Magic might not be involved," I told Stella as we reached my car. Unlocking it, I opened the door for Nana. "We will find her, Stells."

Determined to unearth the truth behind Rosemary's

disappearance, I started the car. We made our way towards the flower shop that had provided the bouquet found in her room.

The quaint little shop stood nestled between two towering buildings, a burst of color amidst the monochrome cityscape. Its facade was adorned with cascading ivy, tendrils reaching toward the heavens in a silent plea for sunlight. There was something magical about the look and feel of the place. There was no way the plants would survive the winter. How did they manage to make it look like this so early in spring?

A wooden sign, weathered by time and adorned with delicately painted flowers, hung above the entrance, declaring it as "Petals & Posies."

As we pushed open the door, a symphony of scents enveloped us - a cacophony of floral notes dancing in the air. Sunlight filtered through the windows, casting intricate patterns of light and shadow across the polished wooden floors and adding to the atmosphere. Shelves lined with blooms stretched towards the ceiling, each blossoming a vibrant burst of color against the backdrop of plain white walls.

If I wasn't mistaken, the air hummed with an other-worldly energy. It was a faint undercurrent of magic that prickled at my senses. *'Not everything is related to magic, Phoebe! Stop looking for what you expect to see.'*

Keeping that in mind, I looked around without searching for anything specific. The shop was a veritable wonderland of botanical delights, with blooms of every shape and hue adorning the shelves like jewels in a treasure trove. There was definitely something there. Without being obvious and giving my magic away, I opened my senses a little.

Behind the counter stood a woman whose presence seemed to radiate mixed messages, smiled up at us. "Welcome to Petals & Posies," she said, her voice soft and melodic. "I'm Evelyn, the owner. How may I assist you today?"

Evelyn was a woman of striking beauty and quiet confidence. Her gaze was steady and unwavering. Her eyes, a mesmerizing shade of emerald green, held a depth that seemed to hint at hidden mysteries. Her long, flowing hair cascaded down her back like a waterfall of obsidian silk.

As Nana and I approached the counter, I couldn't shake the feeling that there was more to this woman than met the eye. My magical senses tingled with a faint energy, subtle yet unmistakable. It was a strange sensation. Almost like standing on the edge of a precipice, teetering between Darkness and Light.

Nana wasted no time in getting down to business. "We're here to inquire about a bouquet of flowers that was delivered to a resident at the Willow Creek Assisted Living facility," she said in a firm but polite voice.

Evelyn's gaze went distant as if she was remembering something. "I'm afraid I can't help you with that," she replied evenly, her voice betraying no emotion. "I didn't deliver anything to that location."

Stella, who had been browsing the floral arrangements, looked over with a puzzled expression. "We know it wasn't you personally. Reports indicate it was a man who delivered the flowers," she interjected, her voice tinged with frustration. Can we speak to your employees?"

Evelyn's facade remained calm. "I'm sorry, but I have no recollection of such an arrangement," she insisted, her tone now tinged with defensiveness.

I couldn't shake the feeling that something wasn't quite right. I followed my magical senses. They tingled with faint energy that I discovered lingering near the backroom like a whisper in the wind. It was a strange sensation, both unsettling and alluring. There was nothing about Lyra that was alluring. Then again, I could be biased.

Turning to Nana, I murmured softly, "There's something... off about her and the shop."

Nana's gaze hardened, her eyes narrowing in suspicion. "I agree," she replied, her voice low and intense. "Something tells me this is just the tip of the iceberg."

With a sense of determination, Nana turned back to the owner. "You're hiding something," Nana said. Her tone was sharp with accusation, and her words rang out with unwavering resolve. "And we're going to find out what it is."

It felt as if Nana had laid down the gauntlet, and the atmosphere cracked with tension. The petals and leaves seemed to hold their breaths, waiting for Evelyn to respond. Her composed facade never faltered as she looked at us.

"I don't know what you're talking about," Evelyn insisted.

Nana scoffed as she prowled closer to the woman. "We know you are responsible for the flowers that led to Rosemary being kidnapped," Nana said firmly, her words cutting through the silence like a blade. "Let's cut to the chase. What are Lyra's plans, Evelyn?" Nana's demand for answers rang out like a clarion call, her voice commanding attention.

Evelyn lifted a shoulder and smiled at Nana, although there was a flicker of fear there. She was afraid of Nana. "I... I don't know what you're talking about," she stammered, her voice trembling.

Stella's frustration simmered beneath the surface and her patience was wearing thin with each passing moment. She grabbed Evelyn's shoulders. "Please," she pleaded, her voice tinged with urgency. "My mom isn't part of the magical world. We need answers. You wouldn't want an innocent woman hurt, would you?"

Evelyn's eyes met Stella's, but she remained stubbornly silent. Her gaze flickered between Nana and me like she wished she could help, but there was nothing she could say. It was clear she knew nothing about this delivery. That was some powerful magic. I prayed it wasn't a new skill Lyra picked up. Otherwise, we would be hard-pressed to find clues.

Nana stepped forward, her presence commanding attention as she fixed Evelyn with a steely gaze. "You think you can outwit us, Evelyn?" she challenged, her voice low and dangerous. "You think you can stand against a Pleiades witch like Phoebe? You're on the losing side, and you know it."

Evelyn's eyes widened in alarm, a flicker of fear dancing in their depths. "I... I don't know what you're talking about," she repeated, her voice barely above a whisper.

But Nana wasn't about to let her off the hook so easily. "You know exactly what I'm talking about," she insisted, her voice ringing with conviction. "And you will tell us everything, whether you like it or not."

CHAPTER 2

*N*ana's demand turned the air thick with tension in Petals & Posies despite the sweet aroma of flowers. The vibrant blooms mocked the gravity of the situation. Evelyn stood before us with her hands trembling as she clutched the counter for support. Her eyes wide with fear and defiance, flickered nervously around the room seeking an escape that didn't exist.

Nana's gaze was as sharp as a blade as she cut through the pretense. "We know Rosemary was kidnapped, and we know you're involved," she declared, her voice as unyielding as granite. "What are Lyra's plans?"

Evelyn's lips trembled and her voice was barely a whisper as she stammered, "I don't know what you're talking about."

Nana stepped closer. Her presence was almost predatory as her eyes never left Evelyn's. "You think you can outwit us? Lyra doesn't stand a chance against a Pleiades witch like Phoebe. You're on the losing side, Evelyn."

Evelyn's fear was tangible. In fact, it was a palpable wave that seemed to emanate from her very core. "I really don't know anything," she repeated. Her voice cracked.

Frustration gnawed at me, and I let my magical senses sweep through the room, searching for any clue that might crack Evelyn's resolve. My attention was inexplicably drawn to the backroom, where a subtle whisper of magic called to me. Without asking for permission, I followed my gut.

"Hey," Evelyn called out. "Where are you going?"

Ignoring her, I entered the dimly lit space. It was cluttered with boxes and shelves that were overflowing with vases, ribbons, and an assortment of floristry supplies. Dust motes danced in the beams of light that filtered through the small windows, adding an eerie stillness to the room.

Footsteps echoed behind me, and I heard Nana shut Evelyn down and keep her from getting in my way. Nana was fierce for a ninety-year-old woman, and she only became more agile and spry when she gained her magic. She seemed to move better and appear younger the more she used it.

My fingers brushed against a stack of old invoices and forgotten trinkets until they landed on a crumpled piece of paper. It seemed out of place, almost too mundane amidst the chaos. I knew it meant something when I felt it pulsate faintly with an energy that made my fingertips tingle. I unfolded it, and an address stared back at me. It was scrawled hastily in a shaky hand. It tugged at my intuition. It was a magnetic pull I couldn't quite explain.

"I found something," I told them as I turned and waved the paper in my hand. "I have no idea what is at this address, but it feels important."

Stella leaned in and squinted at the address. Her face was a mask of concern and confusion. "Why would this slip of paper have magic? It doesn't make sense."

Evelyn's eyes darted to the paper. There was no indication she knew what it was. Nana got in Evelyn's face and barked, "I know you're hiding something. This address means something. And we're going to find out what."

Desperation seeped into Evelyn's voice. "I don't know anything about that address. Please, you have to believe me." I believed the woman. She didn't know anything about this.

Nana's patience was wearing thin. "Enough with the lies. We're done playing games. You know more than you're letting on, and if you don't start talking, things will get much worse for you."

Evelyn's breath hitched, and her eyes filled with unshed tears. "I... I can't remember. There's this blank, and I get the feeling I will be hurt if I say anything. Not that I have anything to tell you."

Nana's expression softened just a fraction as she sensed the genuine terror in Evelyn's voice. "Help us, and we can protect you."

Stella's frustration boiled over, and her voice rose in desperation. "Evelyn, please. My mom's life is at stake. We need to know what is at this address. Was she taken there?" Evelyn remained silent as tears brimmed in her eyes.

With a heavy sigh, Nana turned to me. "It would be nice to have more information, but she's not going to talk. We'll follow this lead anyway." Nana turned back to Evelyn and snarled, "Know this. We will uncover the truth. And when we do, it won't bode well for *you* or for Lyra."

Leaving the shop, the crumpled piece of paper felt like a ticking time bomb in my pocket. Armed with the mysterious address, we set out into the unknown. I considered taking Nana home. She was ninety, but she would be pissed if I tried at this point. And being almost twenty weeks pregnant with triplets, I didn't need to add that battle to my agenda for the day.

As we drove towards the outskirts of Camden, Stella

clutched the paper tightly. Her eyes flicked between the parchment and the ever-changing scenery outside. "We have to find her, Phoebe. I would never forgive myself if anything happened to my mom."

I reached back, and she put her hand in mine. I gave it a sympathetic squeeze. "We won't stop until we get her back." I pulled over a couple of houses down from the address and parked the car.

"You need to prepare yourself that Lyra has changed your mom like she did Mollie. But she will still be your mom, and we will be there for you both," Nana told her as we got out of the car. Nana's gaze remained vigilant, and her steps were deliberate yet cautious as she headed for the house. "Stick close and stay alert," she cautioned. I appreciated her diversion from the topic. I knew her warning was necessary, but I couldn't comfort Stella at the moment. We needed to remain alert in case Lyra was nearby.

I typed out a quick message to Aidon about where we were. Lyra could be close, and I promised him I would keep him apprised. "This area is rife with ancient wards and magical barriers," I informed them when I felt the magic around us. "We can't afford to let our guard down—not with Lyra involved."

Stella shook her head. "We can't have you taken. The gods only know what Lyra would do to you in your current condition."

The thought sent a shiver down my spine and made my steps falter. I couldn't be stupid. But if we could stop Lyra, didn't I needed to take the chance? I was relieved when Aidon responded that he was on his way. I told him where we were and what I sensed about the house. I sensed its emptiness even before we stepped onto the property. The air around it felt stale and abandoned. It was a stark contrast to the vibrant energy of the forest that surrounded it. I let Aidon know Lyra was likely in the woodland beyond the house and that he needed to follow my scent.

A sense of foreboding settled over me as we neared the woods. "Keep an eye out for any clues about where that bitch is hiding," Nana instructed. "There's got to be something. Being beaten by you guys time and again has thrown her off her game."

We nodded and proceeded with caution. Sure enough, as we ventured deeper into the forest, we began to notice strange symbols and runes etched into the trees. They glowed faintly with residual magic that made my stomach churn. I nearly threw up when I brushed my fingers against the rough bark. It was clear that this place had been enchanted by Dark magic to keep its secrets hidden from prying eyes.

At one point, the path split into three. Each direction was shrouded in a dense, swirling mist. I felt a tug at my core, an instinctual pull guiding me toward the middle path. "This way," I said, my voice confident. "I can feel it. This is the right direction."

Stella glanced at Nana, who nodded slightly in approval. Trusting my instincts, we proceeded down the middle path. The air grew cooler, and the mist thicker. At one point, it obscured our vision and made it difficult to see more than a few feet ahead. The silence was oppressive, broken only by the occasional rustle of leaves or distant animal call.

We encountered some magical barriers. They were Dark shimmering veils of energy. I pointed out the wards. "We need to be careful dismantling these. We don't want to alert Lyra," I told Stella and Nana.

"Let me handle them," a familiar voice said from behind us.

A grin spread over my face as I turned to look at my mate.

His handsome face made my heart race as warmth spread throughout me. "Aidon!" I whisper-yelled.

Nana jerked her chin to the barrier. "Have you discovered a way to break them without warning the creator?"

Aidon smiled as he embraced me and ran a hand over my abdomen. "I worked with my father, and I believe we came up with a way to obliterate them with our power without alerting the witch responsible."

Aidon used his formidable magic to dispel the weaker wards first. Next, he moved to the runes and took care of them. His magic rippled through the air like waves of Darkness, tendrils of inky energy dancing around his fingertips as he worked. The power he wielded felt ancient and primal. It was definitely a force to be reckoned with. As he focused his energy, the runes began to shimmer and fade, their hold over the forest weakening with each passing moment.

With a final surge of power, Aidon unleashed a burst of energy that shattered the remaining wards, their magic dissolving into nothingness. The forest around us seemed to sigh in relief as it was released from Lyra's Dark power. The air was suddenly lighter, and the mist began to lift, too.

As Aidon stepped back, a sense of accomplishment radiated from him. The smile he shot me oozed satisfaction. "That should do it," he said, his voice resonating with quiet confidence. "Now, let's find this witch and put an end to her schemes once and for all."

"Don't forget about finding my mom," Stella interjected through a clenched jaw. My normally bubbly best friend was pissed and worried for good reason. I knew exactly how she felt. My mom had been kidnapped by Lyra not long ago.

"That's our top priority," I assured her before pointing to a tripwire nearly hidden beneath the undergrowth. "Careful. They're not just relying on magic to keep people out."

We navigated the traps carefully, making slow but steady

progress. At one point, we encountered a barrier so strong it nearly repelled us entirely. Dark energy pulsed from it so strongly that it made my skin crawl.

Nana shuddered as she moved around it, saying, "This one is different." She held her hand hovering over some runes that seemed to power it. "She's found far more ancient and powerful magics. We need to be careful."

Aidon stepped forward with narrowed eyes as he assessed the barrier. "It's a binding ward, meant to keep something— or someone—in. Or, more likely, she doesn't want anyone to reach her," he explained. "We'll need all our strength to break it."

"Is it safe? I don't want her to bolt before we can catch her," I replied.

He squeezed my hand and nodded. "Channel your power into me, and I will cast it. She didn't feel me break her initial wards, or we would be overrun by her minions by now."

"Good enough for me," Nana said as she took his other hand. Stella grabbed my other one, and we called up our powers. Pooling our magic, we concentrated on the barrier while funneling our power to Aidon. Our combined energy clashed against the Dark magic. The strain on Aidon was immense, but I felt nothing, and from the looks of it, neither did Stella or Nana. Slowly the ward began to weaken, and cracks formed in its shimmering surface. With a final push, the barrier shattered. The residual energy dissipated into the air, and we stood there silently for several seconds.

When nothing came after us, we continued forward. My sense of urgency grew with each step. Apprehension set in when the path led us to a hidden cove. Its entrance was obscured by vines hanging from branches that glowed with a dark light. I was not expecting the pristine foliage when we passed through the vines. There was even a large pool that a waterfall poured into. Squinting, I looked around the area for any sign of Lyra. Beyond the waterfall, I saw a cave mouth. It was dark and foreboding. The exact place I expected to find Lyra hiding.

Stella looked at me with determination etched on her face. "What do you think is waiting for us inside?"

Nana's eyes glinted with amusement. "Whatever it is, we need to be ready for anything. It won't be friendly."

Aidon stepped through the waterfall first. The cold spray was a stark contrast to the warmth of the forest. It was difficult for me to maneuver because the cave entrance was narrow, and I was the size of a barn. Aidon gave me a look, and I nodded to reassure him, then I fell into step behind him. Nana was behind me, and Stella brought up the rear. We were dripping wet, and the light from outside vanished. Fortunately, we weren't plunged into complete darkness thanks to some bioluminescent fungi clinging to the walls.

The air grew colder, and silence pressed around us. Aidon slowed and held up a hand. Peeking around his shoulder, I noticed that the narrow passage had opened into a vast cavern. Its ceiling was lost in darkness. What drew my attention was the stone altar in the center. It was covered in ancient runes and symbols that pulsed with a faint, ominous light. And a red substance that made a vice tighten around my chest.

"This place feels wrong," Stella whispered, her voice trembling slightly. "I want to move on quickly."

My magical senses were on high alert. Every fiber of my being was tuned to the faintest hint of danger. Aidon and I approached the altar to get a better look. A wave of dark energy washed over me. It made my babies uneasy, and the three of them began turning in my womb. The energy felt like Lyra, but I couldn't be sure. She was good at masking her identity.

Nana and Stella flanked me and along with Aidon, were

scanning the cavern for any signs of movement. "Phoebe, what do you sense?" Nana asked in a low murmur.

"It's strange," I replied, reaching out with my magic. "There's dark energy here, but also something else. Something that doesn't quite fit."

Moving closer, I noticed a piece of parchment tucked into a crack on the altar. It was covered in blood. Swallowing back my nausea, I carefully lifted it. Opening it, I saw a hastily scrawled note and an address. It was practically identical to the note from the floral shop that had led us here. Why have another note with the address? That made no sense.

"This must be important," I said, showing the note to the others. "But I still don't understand its significance."

Stella examined the note, her brow furrowing in thought. "We need more information to understand what it means."

Nana's eyes softened with a rare hint of compassion. "We'll find the answers, Phoebe. We have to. For Rosemary, and for everyone else caught up in this."

We searched the cavern thoroughly before deciding there was nothing else there. I snapped a few pictures with my phone before we went back the way we'd come. We emerged on the other side of the waterfall again. I was about to suggest we go home and regroup when Nana grabbed my arm. "There's something here." Nana let go of me and was walking around the pool before I got myself together.

Stella, Aidon, and I shared a look and then caught up to her. I opened my senses but had no idea what she had picked up on, so I let her lead the way. Her magical senses discovered a concealed entrance. The door was barely visible among the thick roots and foliage. With a whispered incantation, the hidden door creaked open, revealing a dark, narrow staircase descending into the earth. "She's down there," she murmured.

"I hope you're right," Stella replied. "I'd hate to walk into a trap."

"Stay behind me," Aidon told us. As expected, the air grew colder and the darkness deeper as we descended. The walls were rough-hewn stone, damp with moisture, and covered in moss. It looked like we were in a castle dungeon, but there hadn't been anything but forest above. We reached the bottom, stepping into a dimly lit hall that stretched out in front of us.

Stella's voice was barely a whisper. "What is this place? It feels... wrong."

Nana's jaw tightened as we reached a fork in the hall. "Looks like an underground network. Lyra has hidden herself well." Three options branched out ahead of us.

Nana pointed down the path to the right. Aidon went first. The further we went, the stronger the sense of malevolence became. It wasn't long before we reached a large chamber illuminated by flickering torches. The sight that greeted us was nothing short of horrifying. My hand went to my stomach, and bile burned the back of my throat.

Witches of all ages were huddled together in makeshift cages. Their expressions were vacant and defeated. Their auras were dulled and suppressed. My heart ached at the sight of their broken spirits and the cruel chains that bound them. Aidon yanked me and Stella to the side to avoid being seen by the tall, gaunt man patrolling the area. His presence radiated a cold, unfeeling menace. "We've got to do something," I whispered. My voice trembling with rage and sorrow. "This is monstrous."

"Do you see my mom?" Stella's voice broke as she asked it.

Nana's eyes blazed with fury. "I didn't see her. We need to be smart before we rush in there. We can't risk getting caught before we free them."

My hand smoothed over the babies that kicked me from

the inside as if they agreed with Nana. We were hiding behind a stack of crates and had a moment to plan. Nana beat everyone to the punch when she said, "I'll create a distraction. Phoebe, you and Stella, start freeing the witches. Aidon, you help me fight and keep an eye out for Lyra. We need to move fast."

With a nod, we prepared to execute our plan. Nana stepped into the open, casting a powerful spell that sent the gaunt man flying across the chamber. Chaos erupted as guards rushed from other areas to respond. It was difficult for me not to help. Nana was a badass and held them off with a barrage of spells.

Knowing Aidon was at her back, Stella and I moved swiftly. With a flick of my wrist and a whispered spell, I broke the first lock. Stella had the second undone. We helped the witches inside to their feet. Their eyes began to spark with hope as they realized they were being rescued. "You're safe now," I reassured them, my voice filled with conviction. "We're getting you out of here."

As we worked, a young witch grabbed my arm. Her eyes were wide with fear and desperation. "They took my sister," she said, her voice shaking. "Please, you have to find her."

My heart clenched at her plea. "We will," I promised, thinking of Stella's mom. "We'll find them all."

The witches ran to the exit having to dodge the magic that was now flying around the room. Stella and I continued our work, and when the last of the witches were freed, we went to help Nana and Aidon. Nana was breathing hard and sweating but smiling like a loon as she tossed fireballs and magical bombs at the guards. Aidon was smirking and fighting alongside her. He was like a whirlwind, covering all of her sides to ensure she wasn't hurt. He knew how much she meant to me.

Joining the fight, Stella and I tossed spells and dodged

Dark magic. The guards were skilled but not up to par with two middle-aged witches and one old granny. It helped that we had a god on our side. But even without Aidon, we could have taken them.

Once we'd defeated all of the guards, we explored more of the halls in the labyrinth. "We should make sure those we rescued get away before we search much more," Nana pointed out. "I'd hate to rescue them only for Lyra to grab them a second time."

"What about my mom?" Stella asked.

Nana grabbed her hand and looked into her eyes. "We will find her. But all of this will have been for nothing if we don't ensure they get to safety."

Stella nodded, and we headed back to the narrow staircase. The fresh air and sunlight had revived some of their spirits. It had to be a relief to be out of that dark, oppressive underground room they had been trapped in. We gathered the freed witches around us. "We need you to get to safety," I told them, pulling out my cell phone. "I am going to have my friends pick you up on the street not far from here." Nana pointed the way that would take them to the road where we'd parked.

Their gratitude was overwhelming, and they all started thanking us at once. I took a moment to send a message to Layla, Tseki, Selene, and Murtagh to bring as many cars as possible and pick up the witches. I was grateful to have such loyal friends I could rely on. Nana had no patience for the adoration and told them to get moving before Lyra and her friends returned. We watched for a few minutes as Aidon led the group through the forest. I watched until he disappeared behind some trees.

It was a relief when Aidon returned not long after, but there was still a heavy weight in my heart. This had become more than just a rescue mission for Stella's mom. It was a fight against a horrific injustice that had to be stopped. "We need to find the others," Nana said as if she'd read my mind. "This is just the beginning. Lyra and her followers need to be brought to justice. But not before I give her a piece of my mind."

CHAPTER 3

I swiped the sweat from my brow, the dampness clinging to my skin despite the coolness of the underground dungeon's air. A sense of foreboding settled over me like a heavy cloak when we stepped into the dimly lit chamber where we had rescued the captive witches. The bodies of Lyra's guards and the empty cages stood as a reminder of what the evil the Tainted witch is capable of doing. The torches lining the walls flickered with a feeble light and cast long shadows that danced in the corners of the room.

Nana's footsteps echoed behind me. The sound reverberated off the stone walls as she prowled looking for something. She refused to leave with the other witches, saying she was going to help find Stella's mom. My mom would have come with us, but Rosemary's disappearance hit too close to home for her. She'd been in a similar situation not too long ago and came away from the experience as a tribred.

Nana's eyes were sharp and alert as she scanned the darkness ahead. "Where the hell is she hiding? She's either a genius or a coward," she whispered like she was talking to herself more than anything.

Stella moved ahead and trailed her fingers along the rough stone as she searched for hidden passages or secret compartments. It was the last place we had to check underground. Her brow furrowed with concentration with faint lines of worry etched into her features. "There has to be something here," she muttered, her voice echoing in the cavernous space. "There is no way Lyra would leave so many victims behind. She needs them for whatever it is she is doing."

"She's building an army," Aidon replied. "It might seem like she stopped after we rescued Mollie and the others, but she hasn't. She failed to control Mollie's mind, but she knows that most aren't as strong as the Dieudonne women." Aidon's presence beside me was a reassuring anchor in the darkness, even if his words chilled me to the bone.

"I kinda hoped she'd moved on and was doing something different. I know it was stupid," I admitted and leaned into his side. I relied on his solid presence to support me. His eyes glowed faintly with his power. It was always simmering just beneath the surface and flared as he swept the room with a keen gaze.

We fell silent as we finished sweeping the walls and floor of the dungeon. Unfortunately, we didn't find a damn thing. Our search yielded no clues as to the whereabouts of Rosemary or Lyra. With heavy hearts, we retreated into the forest. The weight of our failure pressed down on me like a ten-ton truck. I wanted to find Stella's mom safe and sound. The longer she was with Lyra, the higher the chances that something bad was going to happen to her.

The setting sun painted the trees with shades of gold and crimson when we emerged from the underground chamber and returned to the forest's edge. "We have to keep looking," Stella said desperately. "Lyra has to be around here."

Nana nodded in agreement. "We're clearly missing something," she said while scanning the trees for any hint of movement. "There's no doubt the stone altar is used for rituals. Bad guys never go far from places like that. It takes too much time to set them up and enchant them with the proper energy."

Aidon's jaw clenched with frustration, and his hands curled into fists at his sides. "Let's keep looking then."

I twined my fingers with him, and we pressed on. Each step was fueled by the hope that we would soon uncover the truth and bring Stella's mom home safely. We walked for what felt like forever before we came across a secluded cabin. It wasn't because it was all that far from the cave and underground dungeon. It was because we'd checked other areas first and went in that direction last.

The cabin was nestled in a small clearing. It looked like it had seen better days. Its wooden walls were covered in moss and ivy. The windows were dark and covered in enough grime to obscure the glass. It was impossible to see if anyone was inside just by looking at them. Aidon and I exchanged a glance, silently agreeing to use our powers to scan for any presence inside.

Aidon closed his eyes and extended his senses, his brow furrowing with concentration. I did the same, reaching out with my Pleiades heritage to feel for any trace of magic or life within the cabin. After a few moments, we both opened our eyes and shook our heads.

"I'm getting nothing," Aidon said. His voice was laced with relief and frustration.

"Neither do I," I confirmed. "Let's check it out."

We approached the cabin cautiously. The wooden steps creaked under our weight and made me hold my breath. I didn't want to fall through and hurt myself. Luckily, they held and I got to the porch as Aidon pushed the door open. My hand flew to my nose when we stepped inside together. The dust tickled my nostrils and the musty smell didn't help any.

The interior of the cabin was small and rustic. It had a single room serving as both living space and kitchen. A stone fireplace dominated one wall. Its hearth was cold and empty. A worn wooden table sat in the center of the room, surrounded by mismatched chairs. Against the far wall, a threadbare couch sagged under the weight of years of use.

Nana crossed the room and collapsed onto the couch with a sigh. Exhaustion was evident in the lines of her face. "I need a break," she said wearily. "Just for a few minutes."

Stella nodded. Her own fatigue was as apparent. "We all do," she said, sinking into one of the chairs at the table. "It's been a long day."

"We'll take a moment to regroup," Aidon said, his voice steady. "I'll keep watch while you three sleep. And before you argue, I'm a god and can afford to lose some sleep."

"I don't need sleep just yet," Nana said as she got up and joined us at the table. She proceeded to spread out a series of documents. "We should talk this through. Lyra's been careful. Bring up that map Mollie started." I did as she asked and handed her my cell phone. My mom had been documenting areas where Lyra had been active. Nana traced a finger over a map marked with various locations. "There's a pattern here if you look closely enough."

Stella leaned in so she could study the small screen, her brow furrowing. "She's not just a power-hungry witch looking to dominate others. She's changing witches into powerful creatures she can control and doing it right under our noses."

"Exactly," I replied as I noticed what Nana had seen.

"She's going to try and use her army to force me to give her my powers."

Nana nodded, her expression grim. "We've tracked her movements up and down the East Coast, from Maine to North Carolina. We don't know exactly where the remote island where she held you and Stella captive is located, but it might not be far away. She's been active in all these locations, transforming countless witches into her loyal followers."

The revelation sent a shiver down my spine. Facing an enemy driven by pure evil was one thing, but this... this was different. She was cunning and devious. "So, she's not just the enemy we thought she was. She's worse. She's building an army of powerful beings under her command."

What she'd done blurred the lines between enemy and ally. We couldn't be sure who was on our side and who was working for Lyra. "If Lyra's goal is to control, why is she targeting these specific areas? And why did she hold us on that island?"

"She wanted you out of the way so she could send her army after your family. With those you love in danger, you're far more likely to give up your power. And if you still refuse, she could kill them and make you watch until you give in," Aidon postulated.

"That's horrendous," I said, making a face. "And probably true." I ran a hand over my stomach. Feeling my babies safe and sound in my womb soothed some of the horrors that washed over me. I would give her whatever she wanted to save anyone I loved.

Nana sighed and leaned back in her chair. "We won't let that happen. Now, she must believe these locations are strategically important. Maybe there's something about the East Coast and that island that makes it easier for her to operate undetected. Or perhaps she's using these places to gather more power."

"My gut tells me it's both, which makes it easier for her to target me," I replied. "I can't think of a better explanation."

No one had a better theory and the room fell into a heavy silence as we absorbed the implications of our discoveries. Aidon went out and gathered wood before starting a fire in the hearth. While he did that, I tried to look at this from all angles. I couldn't shake the feeling that we were missing something. Like a crucial piece of the puzzle that would make everything clear.

"Phoebe," Stella said softly, breaking the silence. "What do we do now? If we know her pattern, can we predict where she'll be next?"

"Being able to stop her before she hurts anyone else is the goal," I replied. "I agree with Nana that she has to be close, so let's think about the house and the forest. There might be a clue there."

We spent the rest of the night planning our next steps. Our minds raced with possibilities and we shared strategies until it got so late none of us wanted to leave. We would want to be back out there to resume our search in the morning. Aidon kept the fire crackling in the hearth, and he brought the snacks he had in his car. It was a dinner of protein bars, beef jerky, crackers, and candy. And it hit all of my pregnancy cravings, so I was happy. Nana kept complaining about needing a real meal.

Aidon put the fire out when dawn broke the horizon and we headed out to search more for Lyra. The fresh morning air was a stark contrast to the heavy atmosphere of the previous night. It was enough to fill me with a renewed sense of purpose. We set off in a direction that would hopefully lead us to Lyra. The forest around us was alive and active, while the ancient trees stood as silent witnesses to our journey.

Nana began to chant the ancient incantation that would

hopefully unlock Lyra's secrets. We'd discussed doing this the night before and decided it was worth a try, with Aidon adding his power to try and hide her spell. I took Nana's hand, and we formed a tight circle. We joined in a web of shared energy.

With each word of Nana's incantation, the air around us began to hum with more power. The atmosphere shimmered with latent power as mine rose in response and tingled beneath my skin. And then, as Nana's voice reached a crescendo, the flowers before us began to glow with an otherworldly light. The petals came alive. Their colors shifted and swirled. My heart raced with excitement as the spell took hold. Each pulse of energy sent shivers of anticipation down my spine.

In a burst of dazzling light, the spell showed us a hidden magical signature. It was faint but unmistakable, dancing across the petals of the bouquet like a constellation in the night sky. The flowers around us seemed to come to life, their petals lifting gently into the air and floating away, forming a delicate trail. Lyra was definitely in the area.

I watched the petals with wide eyes. "This could be the ticket. It might be the way to stopping her."

We set out to follow the trail of floating petals. It seemed as if they were going to lead us to the rest of the secrets. Hopefully, they would lead us to the truth behind Rosemary's disappearance so we could find her. The forest enveloped us in a symphony of nature's whispers as we ventured deeper into its embrace. Shafts of sunlight filtered through the dense canopy above and cast a dappled mosaic of light and shadow upon the moss-covered ground.

We made our way through the labyrinth of twisted roots and tangled undergrowth. Our eyes were sharp and keen as we all scanned the surroundings with unwavering focus. If this was leading us to Lyra, the chances were high that there would be guards before we reached her. We searched for any sign of Lyra or her followers. I was prepared in case anyone jumped out at us.

With each passing moment, I became more and more tense. My nerves were strung so tight that I thought they might snap. It didn't help that the essence of the woods tingled with Dark magic. It made it seem as if we were surrounded. And we very well might be. The hairs on the back of my neck stood on end, and I dribbled witch fire for a few seconds before I got myself under control.

The forest gradually began to thin. It gave way to a secluded clearing bathed in the soft glow of filtered sunlight. Dark energies hummed around us and danced on the edges of our perception. Taking in what was in front of us, I noted the clearing itself was a verdant oasis. It looked like a sanctuary untouched by the hand of man. I didn't trust what I could see.

A surge of anticipation coursed through me as we stepped into the clearing. Aidon's grip tightened on my hand. I could feel his desire to push me behind his body. He had a hard time with me being in danger. I understood, which was why I asked him to join us. And I was really glad he'd come.

Stella's gaze swept across the clearing with steely determination. "Let's proceed with caution." Her voice trembled as she held herself in check. I could see the desire to race through the clearing and search for her mother.

We ventured further into the heart of the clearing with bated breath. My senses were on alert for any sign of danger or hidden clues. The air shimmered with latent magic. The Dark energy pulsed with the rhythm of the forest itself. My mind processed that information and what it might mean. Lyra was entangled with the natural world, which was giving her even more power. That wasn't a good thing.

Aidon's voice broke the silence as he whispered, "What do

you think we'll find here, Phoebe?" The situations I found myself in challenged him because they were so out of his scope of experience. Dealing with demons was far different.

I shook my head as a sense of worry coursed through me. "I'm not sure," I admitted, my voice barely above a whisper. "But I have a feeling it's going to be big. And it's something that will lead us one step closer to finding Rosemary." I said the last for Stella's benefit. We all had to believe it, or every time we came up empty, the urge to give up would became stronger. Hope was the only way to combat that.

Stella's voice cut through the stillness. "Then let's not waste any time," she declared, her eyes ablaze with resolve. "We have a Dark witch to find."

The heart of the clearing pulsed with an unearthly energy. It was almost as if the magic behind the scenes was our way of arrival. As if those thoughts conjured her, Lyra appeared from out of thin air. The powerful evil witch looked over our group, and a smirk lifted the corner of her mouth. Her presence was imposing. She was a dark silhouette against the backdrop of the verdant glade. It felt as if the plants should start dying just because she was there. Her eyes were pools of obsidian that seemed to pierce through the depths of my soul. She bore into me with an intensity that sent a shiver down my spine.

The witch's voice sliced through the silence like a blade. Her tone was cold and commanding. "How did you find my sanctuary?" she demanded, her words laced with a potent mixture of curiosity and menace.

Aidon's hand tightened around mine. His touch was a comforting reassurance that I wasn't facing her alone. Stella's expression was a mask of determination. Her gaze didn't waver as she squared her shoulders. Nana stood tall and resolute in the face of the vile witch.

I snorted and shook my head. "You aren't as clever as you

think," I replied. "We're here to get our friend back. You've overstepped by taking Rosemary. There's a cell in Coldwater Creek with your name on it."

The witch's lips curved into a cruel smile. Her eyes gleamed with malevolent intent. "Ah, Rosemary," she mused. Her voice was a chilling whisper that made my stomach churn. "She was a thorn in my side, that one. But no matter. She serves her purpose now."

My heart ached when I heard her words. Anger and fear rose within me. Rosemary, Stella's mom, was reduced to nothing more than a pawn in this witch's twisted game. It wasn't right. My magic wanted to lash out. There was no time for despair or rash actions. We had to find and save Rosemary no matter what had already been done to her.

With a silent exchange of nods, we braced ourselves for the fight that was to come. We would do what it took. For Rosemary's sake and for the sake of all who had fallen victim to the darkness that lurked within Lyra. I ran a hand over my obviously pregnant belly, silently telling my kids, "Protect yourselves while mommy fights the evil bitch."

CHAPTER 4

"No!" I screamed as Lyra stepped toward a portal. She paused and looked back at us. The clearing grew colder, and everything went still as we faced the witch standing before us. She was perfectly visible while her form was also shadowed. It went beyond the dark robes she was wearing as well. It was the fact that her eyes looked like liquid night. They were dark, fathomless, and glinted with a malevolent light as she surveyed us. A cruel smile played on her lips. There was something far more unnerving about her than almost any other being I'd ever encountered. Some of the Titans in Tartarus were worse. The sense of dread that seeped into my bones made my stomach ache.

Aidon's hand tightened around mine in a silent gesture of solidarity and support. Beside us, Stella radiated determination. Her jaw was set in a firm line as she prepared for what was to come. And Nana's eyes blazed with resolve. She might be ninety, but her stance was one of unyielding strength. Having these three by my side made facing Lyra so much easier.

Lyra vanished into the shimmering portal, and another witch took her place. My hands clenched into fists, and I took a step toward the witch. "Who are you?" I demanded, my voice steady despite the fear curling in my chest. "Where did Lyra go?"

The witch smiled, revealing sharp, white teeth. "I am one of Lyra's Tainted witches," she declared, her voice dripping with contempt. "She has given me a gift beyond comprehension. You cannot beat us."

I rolled my eyes. Another delusional freak of nature. "That's what they all say before they succumb to our might."

The witch sneered at us. "Our allegiance lies with forces far beyond your understanding. I have been enhanced so I can prevent intruders such as yourselves from meddling in our affairs."

None of what she said was all that surprising. Lyra had these witches fooled. Not that they were all that bright to begin with. Siding with her was a huge mistake. The one thing this conversation did tell me was that Lyra's influence was even more far-reaching than we had anticipated. I exchanged a glance with Aidon and Stella.

Stella stepped forward, her eyes blazing with defiance. "What have you guys done with my mother, Rosemary?" she demanded. I'd never heard such cold anger coming from my friend. Yes, even with enemies we'd faced in the past. "Where is she?" she thundered.

The witch laughed a sound devoid of warmth. "Rosemary serves a purpose," she said cryptically. "But that is not for you to know. Leave now... while you still can."

The tension in the air was thick and suffocating. This was not a fight we had anticipated, but there was no turning back now. "We won't leave without answers," I said firmly, stepping forward. "And we won't leave without Rosemary."

The witch's expression darkened, and her eyes narrowed. "Then you leave me no choice," she hissed, raising her hands. Dark energy crackled around her fingers. Our surroundings grew heavy with impending danger. Was she calling others to join her?

Aidon squeezed my hand one last time before letting go and stepping forward to stand in front of me. "We're ready," he murmured, his voice a steady anchor. He was responding to the fear I had about my ninety-year-old grandmother being in the middle of a fight. Fear for her and my babies would have paralyzed me if not for him.

Nana had always been my pillar of strength. I was in awe of her strength as she moved to my side, and her eyes locked on the witch. "You've messed with the wrong people."

The witch's eyes flashed with fury as she began to chant. Her voice was a dark incantation that resonated through the clearing. Shadows began to coalesce around her. Before any of us could utter a word, her spell took on twisted, menacing forms. They had clubs for hands and spines running down their backs.

A surge of anger welled up within me. I was getting damn tired of these assholes taking what didn't belong to them and attacking those I loved. "Stay strong," I whispered to my companions. "We can do this."

As the shadows lunged toward us, we braced ourselves for the clash. I called upon my Pleiades heritage and the witch energy coursed through me. I cast a radiant light hoping to push back against the darkness. Aidon summoned his own power. His was a fierce, protective aura that enveloped us. Nana and Stella's magic crackled with intensity before they each threw spells at the shadows.

The clearing was filled with fire, shadows, and enough magic to power a small city. I tried to keep my eyes on the witch, but I lost her amid the shadows she had summoned at one point. There was no doubt she was going to use that to try and get me to race around searching for her. Instead, I remained put and continued throwing everything I could at her shadows.

A Dark spell hit my shoulder from behind. The force of it stunned me, but it didn't get its hook in me, thanks to my babies and their protective barrier. My eyes bugged out of my head, and my heart stuttered to a stop when I caught sight of Lyra while I was in motion. Had she never actually left? Or did she come back after we were distracted?

The answer didn't matter. "Lyra's back," I yelled the warning as I stopped my momentum and turned to face her. Dark magic crackled around her, making her look even more menacing. Her presence alone seemed to twist the very fabric of the forest, warping it into a nightmarish realm. That answered one question. She had returned.

Aidon, Stella, Nana, and I shared a quick, determined glance. We were ready, but so was she. "Let's do this," I murmured. Aidon threw magic at the shadows, closing in with Nana and Stella helping.

Without uttering a word, Lyra launched an attack. I tried to duck but didn't get as low as I should have, and the smell of burning hair made me choke. Her power had burned my hair. More shadows erupted from the ground behind me. I shuddered to think about what it would have done to me if it had hit me like she intended. The darkness twisted and writhed as they lunged toward us. Aidon stepped forward, his protective aura flaring to life. He got there in time to shield us from another onslaught.

Lyra's eyes gleamed with malevolent intent. She knew she had to weaken Aidon first. I lurched forward at the same time she unleashed a bolt of dark energy aimed directly at Aidon's chest. The spell hit him with a force that sent him staggering back. Horror washed over me when I saw his skin starting to turn black where the Dark magic made contact. I gasped as panic threatened to stop my heart. Aidon clutched his chest, grimacing in pain as the Dark magic spread like poison.

"Aidon!" I shouted. Stella and Nana moved to intercept Lyra. Their magic clashed with hers in a spectacular display of light and shadow.

"You'll pay for that," Stella hissed. Her eyes blazed with the fury I would feel if I wasn't so frightened. She conjured a whirlwind of fire, sending it spiraling toward Lyra which forced her to retreat a few steps.

I got to Aidon right as his knees buckled. "No. Help them," he insisted. I fought the urge to stay with him and find a way out of that damn clearing. I needed Clio to heal him. If she even could. He was a god. Lyra shouldn't be capable of really harming him. It was the last thought that made me release him and swivel to help Stella and Nana. He was going to be okay. He had to be.

I added power to the barrier of elemental energy Nana summoned to protect us from being hit. "We need to keep her at bay until Tsekani and the others arrive," she said. "I texted them the first time she appeared." I could have kissed Nana for her foresight.

Lyra's laughter echoed through the clearing, a chilling sound that sent shivers down my spine. "You think reinforcements will save you? I bested your *god*," she taunted. "And my followers, come forth!"

Right then, figures emerged from the shadows. They were twisted, dark beings that radiated the same malevolent energy as Lyra. Her minions surrounded us, their eyes glowing with unholy light. The odds had just shifted dramatically against us.

I turned my attention back to Aidon, my heart pounding.

"Hang in there, Aidon," I whispered. Something wonderful happened then. Energy flowed from our babies and reached out to him. I had to go on the offensive and started throwing spells at Lyra so I missed some of what happened but I did feel how the dark magic resisted their efforts to push it out of Aidon.

"We need to break her defenses!" Stella yelled, bringing me back to the moment. I'd been tossing spells, and she was no longer in my line of fire. I had hit her creatures, though, so it wasn't a total loss.

Aidon grimaced and nodded at me. "I'll be okay. Focus on Lyra. She's the key."

I nodded, my resolve hardening. I stood up, channeling the power Hattie had gifted me. Beams of light shot from my palms, slicing through the shadows and illuminating the forest. She combated my power, and each clash of our magic against her sent shockwaves rippling through the clearing. The force of our spells made everything tremble around us.

The witch who had been there in the interim tried to sneak up on Nana. I spun and threw a magical bomb at her. Her eyes blazed with rage as she summoned a torrent of shadowy tendrils. Each one lashed out at us with deadly intent. Nana dodged and weaved, countering with magic that shattered the tendrils upon contact. Stella conjured a whirl-wind of fire, sending it spiraling toward Lyra. I joined Stella when I saw Nana had things under control. Together, we forced her to retreat a few steps.

"Keep pushing!" Aidon urged. His voice sounded stronger, making it easier for me to pour all of my energy into fighting the witch.

The forest was a battlefield and our magic clashed with Lyra's in a dazzling display of light and darkness. We fought with everything we had. Lyra seemed to have a never-ending supply of minions. I'd lost track of the witch, but I had no doubt she was helping Lyra conjure more shadow creatures. Just as it seemed we might be overwhelmed, a thunderous roar echoed through the clearing. I glanced up to see Tsekani soaring through the sky. Layla and Murtagh were clinging to his back. Yes! Our reinforcements had arrived.

Tsekani landed with a mighty thud. His powerful wings stirred up a gust of wind that sent the shadows scattering. Layla and Murtagh jumped down, their expressions fierce and ready for battle.

Layla and Murtagh both shifted and started shredding shadows with their claws. The wolves were formidable allies, as was Tseki's dragon. I laughed when I heard the witch's shriek cut off. I looked over to see Tseki shaking her in his massive jaws. I didn't even get sick when her body parts went flying. It was astonishing what rage could overcome. The chaos of battle swirled around us like a storm. I had to remain focused on Lyra. Every spell and counter-spell cast brilliant flashes through the clearing.

I barely had time to catch my breath between attacks. The intensity of the fight demanded every ounce of my focus and energy. Still weakened but refusing to stand by any longer, Aidon joined me. Stella and Nana had joined Layla, Tseki, and Murtagh in combating the monsters Lyra brought to bear against us.

I had just crouched to avoid one of Lyra's spells when I noticed Stella's eyes dart around. Her gaze locked onto something half-hidden in the underbrush near Lyra's feet. With a swift and agile move, Stella ran forward, dodging Dark spells and rolling forward. I increased my attacks on Lyra, unsure what my bestie was up to. I was grateful Stella had such keen vision when she snatched up a scroll.

"Phoebe!" Stella shouted when she stopped rolling a couple of feet away. "I found something!"

My heart pounded when Lyra's eyes narrowed with fury.

She hurled a bolt of dark energy directly at Stella, but Aidon intercepted it with a burst of his power. His black lightning was enough to deflect the spell away from my best friend.

"Read it!" Aidon urged in a strained voice. "It might be the key we need!"

Stella nodded, quickly unfurling the scroll. Her eyes darted over the intricate symbols, her brow furrowing in concentration. "This... this is written in an ancient language. I only recognize some of the symbols from my studies," she replied frantically.

"Can you decipher it?" Nana asked as she threw spells from around Tseki's front leg. He'd perched himself above her to protect her from harm. Nana might not have helped raise the others like she did me, but she had become as important to them.

"I'm trying," Stella replied. "It's a spell or... no, a message. It speaks of a hidden power, buried deep within the shadows. A key to unlocking secrets... and a warning. Maybe."

"A warning about what?" I asked. My heart raced with a mix of hope and fear. Aidon and I continued battering Lyra with our magic, but nothing seemed to have touched the Dark Witch.

"Something about the balance of power," Stella said, her voice tinged with urgency. "Lyra is after something more than just chaos. She wants to control... to dominate the realms. This scroll could be the key to understanding her true plans."

"Close, but not quite," Lyra replied with a smirk before she snapped her fingers and stepped back into the portal as it formed. I threw myself at the thing, but it snapped shut less than an inch from my nose.

"Son of a bitch!" I snarled while my loved ones continued fighting the shadow creatures. Layla launched her wolf body at the shadow hoping to catch me off guard. After shredding the thing, she nosed the side of my belly. Nodding, I joined the fight. It didn't take long for us to gain the upper hand on the shadow creatures. A few minutes later, Tseki dispatched the last of them.

Aidon held his hand up. "There's still residual energy from her portal."

Nana brushed the dust from her jacket and looked up at Aidon. "Can you activate it so we can follow her?"

He cocked his head to the side and evaluated the magic in front of him. "I can try. I can teleport in the Underworld, but it's impossible for me here, so it will be a matter of reactivating her Dark power." Aidon stood tall despite the lingering pain from Lyra's dark spell. He gripped my hand tightly. His touch was a reassuring anchor in the sea of uncertainty.

I frowned at my mate. "That sounds dangerous."

"He will need to be careful," Nana said. "We need to find Rosemary while Lyra is slowed down."

Shaking my head, I scoffed. "She wasn't slowed in the least."

Nana rolled her eyes and patted Tseki's leg as he moved closer to her. "That's because you let her fool you. Aidon's magic hurt her. She left rather than trying to take that scroll back because she was close to succumbing."

I nodded and took a deep breath to steady my nerves. "Fair enough." Extending my hand, I felt the power of the portal. I sent my magical feelers beyond. "I can sense the danger. It feels... alive, almost sentient."

Stella glanced at me with her heart in her gaze. "We have to go through no matter what is on the other side. My mom could be there."

Aidon's expression was fierce as he activated the portal. "Keep your eyes peeled and stick together."

With that, we stepped forward. The air around the portal

crackled with energy. The barrier between worlds buzzed with an electric intensity. I reached out and my fingers brushed the shimmering surface. It felt both solid and liquid. It was an impossible contradiction that sent a shiver down my spine.

"I don't like this," I said and looked over at Nana. "I don't suppose I can talk you into staying here with Layla or Murtagh."

Nana scowled and kept her gaze fixed on the portal. "I'm in this until we find Rosemary." That's what I thought.

Tseki shifted and grabbed a bag but didn't bother dressing as he joined us. Layla sidled up to me and Murtagh took up the rear. We moved as one and stepped through the portal. The sensation was disorienting. It was like being pulled through a vortex of light and sound. Colors and shapes blurred around us. And for a moment, it felt as though we were suspended in a void.

Then, with a jarring abruptness, we found ourselves standing in a new landscape. The forest clearing had been replaced by a field that felt both alien and familiar. The air was thick with magic, and the ground beneath our feet hummed with power. There was danger all around us. I felt it in my bones even if I couldn't see it.

Aidon's grip on my hand tightened. "Stay alert. We don't know what's lurking here or where they are. They could be hiding right in front of us," he said as if he'd read my mind.

The sense of danger intensified when we took our first cautious steps forward. Shadows moved at the edge of my vision. Everything vibrated with a sinister energy, and every instinct in my body screamed at me to turn back. I pushed those fears aside. We had come too far to turn back now.

A sudden rustling sound made us all freeze. Out of the shadows stepped figures cloaked in darkness. Their eyes glowed with hatred and envy. My heart pounded as I recognized their power. They were more of Lyra's followers. It was disgusting to see so many had been corrupted and twisted to her will.

"I told you she was hurt," Nana said grimly. "She was expecting us because she couldn't eradicate her trail like usual and knew we would follow."

The leader of the group stepped forward, his face partially obscured by a hood. "This is where your journey ends." Hearing a male voice was startling. Sure, Lyra had used them in the past, but those in her closest group were usually women.

I exchanged a look with Aidon, and then with Stella and Nana. Yeah, this was bad. I threaded my fingers into the fur of Layla's neck. We were ready for this. Whatever lay ahead, we would face it together.

"That's where you're wrong. We're here to put an end to Lyra's plans," I informed him.

The figure laughed, a cold, hollow sound. "We'll see about that."

With a wave of his hand, the others lunged at us. Their forms shifted and melded with the shadows. The battle began anew, but this time, we were exhausted and still recovering. Aidon was better, but I could see some blackened flesh lingering on his shoulder.

I kept my focus on the portal behind us as spells flew and magic crackled in the air. I didn't trust Lyra not to send something through after us. My heart pounded as I turned to see a pack of snarling wolves joining the fight. Were they shifters? Their feral eyes gleamed with malice, telling me they probably were. And they were far bigger than normal wolves. Their muscles rippled beneath matted fur. They were clearly afflicted with Dark magic.

Aidon immediately stepped in front of me as his protective instincts kicked in. "Stay behind me, Phoebe," he said, his voice a mix of determination and concern.

"I'm not helpless, Aidon," I reminded him as I soaked up the moonlight. It always invigorated me.

Stella and Nana moved to flank us, with Layla and Murtagh on the outside of them. "These aren't ordinary shifters," Stella echoed my thoughts. "They reek of Dark magic."

Nana nodded, her hands already glowing with the beginnings of a spell. "No doubt more loyal servants of Lyra who won't stop until we're dead."

The lead shifter let out a bone-chilling howl, and the pack advanced. There was no time for hesitation. Tseki dropped his bag and shifted to his dragon form before taking to the skies. I summoned my magic and relished the familiar hum coursing through me. Despite the pain from his earlier wound, Aidon stood tall and ready. His divine power crackled around him.

The first wolf lunged at Aidon. Its jaws snapped closed an inch from his face. Aidon countered with a burst of Underworld energy that sent the creature flying back. Another shifter darted toward Stella, but she was ready. Her spell released a burst of light that momentarily blinded the beast. She followed it up with a magical bomb that tore it to pieces. My stomach lurched at that one.

Murtagh moved closer to Nana, who unleashed a torrent of magic. She conjured a wall of her witch fire that forced the pack to halt their advance. The flames cast flickering shadows across the field. All of Lyra's minions snarled in frustration and began circling us like predators biding their time.

"We can't let them surround us!" I yelled as I launched a magical bomb at the nearest wolf. The creature yelped in pain but quickly recovered, its eyes now locked onto me with a deadly focus. Layla leaped through the air and landed on the thing's back. Her teeth sank into its neck and tore. I looked away when blood gushed from the wound.

Despite his injury, Aidon fought with relentless ferocity. "Phoebe, stay close!" he called out.

I couldn't move anywhere at the moment. I was surrounded. Stella, on the other hand, used her agility to dodge the attacks from the wolves and Lyra's other witches. I was the size of a Jersey cow and waddled everywhere I went. I was only twenty weeks along but carrying three babies made me as big as I ever got with my other two pregnancies.

"We need to break their formation!" Nana shouted. She channeled her magic into a new spell that summoned a gust of wind. It knocked several wolves off their feet. The shifters backed off and regrouped while the magic wielders closed in. They were relentless, and I could see the toll the battle was taking on all of us. But especially Aidon. He hadn't yet healed, and his face was pale from the effort of maintaining his defenses while depleted.

As I watched Layla silently direct Murtagh and Tsekani, who flew above us, an idea struck me. "Aim for the leader!" I shouted to Stella and Nana. "If we take him down, the others might falter!"

Nana nodded, her eyes narrowing in determination. She focused her magic on the lead wolf while I focused on the warlock who had greeted us upon arrival. We each sent a bolt of lightning crackling through the air at our targets. Stella followed suit. Her bolt hit the warlock while Murtagh took the lead wolf down.

The combined force of our magic made them falter. Hope ignited, and I redoubled my efforts, increasing the power that hit the warlock. Stella and Nana did the same. Aidon joined us, and the pair went down. The remaining pack members were disoriented and leaderless. They retreated into the shadows with the other witches not far behind.

Breathing heavily, we regrouped. The adrenaline of the battle still coursed through my veins as I sent out my magical feelers. I didn't want to get stuck here, so we needed to act fast if we were going to save Stella's mom and get home. I knew all too well how adept Lyra was at keeping one captive and cut off from their magic.

CHAPTER 5

"We need to find your mom and fast," I said as I tried to find a trace of Rosemary or Lyra.

"That portal is going to close, and we can't get stuck here," Aidon agreed.

We hadn't gone far when the shadows around us seemed to come alive. A growl echoed through the forest, and I spun around just in time to see the pack of wolf shifters emerging once again from the darkness. Shit on a shingle! Taking out the leader hadn't done much to stop them.

"Something's wrong," I muttered with my heart pounding in my chest. This went so much deeper than I initially thought.

Layla shifted back and moved closer to me. "They're not just ordinary shifters," she whispered. "In addition to their primal instincts being honed for battle, their minds are being subverted by someone else."

Murtagh nodded. "No rational shifter would continue like this without their alpha. They'd scatter and search for a new one if someone didn't immediately emerge."

The moonlight highlighted their sharp claws and glistening fangs. The first shifter lunged at Aidon with blinding speed. Aidon met him head-on. It sounded like thunder boomed when their bodies collided. Another shifter darted towards Stella, who was bleeding from several small cuts. No doubt she smelled like dinner. I shot a ball of my witch fire at the creature, stopping it before it reached her.

Stella stepped forward with a calm expression, her hands raised in a gesture of peace. She cast some kind of spell that rippled out of her in waves. The wolf-shifters surrounding us stopped their approach. Tseki, who hovered above us, stopped picking the wolves off, and watched Stella.

"Listen to me," Stella began, her voice resonating with a serene confidence that seemed out of place in this tense standoff. "You don't have to do this. We are not your enemies. Lyra is using you for her own dark purposes. She's got my mother. We're only here to get her back."

The wolf-shifters snarled softly. It was a low rumble that echoed through the field. The massive beasts had eyes like molten gold that watched Stella with a mixture of curiosity and disdain. You could see them battling for control of themselves again. For a moment, the snarling softened. I liked to think that Stella's words were reaching a part of them that remembered life before Lyra's corruption.

"You have families and lives worth living," Stella continued, her voice imbued with genuine empathy as her spell continued to pump out of her. "Don't let Lyra's darkness consume you. Join us, and together we can end this cycle of pain and destruction."

The wolf-shifters exchanged glances, and a silent conversation passed between them. I held my breath, feeling a flicker of hope. Stella's charm was legendary. I could see the effect her words were having. One of the shifters, a smaller female with silver fur, lowered her head slightly. I swear her eyes reflected a flicker of doubt.

"We know that deep down, you are not evil," Stella pressed on, stepping closer. "You can break free from her control. There's still time."

The silver-furred wolf shifter took a hesitant step forward with her ears flattening against her head. A larger male let out a deep, rumbling growl that made her stop in her tracks. He stepped forward and bared his teeth. He partially shifted, and he growled, "Our loyalty is to Lyra." His voice was rough and guttural and difficult to understand in this partial state. "We do not betray our master."

Stella's face fell, but she didn't back down. "Please, you don't have to do this," she pleaded, her voice tinged with desperation. "There is a better way."

The male's eyes narrowed. His patience was done. "Enough!" he barked. His voice echoed through the clearing. "Your words are meaningless. Lyra's will is our command."

A string of curse words flowed through my head. Stella had tried her best, but it was clear that the wolf shifters were beyond reasoning. Lyra's hold over them was unshakable. It was bound by Dark magic, not true unwavering loyalty, so if we had time to figure it out, we could find a way around it. But we didn't.

Aidon moved to my side. "It's no use, Phoebe," he said softly. "They won't turn against her."

Stella backed away, her shoulders slumping slightly. "I had to try," she murmured, her voice tinged with sadness. "They aren't acting of their own free will."

I gave her a sympathetic smile. "You did your best, Stella. We'll find another way."

The wolves began to advance once more. Their eyes were locked on us with predatory intent. There was no more time for words. We had to be ready to fight, to defend ourselves against these relentless foes.

As the first wolf shifter lunged, its eyes fixed on me with

murderous intent. Aidon stepped forward, making his body a shield between me and the beast. He raised his hand, and a dark light flared, momentarily blinding the shifter. That sent it skidding and scrabbling for purchase in the dirt. Nana began to chant. I recognized the words. She was summoning the elements to our aid. A gust of wind whipped through the field, throwing leaves and debris into the air. It created a momentary barrier between us and the advancing pack.

"Get ready," Aidon said, his voice tight with urgency. "This is going to be a tough fight."

Stella nodded and conjured her witch fire. The shifters surged past the wind and were only a few feet away. Their snarls echoed through the area and into the forest off in the distance. The hairs on the back of my neck stood on end as they ate up the distance between us. I could feel the Dark magic pushing them forward.

Nana's voice cut through the chaos, her tone commanding yet filled with determination. "Stand back!" she shouted, her words carrying a sense of urgency. I glanced over to see Nana raising her hands, her fingers dancing with sparks of her witch fire. But it didn't seem to be entirely in her control. With a swift motion, she unleashed a torrent of flames, weaving them together into a barrier of fire that crackled with raw power. Damn. I've never been so glad I was wrong about that.

The flames erupted in front of us, forming a wall of heat and light that burned the wolves. Their snarls turned to yelps of pain as they recoiled from the intense heat, their fur singed and smoking. I could feel the heat radiating off it and warming my skin even from a distance. It was a testament to Nana's strength and skill as a witch. There was nothing she couldn't do when she put her mind to it.

I sent out my feelers, looking for a connection to Stella. We still had to act fast. Nana's brow was furrowed in concentration as she continued feeding her fire. Beads of sweat glistened on her forehead. It was the first sign I'd seen of the effort it took her to fight alongside us. Layla snarled and snapped at those who broke through, taking them down. Tseki flew over the flames and attacked from the opposite direction.

As the shifters got past the fire, they snarled and clawed at us. The scent of earth and pine mingled with the acrid tang of magic and burned fur in the air. I wasn't finding any trace of Rosemary or Lyra. Where in the hell could they be? We'd gone through Lyra's portal. She had clearly recalibrated the destination before Aidon reactivated it.

Okay, we needed to get rid of these wolves so we could get home and regroup. We had the scroll. There could be something on it that would help us locate Rosemary. With a deep breath, I focused on the energy that flowed within me. I could feel the power of the universe in the depths of my mind.

Slowly, I began to weave spells together using all of the ancient magic of my Pleiades heritage. The air crackled with energy as the power surged through me and filled me with a sense of purpose. I let it build until it became painful to hold it inside. With a flick of my wrist, I sent shimmering tendrils of cleansing light swirling toward them. Each beam was infused with enough magic to clear the darkness out of the Underworld. Or, so I hoped. The light wrapped around the shifters and sought out the malevolent power suffusing them.

But even as the shifters stumbled and faltered under the weight of my magic, I could sense the presence of Lyra's darker forces lurking in the shadows. The air thickened with malice. It was a sickening reminder of the power that Lyra wielded. The wolves reacted and renewed their fight.

Nana lost control of her flames and they died out as a

wolf knocked her to the ground. I tried to rush to her side but was stopped when a giant paw hurtled toward my stomach with razor-sharp claws extended. A defensive spell sprang to mind but the blow was deflected in a shower of sparks. The shifter was too close to lob a magical bomb at, so I kicked the thing in the side, knocking it into Murtagh, who proceeded to tackle it. Tseki redoubled his efforts now that there was no fire to contend with.

The forest was alive with the chaotic symphony of battle. Nausea churned in my stomach as the varying scents assaulted me. Aidon had conjured his sword at some point and stepped in front of me. His weapon sliced through the enemies with deadly precision. Each strike stopped the oncoming shifters with practiced ease. His movements were a dance of steel and sinew, and his expression was a mask of grim determination. I couldn't help but admire how fiercely he fought to protect me and the babies.

"We can't keep this up," Nana's voice cut through the din and brought me out of my stupor. I started firing magical bombs at wolves closing in around us. "We need to retreat!" Nana's plea was desperate. She was already moving toward the forest in the distance. The rest of us followed suit while still fighting.

Stella's hands moved in a blur of motion as she conjured magical bombs and fireballs. "She's right. We're outnumbered and outmatched. We need to fall back and regroup."

I nodded in agreement. We'd tried, but it wasn't working, and we were getting tired. My heart was heavy with the weight of defeat. "Let's find a safer place to gather our thoughts," I said, my voice strained with exhaustion.

As we began to retreat, the shifters pressed forward with renewed ferocity. Their feral eyes gleamed with hunger. Lyra's control was firmly back in place. We reached the forest and it immediately seemed to close in around us. The trees loomed like Dark sentinels as we fought to escape the clutches of our enemies.

When we were out of the field, Tseki was forced to shift and join us. Layla had picked up the bag and was carrying it in her jaw. I continued casting spells and decided to shift gears to confuse and befuddle the wolves hoping that would keep them off our trail. Pretty soon, the sounds of their howling faded into the distance behind us. Aidon leaned heavily against a nearby tree. His chest was heaving as he caught his breath. "That was too close," he muttered.

I nodded in agreement, my body trembling with exhaustion. "We underestimated them and Lyra's control over them," I admitted. There was a bitter taste of defeat lingering on my tongue. "But we won't make that mistake again."

Nana's eyes blazed with determination as she straightened her shoulders. "She may have won this battle, but she won't win the war. We'll find a way to stop her, no matter what it takes."

Stella nodded in agreement. "We have to stay strong. For my mom's sake, if nothing else."

As we stood there, catching our breath, I thought about how the road ahead would be long and treacherous. Lyra had been at this for centuries, we were learning. She'd had plenty of time to hone her Dark magic. And she didn't care who she hurt to win. We had to be ready for anything. And find a new way home. I doubted that portal was going to be there if we ever made it back to that field.

CHAPTER 6

"There's no time to lollygag," Nana chided us and swiveled a finger in front of Aidon. "Turn around, Big Boy. We will move faster with me on your back."

We all laughed as Aidon inclined his head and then gave Nana his back. He crouched so she could climb on. The howls had us moving again. We ran through the forest with the sounds of the wolf shifter pack echoing behind us. Each cry sent a shiver down my spine. My heart pounded in my chest and my breaths were now coming in ragged gasps as I pushed myself to keep up with the others. Well, Stella was keeping pace with me. Layla and Murtagh were right behind us. It was Aidon and Tsekani who were ahead of us with Nana.

"Just a little further!" Aidon encouraged. "There's a cave up ahead. We can take shelter there."

The forest around us was a blur of dark shapes and shadows. Moonlight filtered through the dense canopy, shining on us every once in a while. Under other circumstances, I would enjoy the scent of pine and damp earth joined with the sounds of the night creatures. Our frantic flight made it hard for me to think about much but getting somewhere safe until Aidon could heal and we could rest. My center of gravity was off, and a few seconds later, I stumbled over a root. I barely caught myself before hitting the ground. Stella's hand shot out to steady me. Layla's wolf nudged my side as if she were there to keep me from being hurt as well.

"Thanks," I said between breaths.

She nodded and smiled at me, saying, "We're almost there, Pheebs." Her eyes darted between the trees for any sign of wolves. The howls grew louder and closer. We shared a panicked look. Her expression said what I was feeling. The sound of those paws pounding against the forest floor was right on our heels.

Just when I thought I couldn't run any further, Aidon pointed ahead. "There!" he shouted. "Do you see it?"

Stella and I nodded as we headed for the dark opening looming ahead. It was barely visible among the thick underbrush. We sprinted towards it with the promise of safety spurring us on. As we reached the cave entrance, Aidon ushered us inside. His gaze darted back the way we'd come to ensure we hadn't been followed too closely.

I grabbed Stella before she got too far inside. "We need to mask our scent and hide this cave."

"Good thinking," she panted.

Nana slid off of Aidon's back and grabbed my hand. "I cast a diversion while we were running, so we have time before they find our scent." Grateful she thought to do that, I took a few deep breaths and centered myself. I had to dispel the frantic energy, or I would muck up the spell. I could cast under duress. However, it was always better to be as focused as possible. When Stella squeezed my fingers, we chanted and cast the enchantment. I sighed when the magic rippled out of us and traveled out of the cave opening.

Trusting our power to hide us, we ventured inside the

cave. It was cool and damp, which was a stark contrast to the chaotic night outside. The walls were rough and uneven beneath the palm that I steadied myself with when I became dizzy. Water dripped from the ceiling and pooled on the rocky floor. I considered opening my mouth beneath the stream to get some hydration. It wasn't long before the faint light from outside barely penetrated the darkness. I conjured a ball of my witch fire to light our way.

We entered a cavern of sorts, and Nana collapsed onto a nearby rock. She was the only one of us not panting heavily. "We should be safe here for a while," she said. "But we can't stay too long. They'll find us eventually." Tseki finally pulled clothes out and got dressed while Layla and Murtagh shifted back and did the same.

Stella nodded. Her eyes reflected the same resolve I felt. "We need a plan. We can't keep running forever."

I swiped the sweat from my brow, trying to calm my racing heart. "We know Lyra is behind this," I said as I ran a hand over my stomach to soothe my babies. "She's got countless Tainted witches on her side. And she's done some Dark magic on the shifters so she can control them and use them as weapons."

Aidon was standing near the entrance to the cavern and turned to face us. "We need to figure out if she's anywhere near here. She could have sent us somewhere else but if she is here, we might be able to predict her movements. Then we might stay one step ahead."

"We know she's been all along the East Coast," Stella added, her brow furrowed in thought. "From Maine to North Carolina. And there was that island where she held Mollie and the others captive."

Nana's expression was grim as she took a water bottle from Layla. "She's left a trail of chaos and destruction in her wake while somehow always getting away. Wherever she goes, she convinces witches to follow her down the dark path. Or she turns creatures into tribreds. And she bends most of them to her will. We need to find a way to stop her before she creates more of these things that can't control themselves."

Aidon sat down beside where I was standing. The warmth of his body was a stark contrast to the cool cave air. "How can we piece together her pattern? That'll be the key to predicting her next move."

"She's been methodical," I said as my mind raced. "There's got to be a reason behind each location and attack. We just need to figure out what that reason is."

Aidon's gaze turned thoughtful. "We know she has a network of followers. That island... it was remote and hidden. If we can find more places like that, we might find her."

"We're spinning in circles. I can't escape the feeling that the answer is just out of reach," Stella added. "We need to try and rest. We'll need all our energy for what's to come."

Nana nodded and settled herself more comfortably on the rock with Tseki behind her. "Just a short rest. We will need to find food when we move. Phoebe and the babies need it." Murtagh sat behind Stella and Layla acting as their cushion.

I sat down beside Aidon and felt the tension slowly drain from my body. The cave might have been a temporary refuge, but it was enough to allow us to regroup. "Can you conjure anything? I know on the island you were cut off from your powers, but it might be worth a try now," Aidon pointed out.

Stella sat up abruptly and pointed at me. "Yes, you should. We know the average witch can't do that unless she has that special power, but there's a chance you can."

I sighed and straightened my spine. "Alright. Here goes

nothing." I held my hand out and poured all of my power into creating a double cheeseburger with extra pickles. There was a flicker, but nothing happened. Closing my eyes, I pictured exactly what I wanted and focused only on that. My lids snapped open when a weight settled into my palm. The smell hit me next. I started laughing as I held the burger high. "I did it!" I crowed triumphantly. I took a bite and groaned. It was freaking delicious.

Stella rubbed her hands together. "Can you conjure me a lobster roll? Or maybe a chicken pizza?"

I chuckled and handed Layla the cheeseburger. "I'm going to try for a platter of burgers or maybe tacos. No, wait, sub sandwiches."

Layla frowned at me. "Finishing this might help you conjure better."

I shook my head. "You go ahead. I'm going to try again." Concentrating my intent, I pictured a big platter filled with all of the food I'd just rattled off. My hands dropped when a heavy weight settled on them.

"That's a handy trick," Nana replied as she grabbed a sandwich. "No doubt it comes with a cost. But what I really want to know is how the magic works. Does it make all of this? Or take it from somewhere else?"

My stomach roiled when I considered her question. The bite of taco soured in my mouth. "Magic for personal gain is a big no-no." I set the food down.

Aidon shook his head. "Except this is not for personal gain. You are helping us survive and fight an evil witch. Nothing about that is for your benefit alone. Eat. You and the babies need the sustenance."

He was right. I would be of no use if I didn't get some food. I picked up the taco and finished it. Stella, Murtagh, and Tseki dug in as well. Nana grabbed the water bottle from Tseki's bag, reminding me we needed more. I conjured more while Stella asked, "Why do you think she's doing all of this? What drives someone to such evil?"

"Power," Nana answered around a mouthful. "Control. She wants to create an army of followers who will do her bidding without question. The more powerful the witches she transforms, the stronger her hold becomes."

"And the more chaos she can create, the easier it will be for her to take control," Aidon added. "She's not just gathering power. She's also spreading fear and destruction. We need to stop her before she can do any more damage."

The cavern fell silent as we ate and absorbed that little nugget of information. Something didn't sit right with me. Everything they'd said was true, but I couldn't shake the feeling that we were missing something. A crucial piece of the puzzle that would make everything clear.

"Phoebe," Stella said softly, breaking the silence. "What do we do now? If Lyra's out there, still transforming witches and she has my mom."

I took a deep breath and finished the sandwich I was eating. "First, we locate your mom and get her to safety. After that, we need to find Lyra and confront her. We stop her from creating any more tribreds or turning any other witches. But we have to be careful. She's dangerous and won't hesitate to use any means necessary to protect herself."

Nana nodded. Her eyes were steely with determination. "We've got to come at this sideways. Despite our many lessons, she hasn't learned yet that she's messed with the wrong family. We will find Stella's mom, but stopping Lyra's reign of terror once and for all is going to take all of us."

Stella cocked her head to the side as dawning crossed her face. "It helps to stop trying to figure out how we were going to find and stop her when we don't have anything with us. We will need everyone we know."

I held up a hand. "And some creative potions only Mom can cook up. She isn't going down easily."

Aidon shook his head. "She's far more powerful than any witch I've ever encountered. She shouldn't have been able to hurt me even temporarily, yet she did."

I ran a hand over his chest and grimaced when I felt him recoil. He was still healing. That fact drove the point home, and we all fell silent. Nana broke it a few seconds later when she said, "We aren't going to sit here and stew. We haven't looked at the scroll Stella found. That could hold a clue to something."

Stella pulled the parchment from Tseki's bag. It was aged and brittle. I held my breath as if merely breathing on it might make it crumble to dust. Aidon and I moved closer and looked over the ancient symbols on the outside. As she unrolled the scroll, the delicate sound of the parchment crackling echoed in the otherwise silent cavern. Her brow furrowed in concentration, and her fingers traced the intricate patterns of the symbols.

"I have no idea what any of this means," Stella said, her voice tinged with determination.

Aidon leaned in with me and studied the page. The symbols were unlike anything I had ever seen. They were a complex tapestry of swirling lines and geometric shapes that seemed to pulse with latent magic.

"These symbols," Nana began, "are from an ancient language. I recall seeing something about it during one of my research sessions with Nina. Thank the gods we've had to look up a lot of shit for you guys in the past. This has been lost to most modern witches. Let's see if I can remember what any of them mean." She paused as she moved around Stella and looked over her shoulder. "This seems to be a mix of old and new magic. Not entirely one or the other. Whoever wrote this was incredibly powerful."

"Can you understand any of it?" I asked, unable to contain my impatience.

Nana glanced at me. "It's a warning," she said slowly. "And a guide. At least, I think it is."

Aidon moved closer, his presence a steadying force. "A guide to what?" he asked, his voice low and steady.

"I'm hoping to Lyra's next move," Nana replied. "It's a map, but not a physical one. It's a map of her intentions, her plans. She's been activating these ancient wards along the East Coast, from Maine to North Carolina. Each symbol represents a location where she's been active, places she's marked with her Dark magic."

I felt a chill run down my spine. "She's working to something bigger. And I can see why she's been using others like Zaleria. They were convenient tools. Knowing this, can we use it to predict where she'll strike next?"

Nana nodded. "If we can decipher the rest of it. Something tells me it's not just about the locations. Knowing what I do about magic, we have to consider the timing and the nature of the power she's using. What doesn't seem to fit for me is this here," she pointed to a particularly intricate symbol. "It refers to a remote island. I'm betting it's the same island where she held you captive."

My mind raced as I tried to connect the dots. "That island... was remote. Unless it's in the Atlantic and would form a triangle with the East Coast, I can't see how it comes into play. What if she's using it as a base of operations?"

"It's possible," Aidon said, his eyes narrowing in thought. "We know she was using the place as a battery of sorts. That would fit with whatever big plan she's got cooking. I don't like not knowing what she's up to."

Stella continued to study the scroll. "We dealt her little battery a blow before we left. She can't use it to help her make tribreds anymore. Maybe she's not turning as many into powerful creatures under her control."

I shook my head. "I think her recent BS has been about finding another way. She has Mom's blood and is going to use it to her advantage."

Nana pursed her lips and cocked her head. "She already had a hold on the island once. She could be planning something there. That could be the location of her next move."

Aidon nodded. "Agreed. But we can't go in blind. We need to understand as much of this message as possible."

Nana nodded in agreement. "I'll keep working on it. There's still a lot I don't understand and won't until we get back home.

I smiled at Nana. "We will get there as soon as we have Rosemary. But every piece of information helps, so the more you can study it and try to recall, the better."

Nana continued to pore over the ancient scroll. "These aren't just warnings," Nana said, her voice tinged with realization. "They're riddles and clues. I bet each one points to a hidden location where she's got some hold on the power of the ley lines. That bitch has been leaving a trail. We just need to solve these riddles so we can deal her another blow. She's clearly scrambling after you escaped the island and interrupted her connection. It's why we were able to follow her portal."

Aidon and I exchanged glances. "What do the riddles say?" I crossed my fingers that she could interpret more.

Nana squinted at the scroll as her finger traced the delicate lines of one set of symbols. "I think this one says: 'In the place where shadows dance, and whispers hide seek the heart where secrets bide.' That is a reference to a specific location... maybe a place known for its darkness and hidden truths," she mused.

"The descriptions could be metaphorical," Aidon

suggested. "A place where darkness thrives, and secrets are kept... it might not be a physical location but rather a place of influence or power."

Stella nodded thoughtfully. "That would fit Lyra and the riddle."

Nana sighed and said, "The question is whether that helps us determine where we need to go next. Here's another one: 'Beneath the stars where water flows, find the gate that no one knows.' This one seems more literal. Could it reference an actual gate near a body of water?"

I frowned, trying to piece together the fragments. "Hmmm. We know Lyra's been active along the East Coast. She's been active at countless places with water. Including the house where she was holding Mom. But the stars... that suggests a place open to the night sky. It would have to be somewhere remote and away from city lights."

Aidon's brow furrowed in concentration. "There are places with mystical significance, often tied to natural elements."

"Maybe we can piece it together better if I interpret more," Nana said as she continued to decipher the riddles. She read for several silent seconds. "This one says: 'Where fire meets the storm, and earth gives way to air, the path will be laid bare.' That's four elements. Could it be a convergence point of elemental magic?"

Layla, who had been listening intently, finally spoke up. "Lyra's magic is complex, but it's not like yours. She doesn't know how to weave it with elemental forces. She will need a site that does it for her. Somewhere that will amplify her powers."

My gaze widened. "And there can't be that many places around like that."

Aidon's expression was grim. "You're right about that.

When we get cell service, we should have Mollie and Nina start looking for them."

Nana looked up from the scroll. "There's one more riddle here: 'On the isle where time stands still, the final truth lies waiting still.' That has to be the island where she held you guys. It's remote and fits the description perfectly."

The pieces were starting to come together, each clue pointing us toward a deeper understanding of Lyra's intentions. But the more we uncovered, the more questions we had. My mind was pulled into even more directions making it difficult to pick a direction and go with it. "We need to cross-reference these clues with what we know about her past activities," I said, my mind racing. "If we can pinpoint the exact locations, we might be able to stop her before she completes whatever she's planning."

Aidon's hand tightened around mine. "We'll get through this, Phoebe."

Nana's eyes held a steely resolve. "If we're rested enough, we should head out. The longer we linger, the more chance she has to do whatever she plans with Rosemary."

That got us all up and moving. We packed the water bottles into Tseki's bag. Layla and Murtagh stripped and shifted. At the cave opening, Tseki did the same. I stuffed the clothes into the bag and looped it over his large dragon head. Nana started walking and yelped when Tsekani picked her up on a wing. "Next time, warn a woman, or I will make you impotent. You could have given me a heart attack. I *am* an old lady. Don't let my good looks and spry step fool you. My heart isn't as strong as it used to be."

Tseki turned his triangular head and looked at her through one of his eyes, then snorted. Smoke left his nostril as she clambered onto the middle of his back. "You're riding like a queen," Stella told Nana.

She sniffed and lifted her chin as the rest of us stepped

out into the forest. We began the search for any of the clues from the scroll, a hint of Lyra's presence, or that of Rosemary. The sigils from the message were etched into our minds. Although I doubted we would see anything so straightforward, one could always hope.

We traveled through the forest in search of anything that resembled the clues. I hadn't forgotten about the wolves and kept an ear out for them. I guessed they'd retired for the night, given how close to dawn it seemed to be. We came across a clump of trees where shadows were dancing. The area beyond the cluster was obscured by fog. As we approached the hidden location, the ground beneath our feet vibrated with Dark magic.

Stella paused, her eyes scanning the surroundings. "Feel that? We're close to something."

Aidon's grip on my hand tightened. "We need to breach that barrier. Be on alert. We don't know what we'll face once we do."

Nana kicked Tseki's side and led the way. From the dragon's back, she started chanting and tracing symbols in the air with her fingers. Stella looked at me, and we joined her. She was unraveling the first of the enchantments. There was a faint shimmer as it started to dissipate under our assault. Time seemed to distort before the veil peeled away.

With the barrier gone, we moved forward cautiously. We made it past the fog, and the forest disappeared, leaving us with a difficult choice. "Which way do we go?" I asked as I looked over the options. A sense of foreboding overwhelmed me as we contemplated which way to go.

CHAPTER 7

*T*he scent of pine and damp earth surrounded us as we stood at the edge of the enchanted forest. The paths diverged before us. There were three distinct trails. When I tuned into my magical senses, each one promised to bring us closer to unraveling Lyra's nefarious plans and finding Rosemary.

"We should split up," Stella suggested. "We have to search them all."

"We should send a witch with someone else," Nana added. "I'll go with Tseki and take the path to our right."

I glanced at Aidon, feeling a mix of apprehension and resolve. He nodded in agreement. "We'll meet back here in a couple of hours," I said as I pulled out my cell phone and checked the signal. To my relief, I had one. "Stay safe and keep in touch." I waved the device at them.

Nana's eyes reflected the wisdom and strength of years. "Be careful but trust your instincts."

Stella's gaze was fierce. Her determination was a palpable force. "We'll find her, Phoebe. And we'll stop Lyra." Murtagh and Layla flanked Stella. They knew Aidon was going to go with me. I felt better knowing they had fierce protectors as well.

With a final nod, we turned and set off on our respective paths. Aidon and I headed east. Within a few minutes the forest closed in around us again. The canopy above was dense, allowing only slivers of moonlight to pierce through. The air was cool, crisp, and filled with the sounds of rustling leaves and distant bird calls. I wanted to be relieved that the wolves seemed to have lost our trail, but I couldn't relax.

As we walked, I couldn't shake the feeling of being watched. Opening my senses further, I noted that the forest was alive with magic. Energy pulsated around us. It was ancient and a touch on the malevolent side. It was almost as if the forest had been fighting Lyra's influence. The trees whispered secrets. Their branches swayed gently like they were trying to say something. Aidon was as alert as I was. Every rustle and movement heightened our awareness.

After a while, we came across a narrow path lined with wildflowers. The petals lifted off the flowers and floated gently in the air as if beckoning us to follow. Aidon and I shared a look. Both of us clearly thought the same thing. Following them would take us in the right direction. "I'm with you always," Aidon promised as he squeezed my hand.

"I love you," I told him simply as we took the path to a small clearing. It was bathed in the soft, golden light of dawn. In the center stood an ancient stone altar. We closed the distance and got a better look at the altar. It was covered in intricate carvings and runes.

We approached the altar cautiously. My heart was trying to pound out of my chest. The air around it was charged with magical energy. It made the runes glow faintly and felt on the dark end of the spectrum. I was about to reach for the altar when my phone vibrated. The screen lit up with Nana's name. Answering the call, I pressed it to my ear. "Phoebe, I've found something," Nana said excitedly. "A tree on this path is covered with markings similar to the ones in the scroll."

I smiled, feeling a renewed sense of hope. "Great job, Nana. Keep investigating. I've found an altar with runes that I think is significant."

Another call came in, and I added Stella to the conversation. "Hey, Stells. Nana found a tree with symbols, and I found an altar. You get anything?"

"I'm at a clearing with a circle of standing stones. There's a powerful magical presence here. It's got to be connected to Lyra's magic," she replied.

"We're getting closer. Stay vigilant," I told them. "We should regroup sooner than the two-hour mark."

"Agreed. We already have more to investigate," Nana interjected. "I'll head back after another half an hour." Stella and I promised to do the same and hung up.

With a deep breath, I turned my attention back to the altar. We needed to decipher the runes to uncover their meaning. The ancient language was complex and not familiar to me. I smiled at Aidon. "Do you know what this means?"

He pressed a kiss to my lips before returning his focus to the altar. He had thousands of years of knowledge and experience to draw from whereas I had just over four decades. Time passed in a blur as he worked. I conjured an ice cream cone and canteen so we had water. The babies had a sweet tooth and it was for the greater good that I feed it. At least that was how I reasoned it. I got cranky when my blood sugar dropped.

Aidon didn't notice as he was wholly absorbed in the task at hand. Finally, he paused and looked over at me. "This points to the riddles we discovered on the scroll. It's basically a similar version of it, except there is a little more detail here."

"Take pictures, and we can add it to what we know and anything the others find," I told him with a smile before we turned back towards the forest.

The trees loomed tall and ancient around us. I glanced up and admired the way their branches intertwined to form a natural cathedral. Shafts of sunlight pierced through the canopy, making it look almost like stained glass. We took the path back much faster than we had on the way in. We were already familiar with what was around us.

When we finally emerged from the forest, some of the tightness eased from around my chest. Nana, Tseki, Murtagh, Stella, and Layla were there waiting. Despite having talked to them, I was still worried something might have happened to them. "What did you find?" I asked, stepping into the clearing.

Nana spoke first, her voice steady. "The markings on the tree I found are definitely linked to the sigils in the message. They're protective runes. Whatever Lyra is hiding, she doesn't want anyone to find it easily."

Stella wrung her hands together. Worry had etched deep lines into her face. We would find her mother, I just hoped we weren't too late to save Rosemary from Lyra's vile machinations. "The standing stones are a focal point for magical energy. It felt like it might be part of the network Lyra is using to channel power."

I shared my findings about the altar and the runes, each piece of information slotting together like a puzzle. Aidon's head bobbed up and down as we all spoke. When I finished, he lifted a hand and said, "We're close. Let's go back to the standing stones. If it is connected like Stella believes, it might take us to Lyra. Circles like that are often primed for portals."

Stella's expression brightened. "Maybe we will find my mom." She was practically running down the path she had taken.

"At a minimum, it will get us one step closer," I promised her. My heart twinged when she shot me a sad look. I know she wanted to hear that we were going to find her mom, but I never lied to her, and I wasn't going to start now.

A trail of shimmering magical energy pulsed around us as we followed the path. The power weaved through the trees like a silvery thread. This time, I felt it pull me. It was a subtle but insistent tug that urged me onward. My heart pounded with anticipation, and a mixture of excitement and dread coursed through my veins. I wanted to rescue Rosemary. However, I wasn't ready to face Lyra. I was five months pregnant with triplets, and the thought terrified me. Yes, my babies had an innate ability to protect themselves, but was it enough against a being as evil as Lyra? I had my doubts.

Before long, the forest began to change. The trees grew taller and more ancient, their gnarled branches forming a dense canopy that blocked out the sunlight. The trail changed again. It narrowed and became lined with wildflowers. Instead of floating like the last ones I encountered, these petals glowed faintly in the dim light. Our steps became careful and measured.

We turned several corners and ended up in a small clearing. Sunlight bathed the center where a circle of ancient stones stood. Nana slid off of Tseki's back as we approached. I felt him shift as I examined the surfaces of what looked like Stone Henge. They were etched with intricate runes that glowed with a faint blue light. Magic hung heavy around us. It was like the altar. Not quite fully dark, but it definitely had a malevolent edge. Unlike what I had found, the energy there swirled around the stones like a living entity.

My heart hammered against my breastbone as I stepped in the middle. The runes weren't like what we had seen on the scroll. This wasn't Lyra's doing. The complex and mesmerizing patterns were older and powerful enough that she couldn't fully convert them to her control. I searched for why there was any of Lyra's power there. My fingers grazed the surface of one of the stones, and I felt something that had been obscured from sight. It was a symbol, and I was betting it was one of Lyra's.

I heard a rustling sound behind me while I was studying the runes. Alarmed, I swiveled around and had balls of witch fire ready to go. Aidon put his hand on my shoulder. "It's okay. We just felt the energy surge. What did you do?"

I gestured to the stones. "This is definitely a focal point for Lyra's magic. I came across one of her hidden symbols. The magic of the stones is too powerful for her to overcome entirely, but she has surely tried."

Aidon moved closer and examined the stones. "These are ancient sigils meant to amplify and channel magical energy. It's why these circles are primed for portal travel. I bet Lyra is trying to use this place to strengthen her powers since she lost the island."

Stella leaned forward and scrutinized the markings. "We need to get this magic going so we can find my mom."

Standing in the heart of the ancient stone circle, there was a tangible, electric energy surrounding us. It leaped out at us with her words. "Our goal hasn't changed," I promised her.

We went back to figuring this out. The weathered stones pulsed under the sunlight. Each rune vibrated with life and emitted its own faint glow. Initially, I thought they were all the same color, but now I could see they weren't. The mingling of ancient magic and Lyra's darker, malevolent power set my nerves on edge and had no doubt irrevocably changed the spot.

Stella moved closer to one of the stones, and her fingers gently traced the carved patterns. "Okay, this is so weird," she said. Her voice was a mixture of awe and apprehension.

"There are concealed symbols. This has to be the shadows, hidden messages riddle. Which ones do we need to feed power into to open the portal to my mom?"

I joined her, squinting at the runes. "I told you they were here," I murmured. "Lyra's magic is piggybacking on something older, something that was here long before she ever came but I couldn't tell you which ones were important to opening a portal." I almost told her that she shouldn't expect us to open anything, but I felt the hum of a portal. I'd used enough of them to recognize the energy. Layla and Murtagh both shifted to their human forms but didn't get dressed. I had to avert my gaze from the naked people. I loved my friends, but I was not as comfortable with nudity as they were.

Aidon thrust his hands on his hips as he scanned the entire circle. "We can activate the portal magic, but I will need to determine which ones to use in conjunction with the masked ones Lyra left," he informed us.

"How do we determine that?" I asked as I joined him in the middle.

Stella turned to face us, determination in her eyes. "Do we just trace the symbols and find Lyra's trail? Shouldn't it be her magic that will lead us to my mom?"

We all looked to Aidon. He shrugged his broad shoulders. "I've never done this before. I'm flying by the seat of my pants and acting on instinct."

I patted his chest and smiled up at him. "Awe, we're rubbing off on you. You're officially one of us now. Let's start poking things and see what happens."

Nana rolled her eyes. "Don't go that far. Look but don't touch... yet."

I saluted Nana and moved to examine the section closest to me. The others followed suit. I was most aware of Layla and Murtagh as they moved cautiously around the perimeter because I could see their naked bodies from the corner of my eye. "How do we know which runes might be important? They feel so different. Is there something in particular we need to search for?" Layla asked with a growl.

Murtagh nodded as his fingernails shifted into claws and back. "I don't like this place. It feels... wrong."

Aidon shifted uncomfortably. "I'm... not entirely sure," he admitted, rubbing the back of his neck. "The only thing that comes to mind to describe the sensation is that it should feel like traveling in a car with your head stuck out the window, you know? Like everything was rushing by too fast, and you can't catch your breath." He paused to gather his thoughts. "There should also be this... tugging feeling. As if you are being pulled toward something. Focus on the runes that seem to pull at you the most. It's not much to go on, but it's all I've got."

Layla inclined her head. "That's helpful. Magic is incredibly confusing."

Aidon chuckled. "You've got that right. Let me see if my power can highlight anything."

We watched Aidon do his thing. His wings unfurled from his back, and he shook them out before sending a wave of his power around the circle. The babies in my belly reacted and started kicking like crazy. "Aaaah!" I cried out as a vital organ was hit.

Aidon stopped, and everyone converged around me with concern on their faces. I shook my head and held out a hand. "Don't worry about me. Your energy supercharged them, and the soccer player in there decided my kidney made a good ball. I'm okay."

Aidon put his hand on my stomach and ran it over the bulge. "Don't hurt your mother. She should always be treated like a queen."

I laughed and smiled like a loon hearing him tell our

babies that. I loved him more than anything. With a quick kiss, he returned to what he was doing. Something caught his attention, and he traced one particularly intricate symbol. He jerked suddenly and let out a curse. I watched as a sharp bolt of energy shot through him. His eyes widened as the ground began to vibrate. "I think I activated something," he said as he brought me closer to his side.

The others closed the distance and surrounded us, at the same time, the stone circle started to glow more intensely. The runes lit up with an eerie, supernatural light. A swirling vortex of energy formed in the center of the circle. Its edges flickered with dark, ominous sparks. The feeling of being pulled was unmistakable. Aidon had activated a portal.

"That doesn't look very inviting," Murtagh muttered as his eyes remained fixed on the energy.

"We don't have much choice but to go through," I said, feeling more of the pull of the portal's energy. "Rosemary could be on the other side of that."

Tseki's protective stance signaled his readiness to defend us if needed. "I agree with Murtagh. This energy feels dangerous," he warned.

Layla stepped forward with her hands clenched into fists. "We came here to find Rosemary. We can't back down now."

Aidon tilted his head to the side. "What if it's a trap? What if Lyra is waiting for us?"

Stella nodded, and her eyes met each of ours in turn. "I can't ask you guys to go through with me. I would appreciate the help, but I understand if you don't want to."

Nana gave Stella a stern look and then graced the rest of us with it. "Standing here debating isn't going to find Rosemary. We've faced worse, and it won't get any better if we let fear stop us now. We're going as a family."

Her words struck a chord in me. "She's right. We have to move forward together. That's where our power lies."

Taking a deep breath, I stepped closer to the portal, feeling its dark energy wrap around me like cold tendrils. The sensation was unsettling and made icy dread flow down my spine. One by one, my friends joined me, their resolve unwavering. Murtagh reached for Tseki. "We've got your backs. Always."

Layla placed a reassuring hand on Stella's shoulder. "We'll find Rosemary. Never stop believing that." She must understand what I did. There was a chance we wouldn't come across her mother on the other side.

Tseki shifted into his dragon form and stood protectively over Nana. The energy from the portal swirled around us. My magic automatically reached for my loved ones and bound us together. Despite the malevolent aura, we were ready to face whatever lay ahead. We stepped up to the portal and braced ourselves for the unknown.

The darkness enveloped us, and a second later, the world shifted around me. My stomach lurched as I felt the ground vanish beneath my feet. The air grew colder and the energy more oppressive. The last thing I heard before everything went black was Nana's voice, laced with urgency. "Hold on to your butts, everyone!" Then, nothing.

*a*s we moved from one section of the forest to what felt like a hidden glade, we were immediately confronted by what appeared to be forest spirits. Their forms floated like will-o'-the-wisps only they were erratic and agitated. And their luminous, fiery eyes were fixed upon us. They exuded an aura of ancient power, wisdom, and simmering aggression that set my nerves on edge.

"Are those elementals?" Layla's voice cut through the tense silence. Her canine eyes narrowed as she assessed the creatures.

"Of a sort, yes. They're the spirit of this forest come to life," Aidon explained. He was so calm despite the unsettling presence around us.

"What is wrong with them?" I asked softly. My gaze flickered between the spirits and my companions. My heart started racing when I noted there was no way out of the glade. I could see the tips of what looked like a circle of standing stones, but they were obscured by trees and shrubs.

Nana's expression darkened with concern. "Lyra's taint is at work on this natural wonder," she muttered as she scanned the flickering forms with a mix of apprehension and determination.

"We should try to get through to them," Stella suggested, her voice carrying a hint of urgency.

"How?" I whispered, feeling overwhelmed by the charged atmosphere. "How do you communicate with entities so ancient and powerful?"

Before anyone could respond, Stella took a deep breath to steady herself before she said, "Great spirits of the forest," she began in a voice that projected confidence. "We come in peace and seek to understand the mysteries that lie within this sacred place."

The spirits exchanged glances, and their forms flickered with deliberation. One of them floated closer. "Why do you seek to enter this glade, mortal? What do you hope to find?" Its voice resonated in my mind rather than my ears. Based on the reactions of the others, they heard it in the same way.

Gathering my thoughts, I met the spirit's gaze squarely. "We are searching for captives who are being held by Lyra. She's a witch who uses Dark magic. She takes innocent beings and uses her power to twist them into creatures she controls," I explained, choosing my words carefully. "We believe she may be hiding nearby, hurting others to further her dark ambitions."

The spirits' forms flickered more intensely. "Lyra's influence stains these woods," another spirit chimed in. My heart ached when I heard its voice echo with a hint of sorrow and anger. "Why should we trust you to enter when so many have sought to exploit our power?"

"We understand your caution," Stella replied sincerely. "But we are not here to exploit. We want to find those she has taken. My mother is among them. But that's not all. We also want to restore the balance and purity in these woods."

I nodded in agreement and gestured around us. "If you

grant us passage and knowledge, we can work together to cleanse this place of her darkness."

The spirits murmured among themselves. It was an odd experience as their voices blended into a harmonious hum that resonated through the glade. Finally, the leading spirit spoke again. Its tone was thoughtful yet cautious. "Your words hold sincerity, mortals. We sense your intentions are true. Normally, we would test your resolve."

I shared a look with my loved ones and then held my breath. Of course, they wanted to test us. Life couldn't be that easy. Aidon's tension ramped mine up. Sometimes sharing a bond and knowing what he was feeling wasn't a good thing. The spirits began to part, creating a narrow path through the glade.

"Unfortunately, it is taking all of our energy to combat the Darkness that threatens our borders. Lyra damaged us fundamentally. Her influence has Tainted the very essence of our home," the leading spirit intoned. "But remember that we are guardians of this forest. We cannot do what we would usually but that does not mean we are helpless."

I wondered what Lyra had done to them and almost asked before catching myself. "Thank you," I said gratefully, bowing deeply. "We will not let you down."

Stella held up a hand. "Before we go, can you tell us where Lyra is located? We can remove her influence from your forest if we can find her."

The spirit sighed, its form flickering. "Lyra's corruption runs deep. She has twisted the natural magic of the forest, bending it to her dark will. Creatures that once lived in harmony now turn against each other. Trees wither and die, their life force drained to fuel her malevolent spells."

Stella's eyes widened with horror. "But why? What could she possibly gain from destroying such a beautiful, ancient place?"

Another spirit floated forward and added, "Power. Control. Lyra seeks to dominate all forms of magic, and the forest is rich with the ancient energies she craves. Her Blood experiments have unleashed unnatural phenomena. We've seen storms that rage without end, rivers that run dry, and plants that grow twisted and monstrous."

Aidon clenched his fists, his expression grim. "She's not just corrupting the forest. She's trying to break its very spirit. This isn't just about power. It's about destroying something that might stand in her way."

A surge of anger and determination swelled within me. "We can't let this continue. We have to stop her before she destroys everything."

The first spirit nodded, its eyes filled with a deep sadness. "It will not be easy. Lyra's magic is strong, and her infection has spread far. You must find the source of her power within the forest and sever it. Only then can balance here be restored."

Stella stepped forward, her resolve clear in her eyes. "We'll do whatever it takes. Tell us where to start." I squeezed her hand, trying to tell her we would not forget about her mother in the process.

The spirits exchanged glances. Their forms flickered as if they were communicating silently. Finally, the tall spirit spoke again. "We cannot locate her. She used Blood magic to hide herself from us. That is how she was able to attack us in the first place. But there was a place deep within the forest. We cannot say for sure if it is still there, but before she cut us off, we felt a nexus of power. We believe it is where Lyra has anchored her Dark magic. The last thing we felt were enchantments going up around it. You must be prepared for a great challenge."

Nana scowled and clenched her hands into fists. "That sounds like the evil witch's work. She thrives on destroying everything good. And she's beginning to really piss me off. She might have been at this longer, but we're smarter. We will make her pay for what she has done."

I grabbed Nana's hand and started down the now-open path in front of us before the spirits changed their minds. Ahead of us was the edge of the stone circle I had seen over the barrier created by the forest spirits. It was similar to the one we'd traveled from. The stones here were just as weathered yet were far more imposing. They were also arranged differently. At least, it seemed that way. I couldn't discern the pattern, given the plant barrier obscuring my view. There was also a different energy, quieter yet more profound than the corrupted grove we had left behind.

"They're protecting the stone circle," Aidon murmured, his voice filled with reverence. "This is why they didn't want to let us pass. I can feel their energy attached to the structure."

Stella stepped closer, her fingers tracing the intricate runes etched into the stones. "The magic feels... purer," she remarked softly.

Tseki shifted back to his human form so he could pass through the space between stones. "They've kept her from tarnishing the magic here completely," he observed before he shifted back into his dragon.

"Let's see if we can find Rosemary," I interjected. "Can one of you mark our journey? I want to be able to get back here later. This will probably be our best way home."

Layla inclined her head. "I would be more than happy to oblige." With that, she shifted into her wolf form and trotted beyond the stones and lifted her leg to pee on a tree.

I shook my head and muttered, "I sure hope that doesn't hurt the spirits further. The last thing we need is to make them an enemy."

Murtagh chuckled and shifted as Aidon patted my shoulder. "Animals are part of the forest. That won't even register with them. C'mon, we've got a dark nexus to find."

Stella nodded, her eyes shining with determination. "Once we find that nexus and destroy it. Lyra's reign of terror here ends. I just hope we locate my mom in the process."

Aidon conjured his sword this time before he was distracted by a battle. The black blade gleamed in the moonlight. "Let's move. We have a forest to save."

We ventured into the forest, and practically right away, an oppressive energy weighed us down. Each step felt like it took us closer to a looming danger. We had just left the grove behind when Nana suddenly halted. Her eyes widened as she scanned the surrounding trees.

"Nana, what's wrong?" I asked as a chill crept up my spine.

The ground beneath us trembled before she could answer. Trees shook, and the earth seemed to come alive. It split open with a low, rumbling growl. My breath caught in my throat when I felt the malevolent energy. Could a demon tear a hole in the veil and bypass the Hellmouths? I was about to ask Aidon when something moved.

I clung to him and watched a massive form begin to rise from the gaping fissure. That was no demon that I'd ever seen. Its body was composed of roots, stones, and clumps of earth. "It's a powerful earth elemental," Aidon murmured. He'd likely felt my curiosity through our bond as strongly as he did my fear.

The elemental's eyes glowed with an ancient, yet fierce intelligence. And it towered above us. "How do we deal with an elemental?" Nana asked as she stepped forward with a steely resolve in her eyes. "And is it with the forest spirits or Lyra?"

The creature opened its mouth and roared. The sound

was like boulders slamming together. The elemental's presence was overwhelming, and its massive limbs creaked as it lunged for us. Each step it took shook the ground, and its form shifted and solidified with a terrifying fluidity. Nana raised her hands and said, "I think we can safely assume it's on the Dark side." Her fingers traced intricate patterns in the air as she chanted. I couldn't hear what she said, and I had no idea which runes she was calling upon. The movements didn't give me enough details.

A soft, shimmering light began to emanate from Nana's finger. It grew brighter as she called upon her magic. "You may have been summoned by Lyra," she told the elemental, "but I will not let you stand in our way!" Her voice echoed with a power that matched the elemental's own.

This was not the Nana I had grown up baking cookies and watching crime shows with. She'd changed a lot since she developed her magic. But she was no less the kickass woman I loved with all my heart. She showed me how to own my power and wield it confidently like she had when she taught me how to apply makeup.

The creature raised a massive arm to strike. I moved to grab her, but Nana moved with grace and precision. Tseki was there to lift her on one of his wings. She created a shield of magical energy that absorbed the impact at the same time she slid into place on Tseki's back. The force of the blow sent shockwaves through the air, making Aidon, Stella and I stumble. Nana didn't twitch so much as a muscle. Her eyes didn't even leave the elemental.

"Go, Nana!" Stella called out. Her voice was filled with the pride I felt.

Nana responded with a fierce nod while her focus remained unbroken. She began to chant in a language other than Latin. While any language worked when a witch cast her spells, Latin was traditional. Most still used it. What mattered was intent. Nana's words resonated with the essence of the earth. I could feel it responding to her magic. Layla and Murtagh snarled and lunged for the Elemental's legs. The creature batted them away as if they were nothing more than flies. They got up on shaky feet and started back for the elemental but stopped when it hesitated. They joined us when its movements became slower and more deliberate. It was as if it were struggling against an unseen force.

"She's binding it," Aidon told us with wide eyes. "She's using its own power against it."

I didn't even know that was possible. I really needed to join Nana and Nina on the research ventures. Nana's chant grew louder, and the light around her intensified. The elemental let out another roar, and its form started to destabilize. Aidon picked me up and stepped to the side as chunks of earth and stone fell away. It was crumbling into dust at the same time the elemental fought to maintain its cohesion.

"You are a guardian of the earth," Nana informed it. There was no denying the authority in her voice. "You are not a weapon for destruction. Return to the ground from whence you came and be at peace."

The elemental fought Nana's command, and she renewed her efforts, this time standing between the ridges on Tsekani's back. They battled for several seconds. And then the elemental collapsed with a final, agonizing roar. Its body disintegrated into a pile of rubble and soil. The ground stopped shaking, and a profound silence fell over the forest. Nana lowered her hands, and the light around her faded. She looked down at us and took a deep, steadying breath.

"Nana, that was incredible," I said, rushing to Tseki's side. "Are you okay?" I blurted when she wavered. That would be a long fall from the back of Tseki's dragon.

Nana steadied herself and smiled at me, though her face was pale with exhaustion. "I'll be fine, Phoebe. It took a lot out of me. I wasn't sure the spell would work because I'd never done it, but Nina came across a passage somewhere that talked about elementals and their role in the magical world. I took a chance from that information and made up a spell."

Stella stepped forward, her expression a mix of awe and gratitude. "That was unreal, Nana. We would have been battered without you." Given how it had tossed two large wolves aside like gnats, she wasn't wrong.

Aidon smiled up at Nana. "You were amazing. Our babies are damn lucky to have a grandmother like you in their lives."

Nana beamed down at us and collapsed to her normal position between Tseki's wings. "We're in for some serious fights if that's what Lyra's sending against us."

CHAPTER 9

*M*y chest was heaving as I tried to catch my breath while also keeping up with Stella. "Do you feel your mom?" I called out.

Stella shook her head. "I wish. I'm not sure what it is."

We raced through the forest searching for the illusive dark nexus. And Stella seemed to be following some cryptic directions. She was plowing ahead of us like a woman on a mission. I was normally the fast walker in our friendship, but I had to hustle to keep up. She suddenly halted, making me run into her back. My little soccer player kicked her, and we both chuckled. Stella sobered quickly, and her eyes narrowed. She focused on a seemingly impenetrable wall of foliage. I followed her gaze, noticing the subtle shimmer in the air. It was a telltale sign of powerful magic.

"Do you see that?" Stella whispered, pointing ahead.

Aidon and I stepped closer. I squinted through the dense undergrowth. There was a barely visible curtain of shimmering magic. It appeared to be a veil concealing something significant. "Yes," I murmured. Energy radiated from it. "Do you think this is the entrance to the nexus?"

Stella lifted a shoulder. "I have no idea, but there is something there. Don't forget they said Lyra's enchantments were powerful."

Aidon examined the magical barrier. "You will have to dispel this magic first. It's intricate and might be dangerous."

I took a deep breath as anticipation built within me. "I expect nothing less. Alright, let's do this."

Stella, Nana, and I formed a small circle. Our hands barely touched as we channeled our energies. We focused on the shimmering curtain. "We need to get a feel for the complex web of enchantments," I told them.

Nana nodded and added, "Once you have that, focus your intent on unraveling the elements. There is definitely Dark magic underlying the thing, so I plan on dispelling each piece as I pull it apart. I don't want to hold any part of it longer than I have to."

Hearing the last bit of advice made me look at how I would handle these situations in the future. "How are you going to do that? Push it into the ground? Or the air?"

Nana tilted her head to the side. "Good question. If we send it in the direction of another of Lyra's spells, they could combine and make an even stronger one. I highly doubt she has buried her wards in the ground, so I'm going to take a chance and direct the energy there."

With that plan in place, I focused my mind. We practically murmured an incantation simultaneously. Our voices were steady and clear. I pushed each thread into the earth as I pulled it apart with my magic. The air around us vibrated with tension as we synchronized our efforts. The shimmering barrier flickered and resisted our combined assault. Sweat trickled down my forehead as I poured more energy into the spell and tried to untangle the threads completely. Half of it was buried in the ground and losing power while the other half clung on. An undignified grunt escaped my lips as I pushed more power into it.

"We're close," Stella encouraged. She sounded as strained as I felt. "Just a bit more."

We broke through with a final surge of effort. The shimmering curtain dissolved and revealed a narrow path that went deeper into the forest. A wave of relief and exhilaration washed over me. Stella sighed and said, "I wish that was the worst of it. Let's move quickly. We don't know what else Lyra has hidden in here."

The way was tight and winding, making us move single file. I was sandwiched between Layla in her wolf form and Aidon. The trail was flanked by ancient trees whose twisted roots seemed to reach out. "Do you think they're trying to warn us or hold us back?" I asked as I pointed to them.

"That's a toss-up," Stella said as she stuck her head around Aidon's side. "That dark energy is all around us, but I'm hoping the forest is still fighting against her."

As if it understood her comment, the leaves on the forest floor rippled when the ground cover fluttered. And strange, luminescent flowers began to glow. They pulsed and then dimmed entirely. Stella inched around Aidon and got up close to my back. "I'm not sure if we are going in the right direction. Shouldn't we have encountered more of Lyra's wards by now?"

A grimace crossed my face and I fought the urge to curse. "I was just thinking the same thing. I don't want to turn back before we explore more. We need to exhaust this lead before going home. We will find her. I know how hard it is to be patient when your mom is missing, but you have to try."

She nodded and we moved single file along the narrow forest path. I inhaled the scent of pine and flowers. It helped ease the feeling as the foliage pressed in on us from both sides. It was unnerving to be surrounded by a living wall of green that pulsed with hidden energy. The forest was alive with the sound of rustling leaves and distant bird calls. It was a symphony of nature that both soothed and unsettled me.

The sudden rustle in the underbrush to our right was our only warning. I barely had time to shout before creatures burst from the shadows. They were a grotesque blend of bear and hellhound. They had the massive, muscular bodies of bears, but their heads were elongated and lupine. They also had eyes that burned like coals and teeth that gleamed in the dim light. Their fur was matted and dark. And they moved with a terrifying, predatory grace.

"Aidon, are they demons you can banish?" I yelled in a voice tight with fear. I hoped we would have an easy solution to this one.

"No," he replied grimly, swinging his black sword to intercept one of the creatures. "They're something else."

The path was too narrow for an effective defense, which is how the creatures were able to drive us into the thick of the forest. The trees and shrubs made it almost impossible to fight. I backed up while keeping my eyes peeled for movement behind us.

Branches clawed at my clothes and face and the uneven ground threatened to trip me with every step. "Stella, now!" I called while raising my hands and summoning my magic. Beams of witch fire shot from my fingertips. I kept them narrow and aimed at the creatures coming after me. One stream struck one of the beasts and sent it reeling. Stella responded with her own spell. Raw power crackled through the air and slammed into another beast, sending it sprawling.

In their wolf forms, Layla and Murtagh darted through the underbrush. Their fangs flashed as they lunged at the creatures. Their agility and speed were incredible. They were able to strike blows that we couldn't. But even they struggled with the confined space.

Layla sank her teeth into one creature's leg. She dragged it into a prickly bush, but it shook her off with a roar. After freeing itself, it swiped at her with a massive paw. Murtagh leaped onto another, biting down on its neck. He nearly had it until the beast twisted and flung him aside. I had to douse my flames when they came too close to the trees. Burning down the forest would make enemies of the spirits we'd promised to help.

Aidon fought beside me. His black sword cut through the air with lethal precision. He parried a swipe from one of the creatures, then countered with a powerful slash that left a deep gash in its side. The creature howled in pain but kept coming, its eyes burning with rage. I threw a magical bomb at it, hoping to end what Aidon had started. I cringed and cast a spell to put the fire out that resulted from the flailing beast.

A cry from above got my attention. I was afraid it was more creatures, but it was Tseki and Nana. They circled but were unable to join the fight. The canopy was too dense, the trees too close together. I saw a flash of dragon flames through the branches, and my heart stopped. Cupping my hands around my mouth, I shouted, "Tseki, no! Don't burn the forest! We have to help the forest spirits, not destroy them!"

He roared in frustration but pulled back, his flames dying out. Meanwhile, the rest of us were being driven further into the woods. The creatures were relentless in their assault. My arms ached from casting spells, and I could see the strain on Stella's face as she fought beside me. Layla and Murtagh were both limping, and their fur was matted with blood. Aidon's sword was slick with the dark, tar-like blood of the creatures, and his breathing was heavy. This was not going well.

"Phoebe, we need a plan!" Aidon shouted, deflecting another blow.

I looked around, trying to find some way to turn the tide. My eyes fell on a particularly thick cluster of trees, and an idea formed. "Stella, we need to use our magic to bring those trees down." Her brow furrowed as she looked from me to the trees. "You want to smash them?"

A wicked smile spread across my face. "Absolutely, but make sure to keep the roots intact in your intent. We will put them back in place."

Together, we focused our magic on the trees. I nudged my spell to weave with hers the second she cast hers. It seemed as if the forest understood what we wanted and cooperated. Without much effort, the ground trembled, and then with a creaking groan, the trees began to fall. They crashed down, smashing a significant portion of the creatures.

"Now!" I yelled. "Attack while they're disoriented!"

Layla and Murtagh surged forward, their wolf forms became blurs of motion. They tore into the creatures with renewed ferocity. Their claws and fangs found vulnerable spots and tore beasts apart. Aidon and I pressed the attack from the other side. His sword and my spells worked in tandem to take the creatures down.

Slowly, the tide turned. One by one, the creatures fell, their bodies crumpling to the forest floor. The last of them let out a final, pitiful howl before collapsing. We stood in the aftermath, breathing heavily. The forest around us was eerily silent, the only sound the distant calls of birds.

Stella swirled a finger in front of her body and said, "We should put these back in the ground before we move on."

"Tseki has it," Nana called out as he swooped down and picked a tree up in his talons. He worked fast, setting them back where they'd been. I heard Nana chant something and felt the ground shift below us. The dirt was cementing them in place again.

I huffed out a breath and conjured an electrolyte drink

for each of us and a large bowl of water for the wolves. Aidon took a drink and wiped blood from his cheek. "We lost the path," he said wearily.

"We'll find our way," I replied. "We just have to keep moving."

"Preferably before more creatures attack," Stella added.

I hated leaving the creatures, but we had no choice. Burning them was out of the question. My nerves were strung taut as we traversed the dense forest. Thirty minutes later, we encountered a ward. I smirked at Stella. "Looks like we have encountered Lyra's protections."

"Next time, I need to keep my mouth shut," she grumped.

"I'll work the ward from up here," Nana called out.

I gave Nana a thumbs up and focused my intent on unraveling the ward and directing the energy into the ground beneath us. This ward was much harder to dismantle than the last one. Aidon held me up when my legs weakened. He also fed me power. I pushed some of that to Stella and Nana so they weren't burnt out during the process. It seemed to take forever before I felt the ward give up the ghost. We moved forward when the last of the dark energy was pushed into the ground.

A wave of energy washed over me and reached out to touch my soul. Next to me, Stella shivered. "The magic here is strong," she said in a voice barely above a whisper. "And it's far more Tainted. Be on guard."

Aidon nodded as he scanned the area with his sword gripped tightly in his hand. "Lyra's influence is everywhere. This has to be the nexus."

A chill ran down my spine as we ventured deeper into the woods. The energy that had initially washed over us now pulsed with a life of its own. The Dark magic there was a living entity. And aware of our presence. It made my power spring to the surface and crackle along my skin.

Here, the corruption was more evident. Vines twisted unnaturally and their leaves were blackened and brittle. The ground was littered with withered petals and the remnants of broken branches. At the center of a small clearing stood an ancient stone altar. It was nothing like the one I'd seen earlier. This was more like a pedestal. There were arcane symbols on it but I couldn't make any of them out. They were worn away, and in some sections, scratched out completely.

Stella approached the altar cautiously. Her fingers hovered over the runes. "These markings… they're a blend of old and Dark magic," she observed. "It feels like Lyra."

Aidon scowled as he crouched next to the stone. "The markings are glamoured. I can feel it."

I stepped closer, feeling the oppressive weight of the magic. It was making me sick to my stomach. "Can you decipher what she's done?" My hand went to my stomach as unease gnawed at me.

Tseki landed, and Nana joined us. Stella's brow furrowed in concentration. "We need to break through the glamour first."

Nana cracked her knuckles and then her neck. "This bitch is going down."

My chuckle turned into a gasp that made me choke as I felt Nana attack the glamour. Stella and I stood there gaping at each other for two seconds. Aidon and the others kept watch while we worked with Nana. The clearing pulsed in response. Energy stung me through the soles of my feet. Refusing to let that sway us, we redoubled our efforts. A few pain-filled seconds later, we broke through the glamour.

"I don't like this place," Aidon muttered. His eyes never ceased their vigilant scan. "The forest is alive, and it's angry."

"I know what you mean," I replied, keeping my voice low.

Nana pointed to the stone. "Lyra's used this altar to

amplify her control over this nexus. She's woven powerful enchantments into the very fabric of this piece."

Disgust filled me, and my upper lip curled. "Then we need to disrupt those enchantments"

Aidon nodded, his jaw set. "Let's do it. What do you guys need?"

I glanced around the clearing, my mind working quickly. "We'll need to sever the connections she's established here. Aidon, use your magic to weaken the vines and roots she's corrupted. Stella and Nana, I'll need your help to channel a counter-spell. We need to purify this place."

"Easy enough," Stella replied with a smile.

Layla, Murtagh, and Tsekani stood guard while the four of us went to work. Aidon's magic flared to life. His power surged through the ground as he targeted the twisted roots and vines. Nana, Stella, and I stood before the altar. Our hands joined as we channeled our combined magic into a spell of purification. An acrid smell burnt my nostrils and made my nausea even worse. I had to resist the assault on my stomach with every fiber of my being.

With the help of Nana and my best friend, I didn't falter. Our determination burned brighter than the darkness surrounding us. Slowly, the corrupted vines began to heal. Their destructive grip loosened. The oppressive atmosphere lifted slightly. And for the first time since entering the clearing, I didn't feel like I might hurl.

We continued pushing our cleanser out, and finally, the last of the corrupted magic dissipated. A soft glow emanated from the altar, and a hidden compartment slid open. There was a charm that was steeped in Dark magic sitting inside. A bubble spell left my lips automatically and surrounded the thing. Nana opened her purse and used telekinesis to lift it. "This belonged to Lyra. We might be able to use it to scry for her location."

"This is the first time we have something personal of hers. We might actually be able to find her," I replied.

Aidon stepped forward. "If anyone can do it, you can. Let's get out of here and regroup. We have work to do."

As we turned to leave the clearing, a creature emerged from the shadows. Its form was barely recognizable as a deer. Its eyes glowed with the same unnatural light as the bear thing. This, too, looked like it had mange. It let out a low, mournful sound before disappearing back into the twisted foliage.

"We can't leave without finding the source of this corruption," Stella interjected. "We promised the spirits we would, and that altar wasn't it."

Nodding, I pinched the bridge of my nose. "As much as I want to go, you're right."

"Look for anything that feels like decay," Aidon instructed. "Or a stronger version of what those creatures feel like."

We each took a different section of the clearing and surrounding forest. As I worked, the stench of decay became almost unbearable. The twisted flora seemed to close in around us as it returned. Stella was right. We hadn't discovered the source. It was all reverting to Lyra's dark nexus. It felt like the energy was trying to trap us within the nexus's malevolent embrace. This was not a place I wanted to be as pregnant as I was.

"Over here," Stella called out from somewhere in the woods to the west. We hurried to her side and found ourselves standing before a crystal monolith. Its surface was slick with fresh blood and dark, pulsating runes.

"Holy crap, you found it," I said. A shudder wracked my body. "And the babies don't like it." I bent over and tried to breathe through my mouth. "They really don't like it."

Aidon wrapped an arm around me. "Dismantle the thing. Now!" He told Stella and Nana.

Stella looked over at me. Panic flitted across her face, and she grabbed Nana. "We need to channel our magic together. Phoebe, if you can focus on purification. Aidon, use your power to weaken the Dark magic like you did on the altar. I will guide the spell. It's going to be harder this time."

We joined hands, forming a circle around the monolith. Layla leaned her lean frame against my legs while Murtagh pressed against Stella, and Tsekani pressed against Nana. I poured every ounce of my magic into purifying the monolith. I felt a trickle of it from Layla and then the others as well. Energy crackled around us as we began to chant. Our voices rose and fell in unison. The runes on the monolith glowed brighter, resisting our efforts. We persisted and kept funneling all the energy we could into the spell.

I closed my eyes, feeling the power of the Pleiades flow through me. A pure, cleansing light emanated from my core. It spread outward to combat the Dark magic that pulsed from the monolith. Aidon's energy intertwined with mine to create a steady, grounding force that bolstered our efforts. The babies even put some of their energy into the mix. Stella's voice rose in a powerful incantation. Her words wove through our magic and guided it with precision.

The runes on the monolith flared angrily, and the blood on its surface bubbled as if in protest. The ground beneath us trembled, making me stumble forward a step. Layla caught me before I hit the crystal. A low, ominous rumble echoed through the woods. Sweat dripped from my brow, and I could feel the strain in my muscles as I pushed harder. It wasn't easy to keep drawing on every ounce of power I had.

"Keep going!" Stella urged. "We're almost there!"

Aidon's grip on my hand tightened. His energy surged in a powerful wave that merged with ours. With that, the runes began to crack. Thin lines of light spread across the surface of the monolith like fractures in glass. With a final collective push, the runes shattered. It was a marked difference this time with the dark energy dissipating. The woods sighed in relief as the oppressive weight lifted from the air.

"We did it," I said, my voice trembling with exhaustion and triumph. "We broke the spell."

Stella nodded. Her face was flushed with exertion but lit with a fierce light. "We've dealt her a blow. But we need to stay vigilant. This is only the beginning."

Aidon squeezed my hand, and his eyes met mine with a look of regret. "We did good, but we're not done yet. We need to find Lyra and put an end to her plans."

CHAPTER 10

*N*avigating the corrupted nexus was like stepping into a nightmare. We had broken the hold Lyra had so her darkness was no longer poisoning the landscape, but it hadn't healed. And by the looks of it, those forest spirits would need to work overtime to make this place inhabitable in the next decade. Every corner of the once beautiful landscape had been twisted and diseased by Lyra's malevolent influence. The pungent odor of decay was making it hard to breathe, but the underlying evil was no longer there, making it worse.

We cautiously moved through trees that were gnarled and warped. Looking up, I noted it looked as if their branches were clawing at the sky like the skeletal hands of the damned. "Watch your step," Stella whispered as she pointed at a patch of ground that still squirmed with dark energy. "Looks like the magic is still cleaning shit up."

Aidon shook his head as he held his weapon at the ready. Every muscle in his body was taut with vigilance. "There was a lot of disease to cure. That'll take time to root out completely."

His words were ominous. Especially since I couldn't shake the feeling that we were being watched. The shadows shifted and moved around us. If Lyra had other creatures here, they had to be pissed about the change in the atmosphere. A wild animal was most dangerous when it was cornered. My mind had to be playing tricks on me because I kept catching glimpses of movement out of the corner of my eye. "Do you sense that?" I asked, keeping my voice low. "It feels like there is something out there."

Stella shot me a wary look. "Of course, Lyra has more out there. As Aidon said, we aren't done yet. We can't assume it's safe just because we destroyed her foothold here."

Nana scowled as she scanned our surroundings. "We know we have to keep our eyes peeled. But don't forget to look for Rosemary or any clues that might lead us to her. Once we have exhausted our search, we need to find the way out of here."

The reminder was a good one. I didn't think Rosemary was in the nexus, but we needed to continue looking. Thorny vines reached out to snag our clothes and skin as we scoured the area. My foot caught on a root, nearly making me face plant. I needed to pay attention to the uneven and treacherous ground. Aidon caught my arm and steadied me.

I smiled up at him gratefully. "Thanks, Yahweh." Love filled my heart when I looked at him. He had brought so much to my life. I never imagined having a partner like him. He supported me without question and was by my side through thick and thin. Not only when it suited him.

He gave me that smile of his that melted my panties every damn time. "Anytime, Queenie," he winked and then used his blade to hack away at the most obstructive vegetation, creating a narrow path for us to follow.

Loud cracking made my head snap around. It was our dragon making his way through the dense woods. Nana walked beside Tsekaní, who had taken his dragon form. His immense presence broke through the branches and other impediments. He could have taken his human form, but he was focusing on shielding Nana. It was the only reason I wasn't right next to her. Nana was far more capable than most twenty-year-olds, but there was no denying she was ninety and needed extra care.

A sudden rustling in the underbrush made us all freeze. That wasn't one of us. A creature emerged from the bushes. Its form was grotesquely twisted. I grimaced when I caught sight of the foxlike body with elongated, crooked limbs and eyes glowing with a sickly green light. My breath caught in my throat as it snarled and lunged towards me.

Instinct took over. I summoned my magic, channeling it into a shield that materialized just in time to intercept the creature's attack. The creature's teeth clacked against the barrier, each clash sending shivers down my spine with its eerie, unnatural sound. Equally unsettling was the sight of viscous drool dripping from its gaping maw. The latter was likely poison.

The force of the impact knocked me back. My feet slipped on the uneven forest floor until I landed hard on the ground. My hand instinctively moved to my womb, where my babies rested. Their protective energy flared to create a shimmering bubble around my torso. It was a split-second reflex that saved me from the creature's claws.

As I struggled to regain my footing, I realized we were surrounded. More of these twisted fox creatures emerged from the shadows. Their eerie green eyes fixed on us with predatory intent. Stella and Nana were already on the defensive, weaving spells and incantations to fend off the advancing creatures.

Murtagh and Layla, in their wolf forms, leaped into action. They bounded toward the nearest fox creatures with teeth bared and fur bristling. Their combined strength and agility gave us a crucial advantage as they engaged the creatures in fierce combat. They used their natural prowess to counter the creatures' unnatural agility.

Aidon joined the fray, his sword moving swiftly through the dense undergrowth. He didn't go far from me as he aimed at the creatures. I watched him swing at what seemed like random foxes. I tried to puzzle that out as I got to my feet. It hit me when their organized effort fractured. He was disrupting their coordinated attacks.

Tseki's dragon flames lit up a mutated fox momentarily as he unleashed bursts of fire to scatter them. I conjured water when a nearby tree caught fire. "No flames," I called out to him. Nana helped put the fire out before it engulfed the forest. Tseki hadn't gone very far from her side. Leaving them to it, I fought a creature coming at me. The forest echoed with the clash of magic and the snarls of predators locked in combat. Each of us fought with determination, driven by the urgency of our mission and the need to survive this onslaught in Lyra's twisted nexus.

Layla and Murtagh fought around us and nudged us until we formed a cohesive unit. Our movements were not synchronized in the least, but we still managed to push against the relentless tide of adversaries. With each creature that fell, more adrenaline dumped into my bloodstream. I was as jittery as I was when I downed an energy drink. Creatures began taking off when they saw we refused to give up. Survival instincts for the win.

When the last of the creatures still fighting us fell beneath Aidon's sword, the forest around us fell eerily silent. The scent of burnt foliage and the metallic tang of blood made my stomach roil. It didn't take much lately thanks to the pregnancy hormones. Aidon wrapped an arm around me. "Stay alert," he whispered.

Stella rolled her eyes. "We need to move quickly but carefully. There's no telling how many more of these things are out here."

"Lyra didn't create these beasts intentionally," Nana observed as we walked away from the fight. "My guess is that her magic called to the wildlife and twisted them when they got trapped in her nexus."

Tilting my head, I shot Nana a look. "I would agree. There's no telling what we will encounter."

We pressed on, but the mutated creatures were relentless. They seemed drawn to us. We encountered the warped foxes, deer, and even malformed coyotes. All of them had twisted forms, and they emerged from every dark corner. Aidon's sword dripped with blood, leaving a macabre trail. One lunged at Stella, but she was quick, a burst of magic sending it sprawling back into the shadows.

"They're everywhere!" I shouted, dodging a swipe from a coyote creature. As I spun away, I caught sight of Nana. Everything froze for a minute. Nana was fighting valiantly. Her spells were precise and powerful. But with Tsekaní focused on protecting her, his movements were restricted. He bellowed, flames licking the air around him. I could feel his frustration and how much it took him to hold his dragon fire back. It was effective to a certain degree in keeping the creatures at bay. However, Tseki was still unable to go on the offensive.

We were all exhausted and dripping with sweat as we continued through the woods. Nana climbed onto Tseki's back just in time. The creatures seemed to grow bolder and their attacks more frenzied. "I think they're afraid of what's going on," I mumbled as I fought a mutated bear. The way they fought screamed of being driven by their fear of the magic doing things to them they couldn't control. It likely reminded them of what happened before.

Aidon waved us forward. "There's a break. Hurry and get out of this area before they return." We took the stairs, hoping to escape.

He didn't have to tell us twice. Layla and Murtagh led the foray with Tseki and Nana right behind. Stella and I stuck close to one another until she veered to our right. I looked back at Aidon, who shook his head and started after her. I reached her first. "What is it?" I panted.

"I'm not sure. I saw something sparkle and was hoping it was something like that necklace." Stella was crouched down, pulling at the vines with her hands. As the roots gave way, they revealed a small, hidden entrance. It had barely been visible amidst the natural camouflage.

"Where do you think it goes?" Aidon asked, peering into the darkness. Layla, Murtagh, Tseki, and Nana joined us.

"I'm hoping it's my mom," Stella replied, brushing dirt from her hands. "Regardless, there's something down there. I can feel it."

"You guys should shift. We need to check this out to make sure Rosemary isn't here," I told the shifters behind me. Aidon helped Nana down from Tseki's back. While they turned into their human forms and dressed, Stella and I cleared the rest of the roots and branches from the opening.

We carefully made our way down the narrow passage, determined to uncover whatever lay hidden. The air grew cooler as we descended, and the light from above gradually faded into a dim glow. At the bottom, we emerged into a hidden chamber. Unable to see much, I conjured a ball of light and floated it in front of us.

The sight that greeted us was breathtaking. The walls were adorned with ancient artifacts and arcane symbols. The power coming off of them was a vibration against my skin. It was as if we had stepped into a forgotten sanctuary. It would be easy to think this was a place time forgot. When you dug a little deeper, you discovered the thrum of Lyra's energy beneath it all.

Stella moved forward, her fingers tracing the intricate carvings all around us. "Should we ask Nylah to come and recover these? It's clear Lyra is using them, but is this something Nylah can contain? I'd hate to infect her home, or wherever she stores the relics she guards."

Aidon approached a pedestal in the center of the chamber, where a glowing crystal hovered. It was pulsating with a soft, charcoal light. "This place is filled with magic." That was nothing we didn't all know. "Lyra must have used this chamber for something important."

I wandered to a corner where a collection of scrolls lay, their edges frayed with age. Carefully, I picked one up, unrolling it to reveal delicate script and intricate diagrams. "Do you think these hold some of Lyra's secrets?" My heart raced with the implications.

Nana examined an ornate mirror hanging on the wall. "This mirror," she pointed out, "it's not just a decoration. It's a scrying tool. She uses it to see things far beyond this chamber."

Stella's eyes widened. "I bet she watches us with it. We need to understand everything in this room. These artifacts, these symbols. They could give us the edge we need to defeat Lyra."

I pulled out my cell, took several pictures, and texted them to Nylah before realizing I had no signal. I would send them to her later. Looking at Aidon, I asked, "Do you think we can break that mirror safely? I don't want to leave her a tool like that, and we can't take it with us."

Nana pointed a finger at me. "Good thinking. I doubt we will ever be able to find our way back here. It's been such a convoluted journey."

Aidon winced and shook his head, then pointed at Nana

and me. "You two try unraveling the magic on it first. Destroying relics is a difficult task that often backfires on the magic wielder."

Tseki narrowed his eyes. "What would my dragon fire do to it?"

"That might actually work," Aidon said. "I don't want to try it until we see if they can at least remove Lyra's magic. She's contaminated everything in here and that has changed the magic of these artifacts. As for the scrolls, I highly doubt they have anything directly to do with her. It's far more likely magical spells, prophecies, or other vital information."

"Given all of that, we need to document everything and get pics of the papers while they do their magic on the mirror," Stella replied. "That way, we know what Lyra has at her disposal."

They spread out and began taking pictures of everything. Nana and I stood in front of the mirror. "We should start by assessing the power in this," I suggested. "It will help us decide how to remove her spells."

Nana inclined her head and got right to work. As our magic probed the mirror, the chamber seemed to come alive with a quiet hum of energy. It was distracting until I shut it out. Nana snapped me out of my revere when she said, "A purification spell combined with some elements to boost our power should do it."

"What did you have in mind?" I asked. There was nothing too complex about Lyra's enchantment over the mirror. I had been thinking about the purification spell but hadn't considered anything else.

Nana set her purse on a shelf and opened it. "We need to use some moon water, powdered silver dust to reflect and purify, sprigs of vervain for spiritual cleansing, and a crystal prism to refract and disperse her dark energies."

I smiled at her and took two vials from her as she handed them to me. "Brilliant. What about this for an incantation?"

"By the light of Luna's gaze,
We cleanse this mirror's darkened maze.
Reflecting shadows, now be gone,
Let purity reign, from dusk till dawn."

"Thank the gods it's not in Latin. Saying so much would take away from my intent," Nana griped. That was precisely why I hadn't translated it after I'd thought of the elements that would help hone and direct our energy.

Nana and I set things up for us to cast the spell. First, Nana had us mix the moon water with powdered silver dust. We didn't have a small bowl so I cupped my hands together for her to use. After mixing that, she arranged the sprigs of vervain around the enchanted mirror. Nana was holding the crystal prism and I had the silver mixture as we stood in front of the artifact.

"Now we close our eyes and focus on channeling our magic," Nana instructed. I'd already started that, but I liked that she was taking charge. She had my entire life until magic fell into our laps. It was comforting to have things going back to normal, even if I was more powerful than Nana. It felt right to have her teaching me.

My eyes flew open when I felt the sharp edge of a crystal dip into the moon water-silver mixture. She traced a clock-wise circle in the air in front of the mirror while I visualized the mirror's surface shimmering with a faint, purifying light. She inclined her head, and we chanted the incantation. I visualized the dark enchantment unraveling like wisps of shadow dissipating in sunlight. We kept it up until the mirror's surface was clear and pure.

Beaming at Nana, I pulled her into a hug. "We did it!"

The others came over and joined us. Tseki extended a hand to the mirror. "Do you think it's safe now?"

Aidon bent close and scrutinized the mirror. "I think so, but we should all back up. Just in case."

As a unit, we moved toward the only archway leading out. We needed to keep looking around in case Rosemary was there, so we didn't head for the stairs. Despite knowing it was coming, I still jumped when Tsekani let out a stream of fire and directed it to the mirror. My hip bumped into the shelf, and something fell to the floor. I bent to pick it up while watching the crackle of magic flow over the reflective surface as the heat began melting it.

"Holy shit, it's working," Layla whispered as blobs of the glass dripped to the ground. The gilt frame followed suit.

I handed the book I'd picked up to Stella and took a step toward what now looked like a Salvador Dali painting rather than a mirror. "What the hell is this?" Stella asked.

That got everyone's attention. She was holding a small, leather-bound book like a journal in her hand. Its cover was worn with age. The leather was cracked, and the faint imprint of an intricate symbol was visible on the front. "That's Lyra's mark," Nana observed. I recognized it from the house where we'd rescued Mom.

"This looks important," Aidon remarked, his eyes fixed on the journal.

Stella nodded, carefully opening it to the first page. The handwriting inside was precise and elegant. However, there was an unsettling quality to it, as though each word was a thread in a web of darkness.

"This isn't Lyra's journal," Stella pointed out. "But I would bet it belongs to one of her minions. We might still be able to get a glimpse into her twisted mind from it."

Tsekani held up a hand and then turned to finish off the mirror. Without the Dark magic, the thing melted into a puddle on the ground. It still had power, but she couldn't use it to spy on anyone. And that's all we could accomplish at the moment.

With that done, we gathered around as Stella began to read aloud. The journal entries detailed the witch's role in Lyra's plans. She described how Lyra intended to harness the power of the kidnapped witches, transforming their magic into a source of unimaginable strength for herself while also turning them into creatures she could control.

"She's been at this for years," she growled. A chill ran down my spine as Stella continued to read. The journal spoke of rituals and enchantments, each more horrifying than the last. The witch's words revealed a mind consumed by darkness and driven by a relentless hunger for power. None of this told us much. It was horrific but not surprising.

"Listen to this," Stella said, her eyes wide with horror. "'The witches Lyra has taken will serve as the foundation of her new order. Their magic will fuel Lyra's ascension, and she will reshape the world in her image, giving her loyal followers immortality and power.'"

Aidon clenched his fists as anger flashed in his eyes. "We have to stop her. She's a threat to everyone. She won't hesitate to subjugate the mundies if given the chance."

Nana sighed and said, "This journal confirms what we feared. Lyra's ambitions know no bounds. Too bad it doesn't detail where we can find her."

As Stella continued to turn the pages, we learned more about Lyra's methods. Whoever this was had been around a while and was still with Lyra because she documented how Lyra used Mom's blood to create tribreds and used their power to fuel her evil plans. Each entry was a chilling reminder of the depths of her malevolence.

Hearing all of this reaffirmed my resolve. "We have to find the kidnapped witches," I snarled in disgust. "We can't let her use them like this."

Aidon placed a hand on my shoulder. "We'll find them, Phoebe. We'll stop her."

Stella closed the journal. "I'm not sure if this will be the key to defeating her. But it talks about her weaknesses and fears. In the least, we can use the information to our advantage."

Nana turned and waved her hand. "We'd better continue. We can look through that later."

Stella tucked the journal safely into her bag when the air in the chamber grew colder. An eerie silence settled around us. It was broken only by the sound of our breathing. There was a shimmer in the air, and a witch materialized in the middle of the room. Her eyes burned with a malevolent fire, and her movements were fluid and predatory. She was one of Lyra's Tainted witches. There was no doubt she'd been corrupted by dark forces.

"Stella, watch out!" I shouted when the witch lunged for my best friend. My heart pounded in my chest.

The witch's lips curled into a sinister smile as she stepped forward. "You think you can just walk away with that journal?" she hissed in a voice dripping with malice. "I will have your head for your audacity."

Stella drew herself up and glared at the woman. "We're not afraid of you," she sneered. "And we're taking this journal."

The Tainted witch's hands crackled with dark energy. Aidon and I moved to flank Stella, ready to defend her. The chamber began to pulse with the witch's malevolent magic.

Aidon swung his sword and kept his eyes fixed on the witch. I created a protective barrier around us. The witch laughed then. It was a cold, cruel sound that echoed off the stone walls. "You think a simple barrier will stop me? Lyra's power flows through me. I am unstoppable."

"Well, isn't that precious? Too bad your 'unstoppable' attitude doesn't come with a user manual," Nana quipped with a laugh.

With a flick of her wrist, the witch shattered the barrier. Whatever she did sent shards of energy flying in all directions. Aidon staggered but quickly regained his footing. I reached for Nana and Stella, but the Tainted witch didn't give us a chance to fire back. She launched another attack, dark tendrils of magic snaking towards us. Stella countered with a blast of pure energy, but the witch absorbed it. Somehow her power grew stronger from it.

"Your magic is nothing compared to mine," the witch taunted, advancing on us. I was beginning to wonder if maybe she was right.

"We need to outsmart her," Nana said. "Phoebe, Aidon, keep her distracted. Stella and I will find a way to neutralize her."

Aidon nodded, stepping forward to engage the witch. "You heard her, Phoebe. Let's buy them some time."

I took a deep breath, focusing on the Tainted witch. "You won't get that journal," I declared as I channeled my magic into a bright, blinding light that filled the chamber.

The witch recoiled, shielding her eyes. "You'll pay for that," she hissed in a voice full of venom.

Aidon and I continued to barrage her. I tossed magical bombs at her to keep her attention on us. I couldn't pay attention to what Nana and Stella were doing. I felt them weaving magic together and heard when they whispered a complex incantation.

"I can feel her weakness," Stella whispered. "We just need a little more time."

"You've got it," I told them and threw a magical spear at the witch. She caught it and hurled it back. My magic wouldn't hurt anyone I loved and it did nothing when it hit

Layla in the shoulder. She, Tseki, and Murtagh were itching to shift and attack but they would be at the witch's mercy.

Nana grunted something that made the Tainted witch's eyes go hard. Her attacks became more erratic as her control slipped. "I'll destroy you all!" she screamed. Her voice echoed with madness.

"Now, Stella!" Nana commanded. They shouted an incantation and then unleashed a wave of energy that enveloped the witch. The Dark magic surrounding her dissipated. She fell to her knees and her eyes lost their malevolent gleam.

"She's not so full of it now," Stella said, her voice filled with relief.

The witch looked up at us with an expression of pain and confusion. "What... what have you done?" she murmured.

"We freed you from Lyra's control," Nana replied gently. "You don't have to serve her anymore. And you are no longer fueled by her artifacts or power."

The witch collapsed and started bawling. Her devastation was clear and I didn't feel bad at all. She was part of killing and mutating people and environments to fit her leader's twisted need for power. She was lucky to be alive.

"Let's get out of here," Stella said. "We have to find my mom."

We left the chamber as a group and Aidon blocked the archway with his power so the witch couldn't follow. Lyra's reach was long and her corruption deep. We might be in over our heads this time. The gods only knew what else Lyra had down there.

CHAPTER 11

My nerves were jumpy and I was convinced the journal was acting as a beacon for any of Lyra's other Tainted witches. This tunnel system was a major site for Lyra. The forest spirits were right when they said she put up some powerful protections. She would never leave this unprotected.

We cautiously ventured deeper into the labyrinth in a single file line. There was an undeniable tension lingering among us. It was more than a residue from our previous encounters with Lyra's dark forces. It was the weight of what was at stake. If we failed, this wasn't just about Stella's mom. It was about the survival of life as we knew it.

Stella took a step forward at the same time my eyes narrowed on what I thought were ancient symbols etched into the stone floor. What was that? And what did they do? Alarm bells went off in my head and I reached for Stella to stop her but I was too late. Suddenly, a soft click echoed through the chamber. Stella lifted her foot and looked down at the button she'd pressed accidentally.

Before any of us could react, a shimmering barrier sprang

to life around her. It went from wall to wall and floor to ceiling. Her expression twisted with fear as it isolated her from the rest of us. Nana and I pounded on the shimmering film and called out to her. "Stella!" Our voices echoed in the small chamber.

On the wrong side of the blockade, a sinister laugh echoed before a woman appeared a few feet from Stella who had backed up until she was pressed against the shield. My magical feelers activated instinctually out of worry for Stella. Things had just gone from bad to worse as Stella was now face to face with another of Lyra's Tainted witches. I couldn't get a feel for where the bubble was anchored but there was no mistaking the energy from the new threat. The witch's eyes gleamed with a sinister light as she looked all around us.

"Stella!" I called out renewing my effort to punch my way through the barrier. It remained solid and unyielding. Like everything else in Lyra's nexus, it also shimmered with dark energy. Nana immediately began examining the spell with her signature focused intensity. Before I could do the same, Stella glanced back at us. "I'll handle her," she called out. Her voice was steady despite the dire situation. "Just find a way to get me out of here."

The Tainted witch let out a low, mocking laugh. "You're all alone now, little girl. Your friends can't save you this time."

Stella didn't flinch. "I don't need saving," she retorted. Her fingers moved at her sides, and I felt her power building right in front of me as she prepared to cast a spell. The witch's grin faltered as Stella's magic flared to life. My best friend's energy was a radiant light against the barrier.

Nana slammed her elbow into my side without stopping her fingers from tracing the lines of the barrier. "Snap out of it, Phoebe. We need to dismantle this carefully and fast. It's a containment ward that is designed to weaken its target. Find the damn anchors."

I nodded and turned my focus to my surroundings. I followed the edges of the ward. There were dark runes that glowed faintly along the edge of the barrier. The malevolent energy that pulsated through it matched Lyra's twisted power. "I found them," I told Nana. "They're Lyra's so they're powerful. And I get the sense that they connect to something else."

I examined it closer, looking at the threads of magic. A knot formed in my gut when I noticed the full scope of the thing. Swallowing the bile that burned the back of my throat, I grabbed Nana's hand. "Disrupting the ward in the wrong way will likely harm Stella."

Nana gaped at me. "Of course, it will. No pressure though, right? Lyra is like an open book so this will be easy."

I squeezed her hand and went back to examining the runes. "Find the end of the threads. Destroy the one that pulses fastest first. The others should fall after."

Nana nodded while on the other side of the barrier, Stella and the witch clashed relentlessly. I threw my arm up to protect against the power that came right at me. The ward stopped any from hitting me as their magic erupted in all directions. Stella's spells would have slayed ten elephants, but the witch's attacks were wild and brutal. My heart hammered as I watched Stella hold her ground. I turned my attention back to the task at hand so I didn't see the strain she had to be experiencing.

"Stella, you can do this!" Aidon's voice echoed from behind me. I was glad he was acting as her cheerleader. I couldn't split my focus.

Layla growled a sound of pure frustration. "We need to find a way inside! She can't keep this up forever."

Nana glanced at me sharply. "Focus on that rune, Phoebe. I've got the first one."

I nodded, channeling my magic into the rune Nana indicated. I started by identifying the threads that made up the power in the symbol. When I tried to pull on the end that was strongest, it resisted. Deciding to use tweezers instead of pliers, I took a more delicate approach. When I had a hold of the end, I cast a spell that would worm its way up and into the heart of the rune. The barrier trembled under our combined assault.

Stella dodged a particularly vicious attack and her counterspell sent the witch stumbling backward. "You've got her scrambling, Stella!" I shouted, hoping to bolster her spirits. "Just a bit longer!"

Stella's attention remained fixed solely on the witch before her. She twisted her wrist, sending a bolt of energy directly at the witch's chest. Oh, damn that looked like it hurt. The witch snarled and her Dark magic flared in response. It was a brutal, chaotic dance of light and darkness. And unfortunately, I could see Stella's strength beginning to wane.

Nana's eyes lit up and she gestured to the ground. "There! Those secondary runes are reinforcing the main spell. We need to disable them simultaneously."

Aidon and Layla sprang into action, following Nana's instructions to locate the secondary runes. Aidon attacked with his power while Layla went the old-fashioned route and tried to claw furrows in the symbols to disrupt the power. As we all worked simultaneously, the barrier weakened and its pulse grew erratic.

When she felt that, the witch unleashed a desperate attack. Because she's a badass, Stella met it head-on. Her magic blazed with a blinding light that lashed out at the

Tainted witch. The two forces collided with a thunderous crack and for a moment, everything was still.

The rest of us didn't stop working and we managed to dismantle all of the runes. The barrier shattered, the malevolent energy of it dissipated into the air, and Stella was still fighting. Seeing her unhurt was a huge relief.

"Now's your chance!" I shouted, my voice barely audible over the cacophony of battle. "Take her down, Stella!"

Stella's eyes blazed with renewed determination. She drew on the energy we had unleashed. Her next spell flared to life with a force I had never seen from her before. It blew my hair back and dried out my eyes. Nana and I were rushing forward to help Stella. She moved with her usual grace and agility. She was in her element and ready to kick ass. With quick thinking and strategic maneuvering, Stella launched a counterattack before Nana and I managed to toss so much as a magical bomb.

Blinding beams of light shot from her hands, slicing through the air toward the Tainted witch. They looked like lasers that would cut her in half. I held my breath and prepared my spells to launch. Stella's spells cut through the witch's defenses like a hot knife through butter. The clash illuminated the chamber in brilliant flashes of magic. I lobbed the explosive at the witch. A second later Nana followed suit.

The Tainted witch's eyes widened in shock as her Dark magic faltered under our onslaught. She tried to retaliate by summoning shadowy tendrils. They made me falter and drop my next bomb to the ground. Before it could blow up in our faces, I kicked it toward the dark witch. It was a newbie move, but you would have done it too if you'd seen the way they writhed and snapped at us like snakes. These tendrils crackled with Lyra's vile energy. That in itself was terrifying. Even more so when they lashed out and sought to ensnare and crush us. Stella dodged and deflected them and made it look easy. Her movements were fueled by a worry for her mother and the driving need to save her from Lyra's torture.

I finally made it to Stella's side, along with Aidon and Nana. The tight space made it difficult for us all to converge on the witch and kept Layla, Tseki, and Murtagh behind us. We had to maneuver carefully to avoid obstructing each other's attacks. Aidon summoned the dark flames of the Underworld, sending them roaring toward the witch. Nana called forth binding spells that sought to entangle the witch and limit her movements. While they worked their magic, I focused on disrupting the witch's spells. I channeled my energy to counteract her Dark magic.

The witch's eyes burned with rage and desperation as she retaliated. She conjured a storm of black, crackling energy that lashed out at us. It carried enough power to force us to scatter. The air buzzed with the sheer force of her magic, making it hard to breathe. I threw up a protective shield just in time to deflect a bolt aimed at my chest. The impact reverberated through my bones. Even my babies were jolted awake.

Stella was pissed off this witch was part of imprisoning her mom and she funneled that anger into her magic. It became a whirlwind of light and power. She moved with fluid grace. Each of her movements were precise and calculated. Her spells struck the witch again and again. I added mine and whooped when they weakened her further.

The Tainted witch staggered under the assault and her defenses crumbled. Suddenly, a tendril of Dark magic broke through our defenses and wrapped around Nana's ankle. I gasped when it pulled her to the ground. Aidon reacted quickly and sliced through the tendril with his black blade. "Nana, are you okay?" he shouted. He bent and scooped her up. I continued throwing attack spells at the Tainted witch while keeping an eye on them as well.

"I'm fine," Nana replied though her voice was strained. She pushed on his chest, trying to get him to let her down. "Keep the pressure on her!"

Stella and I nodded. "We are," I promised her. I clasped Stella's hand and twined my power with hers. Our next incantations weren't identical, but they unleashed a torrent of magic that engulfed the witch. The chamber was filled with the crackle of energy and the air vibrated with the force of the spell.

The witch screamed and it was a sound of pure agony. We continued funneling power into our spells and focused on it consuming her. It tore apart her malicious energy, leaving her powerless. When the spells faded, the Tainted witch was gone.

Stella's chest heaved with exhaustion, but her eyes were alight with triumph. Aidon and I rushed to her side, relief washing over us. "We did it," I whispered, the words barely audible as I tried to catch my breath.

But even as we began to regroup, the ground beneath us started to tremble. A low, ominous rumble echoed through the chamber. This fight was far from over. Something deadlier and more powerful was stirring in the depths of the tunnels and had likely been drawn by the clash of magic.

CHAPTER 12

"*Y*ou have no idea what is going on," taunted a scratchy voice. "You're blinded by your obsession and too single-minded to see the truth."

My eyes darted around the room we'd just entered for who had just spoken. Of course, they were invisible. It fit with the elaborate underground tunnel system Lyra had set up. I had no idea where we were in the world, but I was beginning to think it was close to the coast. At least that's what the faint salty-briny smell of the sea made me think.

"Who said that?" I called out with a challenge. "Show yourself. Or are you a coward?"

The chamber we stood in was vast, its ceiling arching high above with stalactites that glistened like jagged teeth. The walls were lined with intricate carvings and ancient runes. They pulsed faintly with residual magic but I couldn't get a good read on them. I was too distracted by the latest of Lyra's minions to confront us.

Aidon stepped forward, his eyes narrowing as he scanned the shadows. "There's something off about this," he murmured, more to himself than to the rest of us. "I can sense a siren's presence, but her voice lacks the alluring quality. Be careful."

A flicker of movement caught my eye, and a figure emerged from the darkness. She was tall and slender, her form shrouded in a veil of evil energy that seemed to writhe and twist around her. Her eyes gleamed with a malevolent light, and a smirk played on her lips as she stepped closer. "You're far more observant than anticipated. No matter. My magical side is far more powerful than you can imagine," she sneered, her voice carrying an edge that sent chills down my spine.

Her dark hair flowed like liquid night and framed a face that was both beautiful and terrifying. It was her eyes that got me. They were an unsettling shade of green and bore into us with an intensity that made my skin crawl. She wore a gown of deep crimson. The fabric of it shimmered as if we were looking at it beneath the water.

Nana snorted and pinned the woman with a look. "Actually, you're ignorant. You've picked the wrong side by following Lyra. And she didn't prepare you for what you're up against."

"You really think you can stand against me?" she growled in a voice dripping with contempt. "You're fools."

The siren-witch wasted no time. With a flick of her wrist, she launched a wave of cloying energy toward us. It was like the tide coming in and I barely had time to react. I raised a shield to deflect the attack. The force of the impact sent me staggering backward. I barely managed to remain on my feet.

"Phoebe, Nana," Stella gasped as she pushed her magic at the siren-witch. I saw the question in her panicked gaze. She wasn't sure what to do. Her power was completely different than facing a pure Tainted witch. There was an element of the ocean in hers.

Nana's eyes narrowed as she assessed the situation.

"We've got this. We're more powerful together. Don't lose sight of that."

The siren-witch's malevolent eyes flickered with a hint of uncertainty. She was momentarily thrown off by our ability to withstand her initial assault. I could see her vicious tendrils wavering. It was almost as if my magic had introduced a note of discord into her symphony of shadows.

Aidon lunged forward. His sword shimmered with a protective enchantment. He swung it in a wide arc, slicing through the spell she threw at him. "Stay behind me," he ordered. He couldn't help his dominant instincts. They'd only gotten worse since I became pregnant.

Layla transformed into her wolf form, her senses heightened as she darted to the side, attempting to flank the siren-witch. Tseki partially shifted. His full dragon would have smashed us against the walls. I glanced at his arm and noticed his scales gleaming in the dim light. That was a handy trick to have. There had been many times I could have used the natural protection against attack.

The witch laughed, a harsh, grating sound. "You really think you can outmaneuver me?" She raised her hands, and the ground beneath us trembled. At the same time, she started singing. The sound was like waves crashing against cliffs. My ears hurt and annoyed me but didn't make it any harder to focus on the Dark tendrils that erupted from the floor. I was all-too aware of them snaking toward us with terrifying speed.

I focused my energy, channeling it into a burst of pure light that disintegrated the tendrils as they approached. "We need to find a way to weaken her," I shouted. My voice was barely audible over the din of battle.

Murtagh's sharp and calculating eyes narrowed, and he nodded. "We need to find out her vulnerability. Knowing that is the only way. She's not one thing or another."

The siren-witch's voice took on a strange, almost musical quality then as she said, "I'm something so much better." The raspy quality was nearly gone now. She said something else I didn't quite catch and I had to shake my head to clear it.

There was no way she had the seductive song of a full siren because I wasn't mindlessly following her. But it was enough to sow confusion. Tseki's scales flickered on his arms and Layla's wolf hesitated in taking a chunk out of the siren-witch's ass. Layla's ears flicked as if trying to shake off a lingering echo. When Murtagh stumbled and his usually keen eyes clouded with uncertainty, my heart sank. She was affecting the shifters.

"Snap out of it!" Aidon shouted, swinging his sword to deflect another blast of evil energy. "She's trying to confuse you!"

Tseki shook his head. His eyes cleared, but then he refocused on the witch. "I... I'm trying to fight it." He growled and started breathing heavily. Fire streamed from his nostrils as he took a step toward the siren-witch. Nana joined him and sent a stream of her dark red witch fire. With the torrent of flame heading toward her, the woman deftly sidestepped. But not before the flames singed the edges of her crimson gown.

That was enough to disrupt the siren-witch's spell and Layla regained her composure. She darted forward and leaped at the witch with her claws extended. Unfortunately, the witch conjured a barrier of malicious energy that sent Layla sprawling to the ground. Nana rushed to her side and had a potion in hand.

I saw a faint, pulsing light emanating from beneath the witch's robes. It was subtle, almost imperceptible, but it was there. "Aidon, aim for her chest! There's something there!" I was betting on it being an artifact. After seeing Lyra's room of treasures, I was convinced that was how her minions were so powerful.

Aidon didn't hesitate. He lunged forward with his sword gleaming as he struck at the witch's chest. He moved too fast for me to follow. I hoped he hit something vital when a loud scream left her lips. The sound was both human and inhuman. The blade had to have made contact. The pulsing light flared brightly before it dimmed. The witch staggered backward, clutching her chest.

"You... you cannot defeat me," she hissed and her voice faltered.

Stella seized the moment. Her magic flared as she cast a spell. Ropes of light wrapped around the witch, holding her in place. "Now, Phoebe!"

I gathered all my strength, channeling it into a single, powerful magical bomb. The siren-witch's eyes widened in fear as the spell came at her. With a final, agonized scream, it detonated. My magic blew her into a million pieces. As the fleshy bits splattered us and the walls, the remnants of her vile energy dissipated into the air.

The chamber fell silent. The oppressive weight of the Dark magic lifted and we stood there, catching our breath. "Next time maybe don't use quite so much force," Nana quipped as she flicked a piece of ick off her shirt.

My stomach roiled and bile burned the back of my throat. "I wasn't about to let her ensnare them again," I said as I gestured to our shifter family members.

The siren-witch had been powerful but there was something else, something more sinister lurking in the shadows. "We need to keep moving," I said. "We have to find Rosemary. Not to mention we don't want to be sitting ducks. Lyra won't stop until she's destroyed everything we hold dear."

We exchanged glances. Aidon sheathed his sword as his

gaze lingered on the spot where the siren-witch had exploded. "You're right," he said, his voice a low rumble. "But there might be something here that will give us a clue. The room is filled with symbols for a reason."

Stella grimaced as she brushed her arms clean. "I'm going to try a cleansing spell before we search the rest of this chamber. I can't go another second with this much evil covering me."

I chuckled and agreed with my best friend. Nana joined us and we cast a spell removing the viscera from our bodies. With that done we fanned out to explore the chamber. The oppressive air began to lighten as the Dark magic that had permeated the space slowly dissipated. My fingers brushed against the rough stone walls and over the ancient runes, cool beneath my touch.

"We need to figure out what these things mean," Layla pointed out. "Otherwise, looking does us no good."

Aidon sighed and pinched the bridge of his nose. "You three keep watch while we decipher this shit. I don't want to be caught with our dicks in our hands."

Nana snorted and lifted one eyebrow. "Speak for yourself. I'd like to see a few of you with your dicks in your hands. But not you. You're mated to my granddaughter and that would be awkward."

"Nana!" I choked as I laughed. "Let's focus on the symbols so we can get out of here."

Nana gave me a look. "Don't be such a killjoy, Phoebe. An old woman has to get her thrills somehow."

My face was on fire as I considered what she'd said. "Fair enough. But you can't ogle Tseki and Murtagh. They're like brothers to me, which makes them like grandsons to you. And *that* gives me the skeeves."

Nana shuddered and said, "Why did you have to say that?

Now I feel dirty." She turned to Tseki and Murtagh who wore expressions torn between amused and honored. "Sorry, boys. Forget I ever said anything. Now, let's see what we have here."

Stella snickered and leaned toward Nana. "We never got to throw Phoebe a bachelorette party. I vote for one as soon as the babies are born. There's a new club in Portland where we can take her."

"This conversation has gone off the rails," I interjected as I checked Aidon's reaction. He found this endlessly funny. It warmed something in me knowing he trusted me without question. That was new for me. With a shake of my head, I refocused. "These feel evil," I observed as I ran a hand over the symbols closest to me. It was like ants crawling beneath my skin. Highly unpleasant.

Thankfully, Nana and Stella followed suit. We silently moved around the chamber deciphering the runes and symbols that adorned the stone walls. It was a delicate dance of perception and intuition. It wasn't always obvious which symbol Lyra had bastardized with her Dark magic.

Stella's magic surged and brushed over the runes. I watched and wondered what she was doing. Nana and I paused to watch her. "I think I understand something," she murmured without moving her gaze from the markings in front of her. "These symbols... I believe they form a sequence. If we find the right order my gut tells me we will find our way to my mom. Or something important."

I gritted my teeth and channeled my magic to enhance our understanding of the cryptic markings. Each rune pulsed with evil power that rubbed against my energy. It felt like a saw cutting through a tree trunk. Every cell in my body rebelled against the discomfort.

A sudden, sharp pain shot through my arm. I gasped, looking down to see a distorted mark forming. What the hell had happened? My babies hadn't reacted. Was it her evil seeping into me? The magic in this place was awful. We had to get the hell out of here.

"Phoebe!" Stella cried out as she grabbed my arm.

"I'm fine," I gritted out through clenched teeth while ignoring the throbbing pain. I couldn't afford to falter now. We hadn't found her mother.

Nana's voice was steady and urgent. "You need to put some salve on that. We will focus on the runes," she instructed me. Her tone brooked no arguments.

I nodded. Aidon was there reaching into my bag before I could lift the limb that felt like it weighed a hundred pounds. "Thanks," I told him as I fought tears. I could feel the malevolence moving into my blood stream.

He pulled out a jar of cream my mom had made that was designed to enhance healing by removing any and all toxins. She had created it when I asked for something to treat injuries that didn't require a healing potion. We could only carry so much. "This woman really doesn't like you," he observed as he gently applied cream over the mark.

"I think I've got it," Stella said in a voice tinged with excitement. "This sequence here points us toward something. We need to find these as we make our way through the tunnels."

Nana's eyes went wide and she nodded. "Yes. It's over here too."

"I think I saw something down the way," Murtagh replied. "Give me a second." Before anyone could stop him, he took off out of the chamber. He hadn't gone far. He was peering at something on the stone wall.

"What is it?" I asked.

He pointed to the first symbol. "It's that marking."

"We need to find the others," Nana pointed out as she continued down the tunnel.

My bladder made itself known a few feet later. I stopped looking back toward the chamber. "What is it?" Aidon asked. "Do you think we missed something?"

I shook my head. "Nope. I need to pee and there is no bathroom."

Stella grimaced and sucked air between her teeth. "You could go back in that cavern. It won't be worse than the body bits now rotting in there."

"Ugh," I blurted. "Nope. I can hold it. There will be another chamber I can use."

Aidon scrutinized me closely. "Are you sure?" I didn't miss the way he looked at my belly where our three unborn babies were cooking.

I ran a hand over the swell. "I'm positive. C'mon," I jerked my chin at the others in front of us. "Get moving."

They got moving but I caught their skeptical looks. With a sigh, I set my sights on our surroundings so I didn't obsess over the need pressing on my bladder. A symbol caught my eye. It was small and etched high in the wall. Upon closer inspection, I noted it wasn't the next in the pattern. It came before a juncture in the paths. An idea began to formulate. These symbols were going to appear at every juncture. If Stella was right, following the ones in her pattern would indeed take us somewhere. Would it be important? Or a trap? That was the vital question that nagged at me as we walked.

"Look," Stella whispered, pointing to a rune carved into the stone. "This is the second one."

Nana nodded, her eyes scanning the surrounding area. "It's on the left wall. The last one I saw was on the right wall. I say we go left and follow it."

Trusting her advice, we took the tunnel to the left. Our footsteps echoed softly in the narrow passageways. The air was cool and damp. It also carried a faint scent of the sea.

The tunnels twisted and turned, forcing us to change course several times as we located the next runes in the pattern.

"Here," Layla said, her voice barely more than a breath as she traced her fingers along another rune. This one glowed faintly. "This way."

We turned down another tunnel. The symbols became more frequent and complex. Suddenly, the tunnel opened into a wider chamber. I didn't feel the ward until after we walked through the opening. I went on alert and cast a shield when another of Lyra's lackeys appeared in the shadows.

Aidon leaned closer to me. "This one feels more like a siren than a witch."

Her beauty was transcendent. I opened my mouth to respond when she started singing. Her voice was a haunting melody that seeped into my soul. There was an irresistible pull to her. I wanted to know her more so I could please her. My feet moved toward her of their own accord. The world around me blurred and all I could hear was her song.

"Phoebe, no!" Nana's voice was a distant echo that barely penetrated the fog clouding my mind.

Stella's magic surged around me. It tickled something in me but the siren's allure was too strong. My heart pounded in my chest as fear and longing battled within. All I wanted was to make this woman happy. I would do anything for her. Wait, what? That was not my thought. I tried to figure out why I was alarmed when a beautiful melody eased my worry.

"She's enchanting her!" Layla growled. I saw her claws flash as she moved to attack. Her steps faltered and she stopped.

Aidon stepped forward and placed a hand on my shoulder. "The siren has you in her thrall, Phoebe. Fight this."

I wanted to do what he asked. I loved him more than anything. Looking into his blue eyes, my head began to clear.

What had happened? Why was he telling me to fight? What was I fighting? Confusion wracked my brain.

The siren-witch smiled and I regained more of my mind. Why had I wanted to be close to her? We should be fighting her so we could continue and find Stella's mom. The siren-witch's eyes glinted with malevolent pleasure. "You think you can resist me?" she taunted. Her voice was a deadly caress. "My magic is far more powerful than you realize." Now that she wasn't singing, I came back to myself.

I was poised to toss a spell at her when she beat me to it. With a flick of her wrist, malevolent tendrils of magic shot towards us. Stella conjured a barrier to repel it. The siren's magic was potent and pushed against my defenses with an unsettling force. If she started singing again, I would be help-less. I looked to Aidon and then Nana. The latter was already chanting an incantation. I felt her familiar power wrap around me.

"Phoebe, fight her!" Nana urged while keeping her eyes locked on mine. "You have to resist!"

The siren's song was a sweet poison. I struggled against the pull. My mind was a battlefield of conflicting desires. Nana's words became a lifeline. I focused on Nana's voice. I drew the strength she was sending my way.

Layla, Tseki, and Murtagh rallied. Their attacks were coordinated as they tried to distract the siren-witch. Tseki loomed protectively with his fiery breath searing the air despite not being in his dragon form. Murtagh bared his teeth at the siren-witch and crouched at the ready.

Aidon moved closer to the siren-witch. His presence was a steady anchor amidst the chaos, and I metaphorically clung to him. It was the best way to stay out of her thrall. "Don't listen to her. Block your ears," Aidon said, his eyes never leaving the siren-witch's. "After that find her weakness."

His words gave me the strength to break free from the

enchantment. The siren-witch's song faltered, her eyes widening in surprise. "Now!" Nana shouted. Her voice was a rallying cry. Without hesitation, Stella and I launched our attack. Our combined magic pushed against the siren-witch's defenses.

The chamber echoed with the clash of spells, like a summer thunderstorm in Texas. The air crackled with light and deadly energy. As our magic surged, the siren-witch's form began to waver. I wanted to cheer when she waffled on her feet.

"Like we told your predecessor. You picked on the wrong people. And you're not as powerful as you think," Aidon said, his voice calm and determined.

I clasped Aidon's hand as Layla stood at my other side. My fingers dug into her fur. Murtagh and Tseki flanked Nana while Stella stood on Layla's other side. I twined my power with Nana and Stella's and then wove it with Aidon and the others. With us bound, I threw a magical bomb at the siren-witch. She let out a final, anguished cry before she was blasted into tiny pieces. Nana grumbled and cast a shield spell before we were showered with blood and guts.

"Thank the gods you were faster this time," Murtagh told Nana with a smile.

"I would tell you to stop that, but it's surprisingly effective," Stella said as she moved through the chamber.

I held up a hand. "In my defense, I reacted before thinking this time. Once I was free of her thrall, I was so pissed at her nearly getting me that I blurted the first thing that came to mind."

"I get it. We take this exit," she said after examining the stone.

We followed the path of symbols etched into the walls. The Dark runes guided us through the labyrinthine tunnels. Each step took us further where the air grew colder and heavier with the scent of the sea. Nana was ahead with Tseki and they both scanned the walls for where we went next.

"Here," Nana said, stopping suddenly. She pointed to a symbol that glowed faintly. "There's something on the other side of this wall," she pointed out. She pressed her hand against the stone and whispered an incantation to reveal the path forward. The wall shimmered and then slowly slid aside to reveal a doorway. That was new.

We stepped through and I blinked in astonishment. The rough stone walls of the tunnel gave way to what felt like the interior of a house. The stark contrast between the two sides was jarring. The room we entered had plaster walls and was warmly lit by soft, ambient lighting.

The floors were covered in plush, intricately patterned rugs that muffled our footsteps. There were bookshelves lined with ancient tomes and trinkets. And comfortable-looking furniture was arranged invitingly in the space. It was warmer there too. It was almost cozy. And it had the faint smell of old books and something floral I couldn't quite place.

I turned, looking back at the rough stone of the tunnel we had just exited. It was like stepping into another world. One that felt strangely familiar yet unsettlingly out of place in the context of the dark, oppressive tunnels. The energy wasn't as differing. Lyra's Dark magic was in the house as well. However, there was also something as powerful as it.

"What is this place?" Stella whispered. Her voice echoed softly in the serene room.

I was busy trying to pinpoint the odd mix of familiarity and alienness. It wasn't all Lyra's influence. Yet, no matter how hard I tried I couldn't determine what else it might be. All I knew was there was something eerie about it.

Before I could voice my thoughts, Stella's eyes widened,

and she took off running through a door on the opposite side of the room. "Stella, wait!" I called after her.

My heart lurched as I watched her disappear through the doorway opposite us. She didn't slow down or respond. I exchanged a worried glance with Nana and the others, then hurried after her. What the hell were we going to step into this time?

CHAPTER 13

"*S*tella, dammit!" I yelled, but she didn't stop. Without hesitation, we sprinted after her, leaving the odd comfort of the room behind. Bursting through the doorway, we found ourselves in a long, dimly lit hallway. Stella was already at the other end. Her figure was silhouetted against the faint light coming from a distant source.

"Stella!" I called again, louder this time. My voice echoed off the narrow walls, yet she didn't respond or slow down. Desperation fueled my magic as I raised my hand and muttered a quick incantation. A soft, blue light shot out, enveloping Stella and freezing her in place. Her eyes widened in surprise, and looked back at me.

"We're making too much noise," Nana hissed as her eyes darted around. With clipped words, she cast a silencing spell. A second later a veil of silence fell over us. Our footsteps became soundless, our breathing inaudible, and our conversations unheard by others outside our group.

We reached Stella quickly. Her eyes were wide with fear and determination as I released her from my spell. "What's got into you?" I demanded.

Stella took a deep breath. Her face was flushed and she was clearly upset. "My mom," she said in a trembling voice. "She has to be in here. Why else would those symbols lead us to this house?"

Nana's eyes softened, though her expression remained stern. "Did you feel her presence, Stella? Do you sense her?"

Stella shook her head, and her shoulders slumped. "No, but... why else would we get here?"

"This could be a trap, Stells. Think about who we are dealing with and how we got here." I placed a hand on her arm, trying to offer some comfort. "You can't go running off like that. We need to be careful so we don't end up at Lyra's mercy. And we have to stick together."

As I spoke, my eyes caught sight of an open door to my right. Inside, I could just see the gleam of white porcelain. Holy shit it was a bathroom! A wave of relief washed over me as I realized just how long I'd been holding it in.

"Guys, I need to pee," I said before Stella could respond. "I've been holding it for far too long."

Nana nodded, giving me a small, understanding smile. "Go ahead, Phoebe. We'll wait here and figure out our next move."

With a grateful nod, I hurried towards the bathroom. With my bladder finally relieved, I rejoined the others. The transition from the rough stone walls of the tunnel to the plastered interior was jarring. I hadn't had a chance to really think about it before. We had been underground, and now we were above it. It was like we'd stepped into another world. The house was dimly lit. The moonlight coming in the windows cast long shadows that danced across the floor and walls.

The house was massive. Much larger than the one I'd inherited from Hattie and it was a mini-mansion with eight rooms and ten bathrooms. The walls were covered with various paintings depicting serene landscapes. I cringed when I caught sight of one that was a stormy sea. It was incredibly caustic to look at.

"We need to find any clues that might tell us more about Lyra's plans and where Rosemary is at," Nana instructed. "But do not go opening doors without us first doing a magical scan. We don't need anyone falling into a trap."

Nodding, we fanned out. Aidon remained close to me as we walked further down the hall. Each of us looked into the open rooms. Stella stepped inside one of them, and I rushed to follow. She was standing in front of a bookshelf, and her fingers traced the spines of ancient tomes. Nana entered the one next door and examined a small writing desk that was cluttered with papers and odd trinkets. I wandered into the room with Nana. An ornate mirror with a tarnished surface drew my attention.

As I studied my reflection, I noticed something peculiar in the mirror's glass. It was a faint glow that seemed to come from behind me. Turning around, I saw a series of runes etched into the plaster. They'd practically been hidden in the room's shadowy lighting. There was a rhythmic pattern that made them seem alive.

"Look at this, Nana," I called softly.

"These seem familiar," she murmured, her fingers lightly brushing over the symbols. "I wish I could remember all of them from that other chamber."

"What did you find?" Stella asked as she came in from next door. Aidon and the others walked in behind her.

"I'm not sure yet," Nana replied with a frown. "But they feel like Lyra's magic."

As we examined the runes, I got the unmistakable feeling that we were being watched. The house had an eerie quality that made my skin prickle. It felt as if the walls themselves were alive and holding secrets just out of reach. It was not a place I wanted to be for long. The problem was that on first glance it seemed to have a couple dozen rooms.

"There's something else here, too," I told the others. "It could be one of Lyra's tricks. I'm not sure. We need to check everything. Aidon, check the far wall," I directed with a jerk of my chin. "Stella, take the left. I'll cover the right. Can you look through the books on that table, Nana? Layla and Murtagh sniff out anything amiss on the south wall. And Tseki, keep watch at the entrance."

Everyone nodded grimly as they went to work. Fear and hope crushed me as I crouched to examine the lower section and the floor. Lyra would have to mark any traps and I reasoned she would put those on the floor. Most people didn't look up or down until it was too late.

"Do you sense anything?" Stella asked in a hushed voice.

"Give me a second," I replied and then closed my eyes. I allowed my magic to flow outward. I told it to search for any disturbances in the energy around us. I squatted like that for so long, I didn't think I could get up on my own. I was about to ask for help when something tickled my senses. "There's something here," I murmured. My fingers brushed against a section of the stone floor that felt slightly warmer than the rest. "Help me move this."

Together, Stella and I used our magic to push a heavy armoire aside. We revealed a small, concealed compartment. Inside was a dusty, leather-bound book covered in strange symbols, along with a few scattered scrolls. Stella reached for the book before she yanked her hand back.

Aidon reached around me. "Let me touch it. I'm tougher to hurt," he replied.

Once it was in his hand, I grimaced and gave him a pleading look. "Can you help me stand up? I don't think I can do it on my own."

Holding the book away from me, he wrapped his free arm

around me and hefted me to my feet as if I were a toddler. "Are you doing okay?"

I patted his chest. "I'm fine. It's not easy getting around anymore, and I'm only halfway there. What is that?"

"It's old magic," he observed as he took a step away from me. He carefully opened the cover. "It contains spells that are a combination of ancient rites and Blood magic."

Stella scanned the pages over Aidon's shoulder. "Can you translate it?"

Aidon nodded as his fingers traced the delicate script. "It will take time, but yes. This could give us valuable insight into how Lyra is controlling the Tainted witches."

Meanwhile, Layla and Murtagh were searching the walls for hidden passages or secret doors. Layla yipped, drawing our attention. Her sharp wolf senses found something. Her nose twitched as she sniffed the air, while Murtagh's keen eyes scanned for any irregularities.

"What have you found?" Murtagh asked softly and then more loudly said, "There's a draft coming from this wall." He pressed his ear to the wall, listening intently. "I hear something. There's a faint echo behind it. Probably a hidden passage. These old houses were made with tons of them."

Aidon joined Murtagh, and they worked to uncover the entrance. Tseki's low growl echoed through the chamber. "Something's coming," he warned. Dragon scales rippled over his skin, at the same time, he moved protectively in front of Nana.

"We need to hurry," I urged my mate. A sense of urgency pricked at the edges of my awareness and made me bounce on the balls of my feet. My magic didn't know whether to surge out of me or simmer under the surface.

Layla bristled and shifted to her human form but didn't reach for the clothes in Tseki's bag. Instead, she glared at me.

"Your magic is prickly. Don't worry. We've got this." With a determined push, Layla and Murtagh managed to shift a section of the wall. The dank, narrow passage that was revealed looked foreboding.

Ever the protector, Aidon stepped forward with his sword at the ready. "I'll go first," he said. His eyes met mine with a look of love and affection. "Stay close, and be ready for anything. Put that in your bag, Tseki," he said gesturing to the book on the chair.

I was right behind him. The warmth vanished, as did the light when Tseki slid the wall shut. We all held our breaths and continued moving away from the room where we'd entered. I'd lost all hope of remembering how we were going to get home from there. I was counting on my brilliant mate to solve that problem for us when the time came. We couldn't ignore the clues as they surfaced.

The walls were narrow, which forced us to move single file. My heart pounded with each step. We were wandering through hidden passages of some freaking house connected to Lyra. This could go bad any second, and my muscles were strung tight as I waited for demons to launch at us from the shadows.

What seemed like a half hour later, we emerged into a smaller chamber. This one was filled with strange, glowing crystals that reminded me of a fantasy novel I read once. Pushing that story to the back of my head, I directed my magical senses to search them for danger. As we moved in to allow everyone to enter, I noticed dark rust-colored spots on a large central crystal. It was etched with more of the evil runes and looked like some kind of ritual site.

"Do you think this is where she performs the transformations?" Stella asked with horror in her gaze.

I stepped closer to the center, and a chill ran down my

spine. "I'm not sure, but we need to destroy this," I said. "If we can disrupt her ability to create more Tainted witches, it will weaken her significantly."

Aidon nodded, raising his sword. "Let's do it."

Nana held her hands up. "Do you think that's a good idea? Will it backfire on us?"

Aidon pursed his lips. "There's a chance of that. Erect a protection shield around it that keeps shit from blowing out but will let my sword in."

"Already done," Nana replied. "I was thinking more along the lines of alerting Lyra."

I gaped at Nana. "I didn't even feel you using magic," I added mine to bolster what she put in place.

Nana gestured up and down my body. "I did it when I felt you probe the thing. I was worried it would react and didn't want to risk you or the babies."

"Thanks for thinking so fast," I told her with a side hug. "Let's remove the power from that crystal. It isn't enchanted, but it is a funnel and is currently storing a significant amount of power."

Stella and Nana nodded, and we channeled our magic into a spell to siphon the power from the thing. The runes flared brightly in response and resisted our efforts. We refused to relent, and I latched onto the power like duct tape. That allowed Nana and Stella's magic to go to work and suck the power from the crystal. Aidon's sword followed their efforts and sliced the thing in half. Those halves shattered when they hit the wood floor. Nana and Stella released the energy, and it dissipated into the air.

"That's one more of Lyra's tools destroyed," Layla said in a voice filled with grim satisfaction.

"She could have felt that," Nana reminded us.

There was nothing else in the room, so we backed out

and continued through the stifling passageway. We were one step closer to uncovering Lyra's plans and putting an end to her reign of terror. My heart raced as we followed the passage until it ended. There were a few rooms along the way, but none of them called out to use when we looked inside. It was the large bedroom at the end that caught me.

We entered and found it surprisingly mundane. A bed dominated one corner. There were also personal effects scattered over the various surfaces that hinted at someone living there. On the dresser lay a shell necklace, delicate and unassuming. When Tseki approached it, the book in his bag began to heat up. He winced, quickly dumping it onto the floor. The book fell open and sat there glowing a bright orange. Intrigued by the reaction, we gathered around it.

"Look at this passage," Tseki said, pointing to the glowing text. The book revealed intricate sketches of coastal landscapes and cryptic notations. As we read through the pages, a specific passage caught my eye.

"Here," I said, my finger tracing the words. "'The cave along the shore holds the key to bringing down the imposter Pleiades once and for all, ending the chaos she has caused'."

Stella's eyes widened. "What does that mean? Who's the imposter Pleiades?"

I swallowed hard as the realization dawned on me. "It's referring to me. No one believes I should have this power."

Nana's face grew serious. "That's not true. Most love you as their leader. Regardless of the author's ignorance, this cave sounds crucial. And if I am interpreting this right, we might even find Rosemary there." I was thinking the same thing. The one thing that would always lure me was the life of someone I loved and cared for being in danger.

Stella's determination hardened. "Then we need to find it. But first, we have to get out of this house."

"Before we leave, we should make sure there's nothing here for us," Layla suggested as she crossed her arms over her naked chest. "Do you think there's any hint in the house about Stella's mom or Lyra? My gut says we should go straight for the cave, but I don't want to miss something here."

"Let me check," I offered and then closed my eyes. I focused on my magical sensors and sent them to search for Stella's mother or Lyra. It took over a minute for me to check the place. The house thrummed with malignant signatures, but none of them felt like Lyra's. And there wasn't a hint of Rosemary.

I opened my eyes and shook my head. "Nothing that feels like Lyra or Rosemary," I confirmed. "We need to find a way out of here."

Nana moved to the window, peering down. "Who's up for climbing down to the first floor?" she asked with a wry smile.

Tseki handed Nana the bag, telling her, "Climb on my back. You too, Phoebe and Stella. I will take you three first and come back for the others." After stripping down and shoving his clothes in the bag Nana was holding, Tseki jumped out the window. He shifted into his dragon form mid-leap.

Nana, Stella, and I scrambled onto his scaled-back. With a powerful beat of his wings, Tseki soared across a manicured lawn and then over the cliffs. He landed gracefully on the shore. Once we dismounted, he flew back to retrieve Aidon, Layla, and Murtagh.

As we waited for their return, a group of hellhounds appeared, snarling and snapping. The beach went from serene to deadly. "Run!" I shouted. We sprinted in the opposite direction with the hellhounds hot on our heels. I worried about Nana lasting very long. Hoping the cave was along this section of the shore, I cast a spell to move our scent out to sea. Hiding would do us no good if they could follow. All we needed was to get ahead of them enough so they lost sight.

We turned a corner, and I almost fainted with relief. There was a cave ten feet to our left. I cast a cloaking spell next. We made it inside before the beasts caught up. The hellhounds prowled outside the cave, confused by our sudden disappearance. They raced back and forth, going a couple of feet inside the cave before racing back out and heading into the waves. I helped Nana move deeper into the cave and out of sight entirely.

We didn't stop until we could no longer hear them. Panting, we finally caught our breath. I looked around the dimly lit cavern, hoping for any clues about where we were. "Is this the right cave?" I wondered aloud. Was it too much to ask that our desperate escape had led us to the right place?

Stella wiped the sweat from her brow, and her breaths were still coming in heavy pants. "Well, it's a cave. Let's hope it's the right one."

Nana glanced around, her eyes narrowing. "We can't just sit here. Let's see if there are any signs that this is the place we're looking for."

Stella sat down on a rock, her head in her hands. "Shouldn't we wait for the others?"

I pondered her question. The sound of claws on the sand decided it for me. "They will find us. Aidon can follow our bond anywhere."

Nana and Stella nodded and we slowly continued our journey. "I thought I felt something earlier," Stella interjected into the silence. "For a moment, I thought my mom was nearby. I don't know. Maybe it was just wishful thinking."

I put a hand on her shoulder, feeling hopeful that we were finally getting close. "She might be in here. If this is the cave in the excerpt, then I have a feeling she's in here."

Nana scowled at me. "That makes no sense. Why would Lyra be hiding in a cave on the beach?"

"I doubt Lyra got her hands dirty and kidnapped Rosemary," I replied.

Stella's eyes glistened with unshed tears. "She might be in even more danger than we thought. Lyra's smart enough to keep her captive alive. I can't say the same about her lackeys."

CHAPTER 14

$\mathcal{M}$y fight or flight mode was working overtime, and I was leaning toward taking off. The cave was a vast, echoing void filled with whispering shadows. Stella and Nana were just as frightened of the tangible darkness that clung to us. It was oppressive and suffocating. The ball of light Nana had floating in front of us glowed weakly. Her spell was barely able to pierce the dense shadows that seemed to press in from all sides.

"This isn't creepy at all," I whispered. My voice was barely audible over the sinister murmurs that filled the cavern.

Nana narrowed her eyes as her witch fire crackled over her palm. "This place is teeming with deadly energy. It's different from Lyra's Dark magic."

Stella moved ahead, and her eyes scanned the shifting shadows. "I hope they're not the ghosts of those that died in wrecks off shore."

I gaped at my bestie. "Why the hell did you have to go and say something like that? Now, I can't get that out of my head."

Nana rolled her eyes at us. "Ghosts are a cakewalk

compared to the shit we've been dealing with. We've been at this for what feels like days. I'm tired, hungry and filthy. Forget the noise. We need to find out what's hidden here. Whatever it is, it's important enough for Lyra to conceal it in this place."

Nana's comment made me wonder how long we had been searching. Being beneath the ground made it impossible to track the passage of time. I pulled out my phone and was shocked to realize it hadn't even been twenty-four hours yet. It seemed like so much longer.

"I wish we hadn't gotten separated from the others," I muttered, more to myself than anyone else. Aidon, Tseki, Layla, and Murtagh had been with us just moments before, but Lyra's malevolent magic had conspired to divide us. Having them with us would make the unseen eyes that watched us less foreboding.

"They will find us," Nana said. Her quiet confidence was reassuring. "In the meantime, we need to understand this cave."

I glanced around and took in the sandy ground and the stone walls. The cave we were inside looked like any beach cave I'd ever seen on television. If you dismissed the creepy whispers. That turned the place into the oddest haunted location on the planet. Hearing the ocean in the background made me think of fresh, clean places. Salt cleansed even Dark magic.

We'd turned down another tunnel when Stella paused. Her gaze was fixed on a particularly dense cluster of shadows. "There's something here," she murmured and reached out cautiously.

I held my breath and kept from snatching her hand back. Instead, I checked to make sure that the protective spell over the three of us was still intact. The darkness recoiled when her fingers brushed it. I gasped and stumbled forward when I saw it had revealed a hidden alcove carved into the stone wall. Inside was an ornate pedestal. Well, it looked more like one of those bar-height tables you'd find in a pub. And even from this distance, I could see the surface was adorned with symbols. Though, I couldn't see well enough to know which ones they were.

My heart pounded against my ribcage so fast I was light-headed. "This has to be what Lyra is trying to hide. We should get a closer look."

Nana was already moving. "There's a spell here. I think those shadows protected it from the salt. We should disrupt whatever spell is anchored here and cause Lyra and her associates more problems."

"I live to put a crimp in her plans," I said as I got a closer look. "Destroy this table and we accomplish that well enough." Some of the symbols were familiar. They were ones for power and protection that were now corrupted and twisted by Dark magic.

Stella circled the thing with her hands hovering a couple of feet away. "Should we focus on purifying the energy? Or do we shatter it to pieces with one of your bombs?"

Cocking my head to the side, I considered the options. "I don't think cleansing will be enough. The runes are engraved into the surface, and so are the modifications. Even if we remove the enchantment, they will still hold power."

"We need a shield first. Shrapnel is not my idea of a good time," Nana interjected.

"I've had protections around us since the hellhounds started chasing us," I replied as we formed a tight circle around the table.

Nana inclined her head and stretched her hands to us. The tips of our fingers almost touched as we began to focus our intent. I pictured what I wanted to happen, adding that the pedestal should crumble at our feet in a pile of small rocks. When Nana dipped her chin, we chanted in unison. The air immediately crackled with energy. The shadows that Stella had dissipated returned and pressed in around us. I almost lost my concentration when the whispers grew louder and more insistent.

Our combined magic pushed against the vile energy while we funneled power into the spell. A radiant light grew between us, and the symbols on the pedestal glowed bright orange as if the artifact was being heated within. The Dark magic resisted our efforts with a fierce, malevolent force. Sweat trickled down my forehead, and my arms shook as I didn't let up. The strain of maintaining the spell was enough to make me start crying. It felt like an eon until the darkness began to waver.

Stella and I smiled at one another and with a final surge of effort, the deadly energy shattered along with the table. It dissolved into millions of tiny rocks at our feet forming a small, skinny mountain in the middle of us. The oppressive shadows finally retreated. However. They didn't vanish. They moved to the corners of the chamber. We stood there, breathing heavily. The chamber was less oppressive now. And the darkness was less malevolent.

I did a little victory dance. "One more blow to the Wicked Witch of the West. One of these days Lyra's going to get tired of us kicking her ass."

Nana was flushed with exertion but glowing with triumph like Stella and me. "I just wish this was the end. We need to regroup with the others and continue our search."

Stella smoothed the top of the pile out. "Take a seat. We can rest for a few while we wait to see if they catch up."

Nana didn't have to be told twice. She sank onto the rocks with a wince. "I'm dying for a tea. And a strawberry kolache. Do you mind conjuring one of each for me, Phoebe?"

My stomach rumbled at the thought of the sweet pastry. Without hesitation, I conjured half a dozen kolaches and three bottles of sweet tea. I sat next to Nana as we ate. Stella remained poised at the entrance, facing the tunnel. We stayed there for about a half hour, and the break was refreshing. Nana was ready to go before I was, and I had to stifle a groan when she stood and prodded my shoulder. "Let's go back to the entrance and see if we can't find the others. It'd be good to have them when we explore this place further."

"Alright," I sighed, wishing I could have more caffeine. Aidon told me it wouldn't hurt the babies, but I wasn't willing to take the chance. I continued limiting myself to one coffee or tea per day. I'd cut energy drinks out completely for the time being.

The tunnels twisted and turned, leading us further into the darkness instead of out. "Do you recognize any of this?" Stella asked, her voice echoing in the narrow passage.

"No," I admitted. "But it might look different with a little less malevolence in here. Let's keep moving."

It wasn't long before the ghosts pressed in from all sides. They floated and swirled like wisps of smoke. Their ethereal forms cast a cold, haunting presence in the cave. The temperature had dropped drastically, causing shivers to run down our spines. I couldn't believe Stella was right about spirits haunting this place. The darkness seemed to amplify their whispers and the bone-chilling cold that permeated the air.

Stella gripped my arm tightly, seeking reassurance amidst the eerie surroundings. I pulled Nana closer to my other side. Their presence helped against the encroaching spirits. Each breath became a struggle against the oppressive weight of the energy that surrounded us. Ghosts had a unique vibration and presence and with this many, it closed in on us in no time.

A sudden scream pierced the air, startling us all. "One of them brushed up against me!" Stella's voice rang out.

Reacting instinctively, Stella, Nana, and I shifted so we were standing back-to-back. I was on high alert, waiting to see what the beings would do next. My eyes stung from scanning the spirits for any sign they could touch us. Stella and I were familiar with what angry ghosts could do. We had to banish one that refused to let a woman leave her house.

"I'm really tired of this bullshit. Why are Lyra and her cronies so fixated on using things in the dark to scare us? It's just pissing me off," Stella whispered, her frustration palpable.

"Because that is the stuff of nightmares. We have all grown up hearing the stories and being afraid of the boogeyman under our beds," Nana replied. How was she so damn steady? I was freaking the hell out.

The ghostly figures grew more distinct as the seconds passed. Their ethereal forms took shape in the dim light. They even hovered closer to us. Their presence was unsettling and threatening, to say the least. It was clear they were not mere apparitions. They were here with a purpose. It just wasn't clear if there was more to their goal than hindering us.

"We need to find Aidon and the others," I said urgently. The ghosts were a formidable obstacle that I could use Aidon's help on. Not to mention I just needed my mate close.

Closing my eyes, I tried to reach out to Aidon telepathically. We'd never communicated that way before, but I tried anyway. *Aidon, we're in trouble. We need you.* I mentally shouted it out to him with all the force I could muster. I waited, but there was no response. It was just an empty void where I had hoped for a connection. I tried again and again but wasn't able to reach him.

Regrouping, I decided to try another tactic. *"Tarja,"* I

called out to my familiar with my mind. My familiar should be able to hear me. I wasn't cut off like I had been on the island. *"Find Aidon and tell him to come to the chamber. We need help."*

"He is already on his way to you. They are fighting the hell-hounds, and he is sending them back to the Underworld," Tarja replied. I practically collapsed with relief when I heard her voice in my head.

"Stay focused," Nana urged. "We can't let them over-whelm us." She was unaware I was talking to Tarja.

"Can you talk to him? Are they alright?" I asked Tarja, setting Nana's advice to the corner of my mind.

Tarja's scratchy sigh was music to my frontal lobe. *"No, I cannot speak with him. He is a god with incredible natural protection around his brain. It takes everything I have to communicate with those in the same house as me. However, I reached out to Layla when you didn't call or return. Your mother is worried about you, Amelia, Stella, and Rosemary. They are making their way to you."*

I nodded even though she couldn't see me. *"Okay. Tell Mom we followed Lyra through a portal and ended up in a cave off a beach somewhere. It looked like it was probably Maine, but I can't be sure. Oh, and let her know Lyra had made siren-witch hybrids. We've encountered two of them."*

"I want you to cast an ear plug spell. Mollie and Nina have been looking into Rosemary's disappearance in hopes of finding a clue about how to find you all and they heard rumors about a siren who is gunning for you. Sirens are extremely dangerous and can enthrall you before you're able to utter one word," Tarja warned me.

My breath caught in my throat. *"Tell me what to do. I'll cast it now."*

"You need to use the spell, impedimentum olfactus sanum. It will protect you. Cast it on everyone," Tarja suggested.

I did as she instructed and promised her, I would call out if I needed more help. The figures moved closer. Their forms coalesced into something almost tangible. I could feel the anger and hatred radiating from them. It made me recoil and wonder what had pissed them off so badly.

"They're testing our defenses," Stella said through gritted teeth. "We need to hold them off until Aidon gets here. He should be able to send them to the afterlife, right?"

I winced and lifted a shoulder. "He does have power over the dead. However, I have never asked him how it worked. I don't know what he can do."

When Stella's palms started to glow, I swiveled to Nana. "Cast a sunlight spell. Maybe if we all join in, we can push them back." Nana grinned and we each cast our own spells. I twisted them together until I created a sphere of light that kept the ghosts at bay. The figures hissed, writhed, and distorted in the light's glow. They surged forward again, testing our barrier with increasing intensity.

"This isn't going to hold for long," I muttered as sweat beaded on my forehead from the effort. Nana had a point about how long we had been at this. The snack and rest had helped, but I was bone tired and needed sleep.

Suddenly, the spirits converged to form a massive, towering figure that loomed over us. Its eyes glowed with an unnatural blue light. "You cannot escape the darkness," it intoned. How did it have a voice at all? "The phony Pleiades will pay for interfering."

Our light flickered, and the ghosts surged forward. Stella shot me a frightened glance. "We have to find a way to break them up again," she whispered.

I focused my energy, drawing on what I could afford without releasing the other spells I had running. "A magical bomb isn't going to work. Any ideas?"

"Untangle them like a ball of yarn," Nana suggested.

Stella and I nodded and funneled power to the new spell. I barely formed the words when I felt the tendrils of my magic snaking into the thing in front of us. I pushed one thread into an opening I found. I imagined it working its way deep into the form and tugging ghosts out one at a time. There was nothing there to grab. It was like the individual spirit moved out of reach. It happened every time I tried to grab something.

But it wasn't enough. The figure laughed a deep, rumbling sound that shook the chamber. "Fools," it sneered. "You cannot defeat the beguiling magic."

"We need to try another approach," Stella ground out.

"Why are they so powerful? Our spell should have worked," Nana mumbled as she tried to work through the problem. Understanding that would tell us where to direct our efforts.

I huffed and braced myself as I redoubled my efforts. "They're insubstantial. I can't pull anything out."

Stella's eyes went wide, and a gasp escaped her. "This is nothing more than a powerful illusion. I'd bet anything they are protecting something they don't want found. Like the shadows earlier."

Nana grinned at that. "Then spells will weaken their hold and reveal what's hidden." Her brow furrowed in concentration. "Let's start with spells to dispel illusions."

I took a deep breath, focusing my mind on the texts I had studied. Raising my hands and channeling my magic, I whispered, "*Lumos Vespere*."

A soft glow emanated from my palms, spreading slowly through the chamber. The spirits recoiled slightly. The massive form wavered, but the power behind it pushed back at me. Dammit! It was not enough to reveal the truth hidden beneath.

Stella stepped forward, her eyes narrowing in determination. "Let me try a general spell." She began to chant without waiting for our response. "*Dispellio Tenebrae.*"

Her magic surged forth, weaving through the air like a shimmering wave. The ghost conglomerate writhed and contorted. We got glimpses of what lay beyond it. Unfortunately, I didn't get much more than a few flashes of white. The true nature of our surroundings remained elusive.

Nana invoked an incantation before Stella's had dissipated entirely. "*Revelare Veritas.*"

Her spell echoed through the chamber and resonated with the very essence of truth. The spirits quivered and shifted. Nudging Stella, I told her, "Cast yours again." She nodded, and I focused on mine. The spell left my mouth. Our magic hit them at the same time, and finally, their form faltered further. We kept pushing energy into it. Slowly the illusions began to fade.

As the ghosts peeled away and the true nature of our surroundings was revealed, a collective gasp escaped our lips. The chamber was not what we expected. The sight before us filled us with horror. It was a chilling spectacle that confirmed our worst fears about Lyra's dastardly schemes.

The ghosts were hiding a macabre scene that defied all reason and humanity. Countless skeletons lay strewn across the chamber floor. There were fleshy, bloody bodies as well. Most were a grotesque mishmash of bones from different creatures and beings. They were all twisted and melded together by the vile touch of Dark magic. My stomach rebelled when I caught sight of one that had the wings of birds fused to humanoid torsos. Averting my gaze, I noted others with the claws of beasts protruding from skeletal hands. It was a horrifying tableau of experimentation and cruelty. And the worst testament to the depths of Lyra's depravity.

We stood frozen in disbelief, our minds struggling to

comprehend the horror before us. Stella's hand trembled as she whispered, "This is the most horrific mass grave I've ever seen."

Nana's face hardened as she scowled at the scene. "These poor souls... twisted and manipulated beyond recognition."

I could feel the rage building within me. It was followed by a fiery determination to put an end to this madness. "No one deserves to suffer like this. Mom would be here if she didn't have a lot of power."

Nana's voice was steady despite the horror around us. "She surpassed evil long ago. I can't imagine most demons doing this for as long as Lyra has."

As we turned to leave the chamber of horrors, I cast one last glance at the twisted skeletons. A silent promise echoed in my heart. We would confront the darkness that had wrought such abominations upon innocent lives. That included Lyra and whoever else was working with her. This kind of evil didn't deserve to live.

CHAPTER 15

"*N*ana, how much further do you think we need to go?" Stella whispered. Her voice was loud in the oppressive silence. We all wanted to get far away from that abattoir.

The cave's interior was a maze of twisting tunnels which made maneuvering in the place a challenge. We tried following our noses to the entrance but none of us had very refined sense of smell. The occasional drip of water echoed eerily through the damp, musty air and was accompanied by the sound of waves crashing against the rocks in the distance.

"Not much longer, I hope," Nana replied as she continued to shuffle forward. "Stay vigilant. We want to avoid being added to that heap of bodies. And we need to find the others."

We moved cautiously, each step measured, until we stumbled upon a chamber. The moment we stepped inside, the air shifted, thick with an unsettling energy. The walls glistened, reflecting our torchlight in strange, shimmering patterns.

"What the actual?" I blurted. My feet carried me closer to

the walls, and my breath caught in my throat as I realized what we were seeing.

The walls were covered in pictures. Not ordinary photographs, either. These seemed to be constructed from water. They were clearly held together by some kind of enchantment. Each image was a perfect, almost lifelike representation. Whoever did this, captured moments and froze them in time, literally.

"This is... incredible," Nana murmured, stepping forward to examine one of the watery images. "I've never seen magic like this."

I gaped at my grandmother. "What? It's horrifying." It highlighted how I wasn't safe anywhere.

"Who could do something like this?" Stella asked.

That answer seemed easy since all of them featured me. "Can witches create these frozen pictures?" I asked. A chill skittered down my spine. These were scenes from different points over the last year or so. They were depicted in exquisite detail. It felt invasive, as though someone had been watching my every move. "This is like a stalker's wall." My skin crawled.

Stella's face betrayed the horror she felt. "Phoebe, look at this."

I turned to see what had caught her attention. There, among the watery images, was a picture of Stella and me in the garden at the rest home with her mother last week. The scene was tender. It had captured a moment of peace and companionship as we shared lobster rolls with Rosemary. Seeing it in this context felt wrong.

"Why would they have this?" Stella's voice wavered, and her hands clenched into fists.

"I don't know," I replied. My heart ached at the sight of so many private moments displayed in this horrible cave. "But whoever it is, they have been watching me for a long time."

They showed the progression of my baby bump. My stomach seemed to have a glow to it in the images after I got pregnant. As if being pregnant with triplets at forty wasn't hard enough.

Nana moved closer. Her face was grim. "This isn't just about you, Phoebe. This is about all of us. We need to find out who did this and why."

Stella's anger turned to sorrow as she stared at the image of her mother. "It's not fair," she whispered. "She was trying to find some peace with her Alzheimer's and now this."

I placed a comforting hand on her shoulder. "We'll get to the bottom of this, Stella. I promise. But we have to stay strong and keep moving forward. We can't let whoever did this win."

Tears glistened in Stella's eyes, and determination hardened her expression. "Let's find the others and figure out what all of this means."

As we turned to leave the chamber, a renewed sense of urgency filled me. This sight confirmed that we were up against something more. Lyra wasn't capable of creating something so beautiful. Not that whoever was responsible was necessarily good. We were up against someone who had been meticulously tracking my every move. This spoke of attention to detail and patience.

The atmosphere was somber as we stood there in a tight circle with the flickering orb of light casting long shadows on the damp walls. I couldn't make myself leave yet. "Why would someone make these images?" I asked.

Stella's gaze darted from one distorted image to another. She lingered on the one of us in the garden. "I still want to know who could even do something like this."

I took a deep breath and let the cool, damp air fill my lungs. "Those answers will lead us to the culprit and hopefully your mom," I said, my voice barely above a whisper. "I can't get past why go to all this trouble."

Nana shook her head as she thrust her hands on her hips. She had that look on her face she got when she was trying to get down to the bottom of something when Stella and I had made mistakes as teenagers. She was searching for a deeper meaning hidden within the swirling water. "I don't know enough about supernatural creatures in general, but my gut tells me a siren is behind this. And not one of the hybrids Lyra made. This takes too much power."

"A siren?" I echoed, looking over the creepy pictures again. The way the water moved to create our likenesses was both beautiful and deeply unsettling. "Why would sirens be working with Lyra? I assumed she'd kidnapped the others and forced the change upon them. That *is* her specialty."

Nana's expression grew even more serious, and her lips pressed into a thin line. "Sirens are known for their manipulative powers. They're driven by destructive impulses. I don't know why they would care about a witch on land. But if Lyra is controlling or has allied with them, it could explain everything." She gestured around us. "Including the magic behind these images."

"This would be a member of the royal family. Their ability to shape water like this is almost unheard of. Only those of that bloodline have this ability," Tarja interjected. I told the others what Tarja had said. She couldn't speak into all of our minds across distances.

"I remember Fiona, Violet, and Aislinn talking about their troubles with a siren in England," I added as my mind raced through everything. I could almost hear their voices recounting the harrowing tale. "It was a difficult ordeal, and they barely made it out. And I believe the Twisted Sisters had a run-in with sirens at a birthday party they threw. Sirens are cunning and dangerous."

Nana walked over to one of the walls. Her steps were deliberate and careful on the slick cave floor. She pointed to a section where a water-damaged mural was faintly visible. The colors were muted, but the shapes were still discernible. The mural depicted a siren whose eyes were incredibly life-like. They even seemed to follow us as we moved.

"Look here," Nana said. She traced the outline of the mural. The stone was cold and damp to the touch, and she shivered slightly as she made contact. "There are runes beneath the image that are partially obscured by moss."

Stella leaned in closer, squinting at the faded symbols. The moss had grown thick, making it difficult to see the details. "What could this mean?" she asked.

I placed a hand on her shoulder, trying to offer some comfort despite my gnawing uncertainty. "I wish I knew, Stella. Do you think we can decipher the symbols and figure out what it says? They aren't witch or Underworld runes."

"These runes could be a clue," Nana started with a low hum, "or even a warning. But whatever they mean, I doubt we will get many answers about Rosemary. These have been here a while."

The siren's eyes seemed to watch us as we spoke, adding to the weight of her words. They glistened in the orb of light almost as if they were alive. We were in the middle of a web of secrets and Dark magic. From the last cavern we were in they were the kind that cost lives. I was with Nana. These markings didn't seem vital to our journey, but I couldn't deny that understanding our enemy better would help us in the long run. The problem was none of us were fluent in siren.

I was jolted out of my thoughts when I heard footsteps echoing down the tunnel. I pressed a finger to my lips, telling Nana and Stella to be quiet, and then crept to the opening. I poked my head out, ready to toss an offensive spell at the newcomer, when I saw familiar faces. Relief washed over me. Aidon, Layla, Murtagh, and Tseki had found us.

"Aidon!" I cried out. The sight of them lifted the heavy weight of fear from my heart.

He rushed toward me, closing the distance in a heartbeat. His arms wrapped me in a tight embrace. And for a moment everything else faded away. The cold of the chamber, the eerie ice pictures, the looming threat of the siren, and the need to find Rosemary. It all dissolved in the warmth and safety of his hold.

"Phoebe," he murmured against my lips. The relief and love in his voice echoed mine. He pulled back just enough to look into my eyes. Without another word, he kissed me. It was a soft but urgent press of his lips against mine. I felt his need to reassure himself that I was truly there.

I melted into the kiss. The fear and tension of our journey eased away. When we finally pulled apart, I rested my forehead against his. I drew strength from the connection we shared. "It's good to see you guys," I admitted.

He nodded as his eyes searched mine. "Me too. What did you find?"

I stepped aside and gestured to the chamber. "A stalker's lair," I replied.

The four of them gaped at the sight and moved forward quietly. Watching their expressions as they looked over the images sent shivers down my spine. We updated them on what had happened and our theories about a siren being involved. Before anything else happened, I cast the magical earplugs for them as well. I wanted us all protected.

Stella, Nana, and I stood in the center of the room while they scoured it. We'd already seen the pictures and the mural. And I didn't want to be any closer to them than necessary. It was Murtagh who first noticed the small, weathered leather-bound book nestled within a narrow crevice in the cave wall. He pulled it free with a grunt of effort. The old leather cover was cracked and brittle in his hands.

"What do you think this is?" he asked. His voice echoed slightly in the chamber. He handed the tome to me. I carefully opened it, noting how the pages were yellowed with age and faintly smelled of mildew.

I squinted at the faded ink, my heart quickening as I realized what I was holding. "It's a journal," I said, glancing up at the others. "It belonged to a mage. Someone who encountered the siren and chronicled their vile rituals."

Stella leaned closer, her eyes wide with curiosity and fear. "Holy shit. I bet he was connected to Lyra."

I nodded and began to read aloud. My voice barely rose above a whisper. "The mage writes about a hidden lair deep within the Chamber of Shadows. He describes the siren performing sacrifices and conjuring powerful spells. 'The siren's lair is a place of Dark magic,' he writes. 'A place where the shadows themselves seem to whisper secrets and the air is thick with the scent of blood and despair'." The words came alive in the eerie silence of the cave

Nana's expression grew more serious with each word. "That sounds like the room we ran across earlier," she said quietly. "At least we know why there was the bloody mess in that cavern."

I continued reading, my fingers tracing the delicate script. "The mage also mentions something about a key to bringing down an imposter Pleiades once and for all. 'The siren holds the key to ending the chaos the imposter has caused.'"

Stella's face paled as she absorbed the implications of my words. "What does that mean, Phoebe? An imposter Pleiades? Could it be talking about you?"

My heart pounded as I considered the possibility. "I'm the only one in history known as an imposter. Why would this be documented so long ago? This is really old. I'd bet I wasn't even born when this was written."

Layla frowned and flexed her claws nervously. "Maybe this is why the siren is working with Lyra. That doesn't explain why it was written before your time, but helps the rest make sense."

Tseki's dragon eyes glowed softly in the dim light. "We need to find this Chamber of Shadows. It sounds like it's important." I pointed to another passage, and I read aloud again.

"'Beware the guardian of the Chamber,'" I recited. "'A beast of nightmares that protects the siren's secrets. Only the brave and the foolish dare to face it.'" I paused and thought about what I'd read. "The room with the abattoir came to mind when I first read this. Now I wonder if it is somewhere else," I added.

"There's only one way to find out. Let's keep moving," Aidon said as I closed the journal and tucked it safely into my bag. "The Chamber of Shadows is our next destination. We have to find it and put an end to the threat the siren poses once and for all."

Stella grabbed Aidon's sleeve as we left the chamber. "We can't forget my mom. We have to rescue her."

Aidon patted her hand reassuringly. "I haven't forgotten that. I know this case has thrown several curve balls, but there is a reason for everything. Growing up with the Fates, I know better than anyone that nothing happens without design or reason."

Stella's face went pale. "You suck at reassuring people. That doesn't make me feel any better."

Aidon chuckled and wrapped an arm around her in apology. We fell silent as we traveled in pairs through the tunnel. The deeper we ventured, the more oppressive the darkness became. I cast a light orb that went from blinding to barely visible and I swore the shadows were conspiring to smother us.

After what felt like an eternity, we arrived at a vast, cavernous space. This had to be the Chamber of Shadows. It was creepy and foreboding, as the name suggested. Our torchlight flickered when we stepped inside. Shadows began dancing on the walls. My heart pounded against my ribcage as I took in the sight before us.

At the center of the chamber was a disturbing tableau. The ground was stained with blood. I crouched and noticed we had left the sand behind and were standing on light-colored slate. I expected it to be covered in dark, corrupted runes and sinister symbols. It wasn't. I could feel the writhing, pulsing energy beneath us.

Nana stopped next to Tsekani. "This feels like the place." She pointed to the blood. "It appears to be the siren's sacrificial site. Now what?"

Layla's claws flexed nervously. "Get rid of the magic here."

Murtagh moved closer to the center. "It smells like death."

A sudden, ominous sound echoed through the cave. The entrance behind us slammed shut with a resounding thud, trapping us inside. My heart skipped a beat and settled in my gut. I turned to see the solid rock wall now sealing our exit.

"Oh, hell. We're trapped," I said, trying to keep the panic at bay. "I didn't feel any power that might have triggered it."

Tseki stood protectively next to Nana. He was vigilant as he looked around the chamber for any sign of danger. "We need to find a way out. This place doesn't feel right."

Aidon wore a grim expression as he inclined his head. "Phoebe, can you sense anything? The source of the power here? Any weaknesses in that magic, by chance?"

I closed my eyes and focused, reaching out with my magical senses to probe the energy surrounding us. I was acutely aware of being trapped. It was difficult to concentrate between that and the way the air hummed with malevolent power. My stubborn nature meant I pushed even harder. I looked for ways around what was keeping me from getting a feel for things.

"It's strong," I said, my voice strained. "If there are weak points, I can't find them. And there's nothing to indicate there was ever a doorway. We're trapped."

CHAPTER 16

"There was a way into this place. The way out is still there. We just need to shed some light on the matter," Nana said in a steady voice despite the strain of the case on everyone. She muttered something and conjured a more powerful orb of light than I had floating with us. Hers managed to push back the shadows and illuminate the room. Without the darkness, the name Chamber of Shadows didn't fit.

As the entities protecting this place were pushed to the outer edges by Nana's light, we saw what looked like a place where a creature of the sea would feel at home. It wasn't filled with symbols, altars, or anything I'd come to expect from Lyra and her Tainted witches. The chamber was dominated by a large, shimmering pool of water surrounded by delicate seashells and coral formations. Its surface rippled with an unearthly light. There was also an ornate, silvery chaise lounge that sat near the water's edge, draped with seaweed and pearls.

"Is this... where the siren lives?" Stella asked with wide eyes.

"It sure seems like it," I said in a whisper. It felt like we were intruding on her private space. And without the oily feeling of malicious magic, it seemed wrong. "It looks like her personal lair."

Layla moved toward the center of the room, where a mesmerizing water orb floated above a plinth. It radiated a cool, bluish light. The surface was smooth like a crystal ball, but it seemed to be made entirely of water. When we got closer, the surface started shifting and swirling with images. It was mesmerizing and beautiful.

"This must be how she sees everything," Aidon observed. "She's got an eye on the world and no one knows it." Scenes of the ocean depths and distant shores played out as he spoke. It was interspersed with glimpses of a siren. Was it the owner of this chamber? The one stalking me? Whoever we were looking at was weaving her magic and plotting schemes.

"What do we do now?" Layla snapped. Her frustration was a live wire lashing out of her. "We're trapped in here." She'd shifted and was now slipping clothes on, although she looked ready to claw through the stone surrounding us.

"We need to stay calm," Nana said firmly. "There has to be a way out. The siren wouldn't trap herself in here."

Murtagh wore a grim expression. "We need to understand what we're dealing with. This lair, this orb... it's all part of her power. There's an answer somewhere here."

"Okay, how do we fight something like this? I know nothing about siren magic," Stella pointed out. "She's got the whole sea at her command, and I have a feeling we're surrounded by it."

"We've faced worse." Tseki's voice was steady and reassuring. "We just need to find a way around her magic."

I took a deep breath, trying to steady my nerves. "If this orb is how she sees the world, maybe we can use it against her. There has to be something in here that can help us make it work."

As we stood around the water orb, the light Nana conjured highlighted more details of the lair as it moved. It landed on delicate glass bottles filled with shimmering liquids. It was the way their contents glowed softly in the dim light that caught my attention. They sat on shelves carved into the stone walls. There were ancient tomes next to the containers. Given the siren's association with Lyra, I bet the books were likely filled with dark spells and forbidden knowledge.

"I can't imagine that this place is filled with her secrets," Nana reasoned. "She would make sure no one could enter the space she kept the heart of her powers. We walked right in here."

Stella's eyes lingered on the orb. "I would agree with Nana, so why did she want us in here. She laid the bread-crumbs leading us here."

"Then we haven't triggered whatever the Chamber of Shadows is supposed to unleash." I shuddered and moved closer to Aidon. I didn't like that thought.

Stella's eyes went wide. "Then let's not do that. The power here... is ancient and potent. Not something I want to tangle with."

Nana's grip on Tseki's arm tightened. "I don't think we're going to get out of here until we get the magic working in here. And that is going to involve those shadows."

Stella sighed and took several steps away from the orb. "I wish I could say you're wrong. We might as well get this over with. My mom needs us." She shot me a wry look and continued, "If we need to use her magic against her, let's show her what she's messing with."

Nana and I chuckled and joined Stella. "I say we start with a simple reveal spell," I told them. "And before you say that's not enough pizazz, let me remind you that we can pack it with a punch."

"As if we'd do anything less," Nana sniffed.

Laughing, we joined hands and started with a spell to unveil anything that was hidden within the room. our voices blending in a chorus of incantations. My fingers tingled with energy as I focused on pouring more power into the enchantment. Our energy bounced around the space and aggravated the shadows. They surged forward and swarmed us. A cry escaped my lips when contact left a red welt on my forearm.

Aidon positioned himself in front of me and took the brunt of their attack. Anger bubbled when I saw him flinching from pain. I added power to Nana's light orb and it brightened. It sent beams of light piercing through the shadows. When they were pushed back, I cast a protective barrier around all of us and Nana and Stella joined me.

"We need to try something different," Nana called out as the shadows darted forward, trying to reach us. They didn't get close enough to hurt us, but they tried. For a moment, they disoriented me. Thankfully, maintaining my magic had become a reflex, and my protection didn't waver.

I closed my eyes for a moment, feeling the pulse of magic around us. "Stella, focus on the water. Nana, keep the light steady. We need to channel the power of the elemental force."

Focusing on the water orb, I tried to tap into its power. Blue sparks danced along my fingertips as I wove my spell. I channeled the magic laced in the elemental forces that coursed through the chamber. It pulsed in response to my efforts to draw upon it. The water orb flickered, and the images within shifted more rapidly. The shelves carved into the stone walls vibrated with the power we were unleashing.

"Go for the ball of water," I told them when I realized they might be concentrating on the pool of water. Stella's energy shifted and then struck the water orb directly. It glowed brighter, reacting to our combined magic. The images within the orb began to swirl violently, the water inside churning with an almost sentient force.

The shadows were even more irritated. They moved so fast it threw me off my guard, and I dropped the spells I had cast. Nana's light dimmed, we lost our protection, and the formless shapes felt like liquid as they scalded my skin. I tried to step away from them, but they were everywhere at once. The searing pain was like being burned by acid.

"Focus, Phoebe!" Nana shouted. Her face was contorted with effort. "You hit on something. Just a little more, and we might be able to get out of here! We need to synchronize our spells."

Stella nodded and jerked away from the shadow wrapping around her. "I'll split my focus on this and on binding the shadows. You two push your magic into the orb."

The air around us shimmered with energy, and the water orb began to glow even brighter. I gritted my teeth against the pain and refocused my mind on the spell. Stella's voice grew louder as she chanted her spell over and over. Oddly enough, her mantra helped me keep my eye on the ball. The shadows pressed harder. Their touch was like fire against my skin. And my vision blurred with tears, but I didn't stop.

The water orb's glow intensified, making the shadows retreat. A spectral form began to emerge from the sphere. The magic we had unleashed swirled around the orb. The air smelled like salt, and the sound of crashing waves was all around us. The spectral form took the shape of a woman. It hovered in front of the stand. The woman's presence was commanding and serene at the same time.

The figure was ethereal, with translucent skin that shimmered like moonlight on water. Her dark hair flowed around her like tendrils of seaweed. And her eyes glowed with an ancient, magical light. She regarded us with a mix of curiosity and malice. I swear her gaze pierced through to our very souls.

"You have disturbed the balance," the spectral form told us. "The prophecy has been set in motion, and your actions have sealed your fate." Her voice echoed through the chamber like a haunting melody.

I had a feeling I wasn't going to like what came next. I hated vague prognostications. "What prophecy?" I blurted.

The spectral form's eyes seemed to pierce deeper as if weighing our very essence. The shadows around us writhed in response. Thankfully, they didn't get any closer. I imagined they were as afraid of the specter as we were. Not that I blamed them. The woman was looming over us.

Her voice cut through the air with an eerie yet soft resonance. "The prophecy speaks of a chosen one destined to confront this looming evil and restore balance to the realms of magic and mortals alike." I had a bad feeling about who that was referring to. I was five months pregnant. I did not want to be the subject of a siren prophecy.

We stood in silence, the weight of her words sinking into us like stones. A chill ran down my spine as the spectral siren continued. Her voice wove a tapestry of fate that hung heavily in the air.

"In the darkest hour when shadows reign supreme and hope is but a whisper on the wind, the chosen one shall rise. Born of light and shadow, they will wield the power to mend the rift between worlds. They will bring forth a new dawn from the heart of night. Nothing will be saved from her influence. Not even the depths of the ocean."

The siren's cold and knowing eyes swept over us. It was like she was seeking the truth within our souls. "The path is fraught with peril, and many will fall before the final battle is won. Trust not in the obvious, for deceit runs deep. The chosen one will be known by their heart, not their lineage. And their strength will come from the bonds they forge."

Aidon exchanged a glance with me. His expression revealed his thoughts aligned with mine. "She is talking about one of us. And you don't want it to be you."

Nana narrowed her eyes at us. "Of course, it's one of us. And the answer is obvious. However, we can't dismiss it. If this prophecy is true, we have a duty to fulfill. The fate of our world could depend on it."

Stella gripped my hand and shot me eyes filled with fear. "I hate prophecies, but Nana is right. The one thing that's bugging me is why the siren is after you. Shouldn't they want to help us rather than stop you?"

A deep sense of destiny awakened within my soul in the moments since the spectral image started talking. It was a calling that beckoned me toward an uncertain but crucial future. "I don't think they want us to succeed. I imagine they're afraid of what their lives will be like if I do."

Nana's gaze remained fixed on the spectral siren. "People are often foolish, clinging to their fears and insecurities. The siren might think that means Phoebe will try to steal her limelight or put rules in place for her life." Hearing Nana say it felt like she was sealing my fate where I wanted to put it onto someone else.

The siren's form began to waver. Her image flickered like a dying flame. "Heed my words, for they are the keys to your salvation. The chosen one must walk a path of sacrifice and courage guided by the light within. Only then can the balance be restored, and the realms be saved from eternal darkness."

Her voice faded after that leaving us with a profound silence. She still hovered there, staring at us without saying a word. It was unnerving and likely added to the sense of destiny that awakened within me. It was strong and real. We were standing on the precipice of something monumental, and there was no turning back.

Layla stepped forward with a scowl. "What the hell does that even mean? While it's fairly obvious Phoebe is the chosen one, how can we be certain? If it's someone else, that person needs to step up."

Murtagh, his usual stoicism cracked by a hint of concern, added, "That's not where we need to put our efforts. We are in this together, so if it is someone else, we can avert disaster. What is more important is understanding more about the prophecy."

"I would agree. It would help to put the pieces together." I turned to the spectral siren and asked, "Can you recite the prophecy to me in full?"

The specter inclined her head and clasped her hands in front of her body. "In the darkest hour when shadows reign supreme and hope is but a whisper on the wind, the chosen one shall rise. Born of light and shadow, they will wield the power to mend the rift between worlds. They will bring forth a new dawn from the heart of night. Nothing will be saved from her influence. Not even the depths of the ocean.

"The path is fraught with peril, and many will fall before the final battle is won. Trust not in the obvious, for deceit runs deep. The chosen one will be known by their heart, not their lineage. And their strength will come from the bonds they forge.

"When the skies bleed, and the seas boil, when shadows consume the stars and the earth trembles with their weight, the chosen one will stand at the crossroads of fate. Their choice will shape the destiny of all realms, and in their hands lies the power to save or to destroy." Her gaze intensified as she told us, "The prophecy is now awakened. Prepare for the trials to come, for the balance of all worlds rests upon the chosen one."

Stella started pacing a short circuit in front of us, staying clear of the shadows hovering around the edges. "It's even worse hearing it all like that. But, I am more convinced this hero is you, Phoebe. Not that you are in it alone. This is bigger than my mom and the siren. We need to get out of here and stop Lyra. She's the evil behind the danger."

I was shaking my head when the pool of water across the room started frothing. The specter vanished, and the water orb stopped glowing a second before a head emerged from the pool. A naked body followed suit. This was no spirit. This person was flesh and blood. My heart started racing when I felt the power coming off of the woman. There was no doubt she was a siren. She prowled forward, swaying her perfectly curved hips. She opened her mouth, and I hastily cast another earplug spell just to be safe.

Her song drifted through the room but cut off when we didn't go all gaga over her. She scowled at us and snapped her fingers. Power whooshed around the room with that, and the shadows surged forward. They were just as liquid and still burned like acid. They swarmed us, their touch searing our skin and sending waves of pain through our bodies.

"Stay close!" I shouted, casting a protective spell. Stella and Nana joined in, their magic intertwining with mine as we tried to push back the relentless evil.

The siren's laughter echoed through the chamber. It was a chilling sound that made my blood run cold. "Pathetic fools," she taunted. "You think your pitiful magic can save you? You've walked into my trap."

"Your plan?" I asked with an arched brow. "Don't you mean Lyra's?" The shadows clawed at us. Their touch was burning through our defenses. Aidon swung his weapon to dispel them, but his efforts seemed futile against their relentless advance.

"Your struggle is meaningless," the siren sneered. "The

prophecy is in motion, and you are but pawns in a game you cannot comprehend."

Nana's light flickered and wavered under the onslaught. "We need to get out of here," she grumbled.

Stella gritted her teeth, focusing her energy. "She's not going to win. We're more powerful."

"You cannot escape your fate," she hissed, raising her arms. The pool of water behind her churned violently.

"You've misinterpreted the prophecy," I said, stepping forward with a confidence I barely felt. "The chosen one will end the darkness and restore the balance between realms."

The siren laughed, a sound like broken glass. "Do you think you can change fate? The prophecy is just words. I am the power here. I am the one who will bring darkness to this world."

Stella's grip on my hand tightened while her eyes remained fixed on the siren. "Why are you doing this? What do you gain from plunging the world into chaos?"

The siren's smile widened. "Power. Control. The satisfaction of seeing mortals and witches alike bend to my will."

Nana's voice was steady, but I could hear the underlying fury. "You won't succeed. We'll stop you."

The siren's eyes gleamed. "You? A group of misfits and children? You have no idea what you're up against."

Aidon stepped forward. "It's you who are mistaken." He let some of his power leak through. It was enough to make the shadows back off.

The siren's expression darkened, and her power thrummed in the air around us. "Then come, *chosen ones,*" she *sneered.* "Let me show you the true meaning of despair."

With a flick of her wrist, runes we hadn't seen on the ground flared to life. I accessed my power and had it manipulate hers. I told it to open the way out. While I was busy trying to use her display to our benefit, the chamber filled with a blinding light. The shadows twisted and danced, forming grotesque shapes that lunged at us.

My loved ones fought the creatures while I worked. They fought back with everything they had. Aidon's blade flashed and cut through shadows. Stella and Nana channeled their magic and bombs exploded inside the darkness, making it dissipate.

"You can't win," I shouted. "We are stronger, and we will bring balance."

The siren's laughter turned to a snarl when I managed to open an exit in the wall. Tseki rushed over and shifted into his dragon form so the stone couldn't roll back into place. The siren bared her teeth at me and growled, "You are nothing!"

But even as she spoke, I could see the cracks in her confidence. If I wasn't mistaken, that was fear behind her eyes. The siren's eyes darted between us and the exit. Her fury was palpable. She took a step back and bared her teeth at me. "This is not over," she hissed. "You may have won this battle, but the prophecy is still in motion. And I will find you alone at some point."

Stella stepped forward with her hands glowing from residual magic. "Good luck with that. Phoebe is never alone."

With a piercing glare, the siren gave a guttural scream of frustration. She turned and leaped back into the pool of water. I sagged as her form disappeared beneath the surface with a splash. The water stilled, and the oppressive darkness began to lift.

I took a deep breath as my heart pounded in my chest. "Is everyone okay?" I asked.

"We're fine," Nana replied as she moved to Tseki's side and leaned against his dragon where it was squished into the exit. "But we need to move before she regroups," she finished.

CHAPTER 17

I grabbed Aidon's hand as he started to leave. "Wait. I have an idea."

Layla groaned and said, "Why do I get the feeling I'm not going to like this?"

I rolled my eyes at her. "This could be the key to us going home in the next hour or so."

Nana straightened. "What are you thinking?"

I smiled at her. "We need to use the water orb. We can turn it into a scrying surface. We aren't leaving without Rosemary, and this will be the easiest way to find her."

Aidon's gaze was steely as he nodded in agreement. His grip hadn't so much as loosened on the hilt of his sword. "We will keep the shadows at bay while you three get to work."

I pressed a kiss to his lips then stepped up to the water orb that floated serenely above a stone plinth. Its surface shimmered with that ethereal light. When we got closer, I swear it pulsed with anticipation. "This isn't the traditional scrying water but it has a unique power," I explained what I had been thinking. "Together, we can channel our magic into the orb asking it to search for Rosemary."

Nana rubbed her hands together with a smile. She was moving far slower than she had been when we entered the Chamber of Shadows. We would need to take a break soon. "Let's do this," Nana said, making me admire how strong the woman was. I may be biased but there was no denying how incredible she was.

Setting those thoughts aside, I focused on finding Rosemary. The three of us formed a circle around the orb. I reached out and clasped Nana's and Stella's hands. We were dealing with a foreign power. The feel of it brushing up against me reminded me we needed to coax it to cooperate. I told them my thoughts and then closed my eyes. I delved deep into the wellspring of power within me and drew forth strands of magic that intertwined with those of the orb. They connected to Stella and Nana next.

I was startled when Stella took the lead and began casting the spell. "Water that flows, water that sees," Stella intoned softly. Nana and I copied her words. "Reveal the path, show us the way. Guide our sight to the one we seek. Unveil her location."

The water within the orb responded to our collective energy. Its surface rippled and swirled with its transcendental glow. The chamber around us seemed to fade away as tendrils of light reached out. They connected our spirits to the magic that was unfolding before us. Images began to form within the orb. They shifted and shimmered like reflections on water.

At first, the images flickered through scenes of unfamiliar landscapes. There was a dense, shadowed forest. It passed too quickly for me to determine if it was the one we had been in when we followed Lyra. Next was a barren, windswept plain. That didn't trigger anything. A tranquil meadow that was bathed in the golden light of a setting sun followed that. None of them showed Rosemary. She might have been taken through there but they weren't the right place. A knot of anxiety tightened in my chest. This might not work. Before I could lose hope, the images stabilized. It settled on a dark chamber illuminated by an unnatural glow. I couldn't see much because it was zoomed in on Rosemary's face.

"Mom," Stella breathed. Her voice was barely audible and her gaze was fixed on the image. "She's alive."

Rosemary's spirit appeared weakened. Her once vibrant aura was now clouded with confusion and fatigue. Even more than usual. Her hands were clasped tightly on her knees as if seeking solace in the evil that surrounded her. The dark circles beneath her eyes were dark purple and made her look even worse.

Seeing her in such a state stirred a deep ache within me. My swell of emotions mirrored the concern etched on the faces of my friends. We stood transfixed. Stella's anger began bubbling to cover the sadness that sparked when she first saw her mother.

"Where is that?" Layla asked. Her voice cut through the tension as she scrutinized the surroundings shown in the orb.

Nana frowned, her brow furrowing in concentration as she studied the details. "It's hard to discern. We can't see enough of the barrier and the surroundings to know for sure."

Aidon's jaw tightened as his gaze fixed on Rosemary's form trapped within the orb. "We have to find a way to break her out of there. She doesn't belong in that place."

Murtagh, his expression grave, stepped closer to the orb, his eyes narrowing in contemplation. "There must be clues we're missing. Something that can help us pinpoint her exact location."

"We need a wider view," Stella growled. Stella's expression was sharp as a blade. If that siren were still standing in front of us, she would be dead. "I can't make out the details. It might help to see if there are windows in the walls. Hell, I would settle for knowing if she was in a house, forest, or cave."

Almost as if in response to her words, the water within the orb rippled and shifted. The image zoomed out to reveal a broader perspective. The craggy stone walls and sandy floors of the chamber came into clearer view. Their rugged textures, wet surfaces, and ancient glyphs were now visible in intricate detail.

"Nice going, Stella," Nana remarked, her voice tinged with satisfaction as she studied the newly revealed scene. "Now we can see the layout of the chamber. And identify those symbols."

Aidon nodded in agreement. "Those are the same markings that lit up on the floor here. We need to find the cavern she's in and breach that barrier," he said, his tone resolute.

Layla stepped forward, flexing her claws thoughtfully. "The barrier appears to be infused with strong magic," she observed. "That'll be on you guys to weaken it." I could hear how much that pissed the shifter off. She wanted to help free Rosemary.

Nana tilted her head. "Perhaps we can disrupt the magic at its source," she suggested. "If we can identify the focal point of the enchantment..."

Stella cut Nana off as she pointed to a faint shimmer near the top of the barrier. "There," she practically shouted. "That seems to be where the magic is most concentrated."

Murtagh's eyes gleamed. "We can create a diversion if there are any guards," he offered, his fingers sprouted claws. "We will protect you while the rest of you work on breaking through."

Nana nodded appreciatively. "We know you will," she told

him with a smile. "Phoebe, Stella, and I will focus on dispelling the magic. We can only succeed if the rest of you provide cover and support."

Aidon squeezed my hand reassuringly, his gaze meeting mine with unwavering resolve. "We're close. This will be over soon," he said quietly in a voice filled with confidence.

I nodded as a surge of determination rose within me. "Let's get Rosemary out of there," I said, my voice steady despite the urgency of our mission.

With a destination in mind, we moved into action. Tseki, his dragon form unsuitable for the narrow confines of the tunnel, reverted to his human guise. His keen eyes scanned the hall. Aidon grabbed my hand while Murtagh picked up Nana. Layla pulled Stella. At Nana's scowl, Murtagh explained, "I don't want the door to close on us. I doubt Phoebe will be able to get those runes active again." That was enough to have us all running. We made it through the exit without issue.

Tseki threw on his clothes while Layla and Murtagh stripped. The oppressiveness of the chamber atmosphere gave way to the familiar, albeit unsettling, surroundings of the siren caves. Scanning both directions in the dimly lit passages, I wondered which way we needed to go. We hadn't gotten directions to Rosemary's prison.

"Layla, Murtagh," I whispered, gesturing to the tunnels at my sides. "Can you track Rosemary's scent?"

Layla nodded, and her wolf started down the tunnel to the right. Murtagh took off to the left. The rest of us stood there watching as they prowled down the passage. Murtagh made a noise that brought Layla up short. When she began trotting back our way, Tseki headed after his mate. He and Murtagh had been together almost a year. They made a formidable team I was grateful to have on my side.

The cave system stretched before us, winding and

twisting like a labyrinth of stone, sand, and shadow. I'd been waiting for the tide to roll in and flood the tunnels ever since we entered it. I wasn't sure if it was magic that kept it at bay, but I was grateful. Initially there was nothing around us. As we got further into the caves, we caught glimpses of other sirens going about their daily routines. Some were eating oysters, others were weaving intricate spells, while more tended to mystical gardens or were engaged in quiet conversation. Each time we came across a group, we pressed ourselves against the walls. Stella and I cast spells so we avoided detection.

Aidon's voice broke the tense silence. "We should head toward the central area of the siren living quarters," he suggested quietly. "If I were keeping someone captive, I'd hide them in the middle of my people."

"I will use spells to help hide us, but I don't want to risk too much. I don't know how sensitive to magic sirens are. And we don't want to alert anyone to our presence," I added.

I cast a spell to quiet our steps while adding an aversion spell that would make others overlook us. With cautious steps, we navigated through the maze of tunnels. It was challenging to avoid patrols of sirens while keeping our senses sharp for any sign of Rosemary's location. My enchantments helped but didn't cover everything.

Finally, after what felt like an eternity of searching, we reached a cavern that seemed more centrally located within the siren enclave. The air here felt charged with a different energy. It became tinged with anticipation and guarded hope. Where was that coming from? Stella gasped softly answering that question. Her hand flew to her mouth and tears welled up in her eyes. "There," she whispered, her voice trembling with emotion.

Aidon stuck his head into a chamber two openings ahead of us. Layla and Murtagh followed with Stella running right next to them. Nana, Tseki and I caught up and my breath caught in my throat. A woman sat hunched in a corner with her back to us. She was surrounded by a shimmering barrier of magic. I would know her silvery and blonde hair anywhere. It was Rosemary. And the water orb had been right. Her spirit was weakened.

"Mom," Stella choked out. Her voice broke with emotion. "We've come to get you out of here."

Rosemary's gaze flickered over her shoulder and lit with recognition. She scrambled to her hands and knees and crawled toward us. Despite the circumstances, Rosemary must have been having a good day because it was clear she knew who Stella was. And that was rare with her Alzheimer's. "Stella? Where am I? Why am I here? I know I forget sometimes, but please don't leave me here."

Stella let out a sob and shook her head back and forth. "We're going to get you out of here and take you home. Don't worry."

I stood on my tiptoes and pressed my lips to Aidon's ear. "We need to ask your mother if she can help her memory. There's nothing the healers can do for her. But there has to be something."

Aidon pressed a kiss to my lips and nodded. "We will deal with that when we get home. You focus on getting her out of there." I read between the lines. There was nothing his mother could do. She could help some, but she could not repair brain matter that was already lost.

I turned back and noticed Rosemary was watching Layla and Murtagh prowl back and forth in front of the barrier. Stella pulled me into her side and pointed to the rune in the corner of the cell. "Let's focus there."

Nodding, Nana and I put a hand on Stella's shoulder. Together, we focused our combined magic on the barrier. We funneled our energy into dismantling the enchantment that held Rosemary captive. Something pushed back at us and nearly blew us off of our feet. I caught myself just in time and made sure Nana stayed upright as well.

"C'mon, we need to get her out," Stella urged anxiously. "Now."

Nana squeezed Stella's shoulder. "We're working on it. Stay focused. We need your help."

I focused my concentration on the barrier. Threads of my own magic intertwined with Nana's, creating a surge of power that crackled through the air. Stella struggled to do much. This wasn't working, but I wasn't going to tell her that. With a determined growl, I extended my hands towards the barrier. If I could get a feel for the resistance, I might be able to gauge how to dismantle it.

Sweat trickled down my forehead as I pressed my palms against the barrier and felt the pulse of its magic against my skin. The barrier was dense. There were layers upon layers of enchanted energy woven tightly together. My fingertips tingled as I probed for weak points. I just needed one place where the magic was less concentrated. I could pull it apart if I found one.

"Nana, focus on the lower left," I instructed when I sensed a slight thinning in the barrier's weave there. "Stella, try to channel your magic into a concentrated beam and aim for the center. We need to disrupt the core."

Nana nodded and her eyes narrowed in concentration as she directed her energy toward the spot I indicated. Her magic was powerful and fresh despite having been at it for over thirty hours. She was a steady force that bolstered me and helped me keep going. I kept poking the hole I found. I got distracted when Stella took a deep breath. Looking over, I saw her hands trembling slightly. She managed to shake it off and aim her magic at the center of the barrier. I went back to work when a beam of light shot from her palms and struck the barrier with a fierce intensity.

"That's it! Keep it steady!" I encouraged, feeling the barrier vibrate under the combined assault. The magic we channeled into it began to create fissures. I noticed a spiderwebbing of cracks shimmer across one corner of the surface. The barrier groaned under our efforts and the cracks spread wider. I could see more of Rosemary now. Her eyes were wide with hope and fear. The sight of her had me pushing harder. I directed a concentrated burst of my own magic into the barrier.

The cavern shook as my magic surged forward. I continued hitting the barrier with unyielding force. The shimmering wall quivered under the assault, but it didn't break. What the hell was it going to take? We were all getting tired.

"Keep pushing!" Aidon's voice rang out, his sword drawn as he stood guard, ready to defend us from any threats.

As if I'd conjured danger, songs echoed in the chamber. It had to come from the sirens that lived there. I had no doubt they'd felt us by now and were approaching to stop us. I tensed for a fight which weakened my assault on the barrier, but I couldn't be caught off guard.

Aidon, Tseki, Layla, and Murtagh sprang into action as soon as the sirens rushed through the archway. Aidon's blade glinted in the dim light as he stood ready. Tseki moved swiftly to guard our flanks. Layla and Murtagh's wolves lunged at the people now trying to stop us. The volume of their song increased. I could feel it trying to work its way past my magical earplugs.

After a scan of the sirens, I realized the one we'd encountered in the Chamber of Shadows was not among them. I was relieved and had to remind myself that these were no less dangerous. Their songs sought to disorient us. When that failed, their expressions twisted into menacing scowls. "You dare defy us?" one of them hissed. Her eyes glowed with malice.

Tseki and Aidon merely laughed. I went back to trying to break through the barrier. If we could free Rosemary, we could get the hell out of there. It was challenging to concentrate when a fierce battle erupted. Our defenders clashed with the sirens with a loud roar.

I checked over my shoulder to make sure those I loved were okay. Aidon's sword cut through the air with deadly precision. Tseki used his agility to dodge the sirens' attacks while countering with powerful strikes. Layla and Murtagh's wolf forms were a blur of motion. Their claws and fangs were lethal against the sirens.

"Almost there!" Nana urged bringing me back to our task.

Sweat dripped down my face as I clawed at the barrier with all of my strength and will. I don't know what Nana was feeling but it didn't seem close to falling. Magical energy sparked and crackled around me. Some of it responded to my command and the rest resisted my efforts. Stella's magic wove in alongside mine. Together our power formed intricate patterns.

"Push harder!" Stella cried, her voice filled with determination.

The barrier groaned under the strain. More small cracks appeared where our magic tore at its seams. Rosemary's face was etched with weariness yet brightening with hope as she sensed our efforts to reach her. Of course, her attention was torn between us and the fight behind us. The cavern was filled with the sounds of clashing steel, snarls, and magical blasts as Aidon, Tseki, Layla, and Murtagh fought to keep the sirens at bay. Unfortunately, more sirens poured into the cavern. The chance of succeeding diminished as their numbers grew.

"Don't let up!" Aidon shouted as he parried a siren's attack before countering with a swift strike.

My heart pounded as exhaustion threatened to overtake me. But we couldn't stop now. We were so close. Gritting my teeth, I focused all my remaining strength into another push. The magical energy around us surged, crackling with intensity. The barrier groaned once more, but still, it did not shatter.

Between one breath and the next, the air grew colder. And I became aware of an oppressive presence filling the cavern. My first thought was Lyra. I spun in a circle searching for the source. I was disappointed and relieved when my gaze landed on the siren from the Chamber of Shadows. She was wearing black clothes this time. It made her look and feel more formidable than the others. The way her aura exuded raw power added to that sense. Her power was stronger, more oppressive. The air around her thrummed with her volatile power, making it harder to concentrate. I gritted my teeth, determined not to let her intimidate us. Her cold and calculating gaze locked onto us. A malicious smile curved her lips as she surveyed the scene.

"You will never free her," she taunted. Her voice was a chilling whisper that resonated through the cavern.

For the first time since we began this journey, I wondered if she might be right. Nana and I were barely holding on. Stella was too emotional to have complete control of her magic. And our protectors were completely overwhelmed by the other sirens. It was not looking good for us.

CHAPTER 18

The prison chamber felt suffocatingly small as we confronted the siren who had imprisoned Rose-mary. Her power filled the space and nudged me. It was her power to compel trying to push at me. What really got me was her wicked smile. It sent a chill down my spine.

"You dare challenge me?" the siren's voice echoed and each word dripped with venomous sweetness. She lifted her hands gracefully, the air around her shimmering with an ethereal glow. "You mortals are fools to think you can stand against my power."

"Mortals?" Aidon raised an eyebrow as he looked over from fighting her fellow sirens. "We've come for Rosemary. Release her now, or face the consequences."

The siren's smile widened and her eyes gleamed with amusement. "Ah, but I have plans for dear Rosemary. Plans that do not involve her leaving this place." With a toss of her long hair, she began to weave a haunting melody. The notes twisted and coiled around us like tendrils of smoke. That hadn't happened last time. And it hadn't happened with the others in the chamber. Those still alive joined their voices with the woman I assumed was the leader.

I shook my head to clear it and quipped, "I can't believe I thought a powerful witch like Lyra was ever teamed up with you. It's clear you're nothing more than her victims."

The leader's scowl deepened and her voice increased in intensity after she ran her thumb over a ring she was wearing. The song filled the chamber. To my horror, the hypnotic rhythm disoriented me. My head grew heavy and my thoughts were muddled by the siren's enchanting voice. Stella stumbled, clutching her ears as if trying to block out the mesmerizing tune.

"Nana, snap out of it!" I shouted. My voice sounded distant and distorted. While I still had the ability to think freely, I focused on my magic. I pictured the magical earplugs and then made them impenetrable by their magic. Her song had gotten an upgrade since we'd last seen her. We were so close to saving Rosemary and getting the hell out of there and I refused to let her win now.

Nana grabbed my hand, squeezed it, and then inclined her head. Together, we cast the spell and included our friends. Layla and Murtagh shook themselves and launched back into attacking the sirens. My head cleared and I cast a magical bomb and threw it at the back of the sirens. Body parts flew into the air, making my stomach roil.

"You will regret defying me," the siren hissed, her voice now tinged with anger. She raised her hands, conjuring tendrils of magic that snaked toward us with malicious intent.

Aidon's sword gleamed in the dim light as he swung it and laughed at her. "Focus on breaking the spell. I want to get out of here."

The lead siren put a hand behind her back and I countered

with a barrier that would deflect the attack I suspected was coming. Behind her, I saw Layla and Murtagh leap through the air and tackle sirens. Tseki unleashed a roar that shook the chamber. It was terrifying in his human form. I'd hate to hear him do that when he was a dragon. With each clash of magic and steel, the air crackled with tension and raw power. Nana, Stella and I tried to unravel the barrier while also fighting the lead siren. She remained focused on us. There were so many others that Aidon couldn't break away and come help us.

"Watch her. I'm not sure what she did a second ago, but I sense something building," I told Nana and Stella.

They nodded in agreement, and we continued to cast. I alternated my spells. One was aimed at the lead siren. The next was aimed at weakening her hold over the prison. She let out a growl and pulled out small, intricately carved onyx sphere from behind her back. My mind was torn between wondering where she'd pulled that from and taking in the glowing arcane symbols covering it. The sphere hummed with a faint, ominous energy. When she set it down, its surface rippled as if containing something alive.

"That's not good," I muttered as I threw a magical bomb right at her. It landed on the sand and made the sphere bounce three feet into the air.

The lead siren smirked at me as she pushed several symbols at once. The frequency changed when she did that. Stella cursed and said, "She activated the damn thing." As she fell into the barrier. I reached for Nana as the ground rolled beneath our feet. Whatever that artifact was, it was powerful.

Aidon cursed long enough to make a sailor blush and his grip tightening on his sword. That made all of us stop and take notice. A sharp crack made me duck and pull Nana with me. Glancing over, my heart skipped a beat when the air began to shimmer and warp. To my horror, a horde of creatures unlike any I had seen before emerged from a newly created portal. Not that it was like any portal I'd ever seen.

They looked like demons with twisted horns and jagged claws. They slithered forth, and their red eyes burned with malice. Next came scaled beasts that had three legs. There were so many of them that Aidon, Layla, Murtagh, and Tseki backed up to join us. We abandoned the barrier for the moment and focused on the battle in front of us. Stella gasped and her hand covered her mouth in horror. "What are these things?"

Nana's voice rang out clear and steady as she barked, "Stay focused! We can't let them overwhelm us!"

Aidon raised his sword, his jaw set in determination. "Everyone, stick together! Take them down, one by one."

I shivered when a series of low guttural growls and hissing reverberated through the chamber in response. The sounds promised death and destruction. This was not going to be a pleasant fight. I inched back and pulled Nana with me. She and I were the most vulnerable. My mind didn't even get started with trying to come up with a spell that would take the enemy out but not hurt any of us because the artifact's glow turned red. And something much worse stepped through.

"Lyra," I hissed.

"You thought you could beat me?" Lyra tsked us. "You stepped right into my trap. And now I have you right where I want you."

Fucking shit!

Layla bared her teeth while Tseki partially shifted. "We can handle this," he growled. His talons slashed through the air as he prepared to fight. This form was difficult for him, but his dragon was too big for the chamber. The Twisted Sisters visit for Nina's birthday suddenly seemed fated. They'd spent a long time talking to him about how they could shift into smaller dragons. He'd been experimenting and discovered his lizard-man form. It just took a lot of his energy to hold for long.

Murtagh lowered his front legs and began growling at the creatures eyeing him. As if that was a signal, Layla howled and launched herself at a cluster of creatures. That kicked things off. Tseki unleashed a deafening roar that shook the chamber as he threw himself into the fray with flames streaming from his mouth.

I summoned my own magic, tendrils of energy coalescing around me as I threw a magical bomb into the middle of the sirens at the back. Aidon went for Lyra and nearly claimed her head. She moved faster than any witch should and managed to put herself in the middle of her minions.

The creatures advanced with swift, coordinated movements. Demons lunged with deadly precision. Their claws slashed through the air. Lyra cast spells that crackled with arcane energy, seeking to ensnare us in her grasp. My magic reacted instinctively and I started flinging shields that absorbed her power. The problem with that was I couldn't stop and send anything to the creatures. At least we'd managed to thin the sirens out.

Stella and Nana's combined magic created a protective barrier that shimmered around us, deflecting the first wave of attacks. Layla and Murtagh struck back with swift and precise blows, their attacks finding vulnerable spots on the creatures' bodies. Tseki's flames engulfed several. Their screams echoed in the chamber as they were consumed by fire. His flames got close to Lyra and forced her closer to Aidon's blade.

My mate fought like a god possessed. His sword was a blur of steel as he parried and struck at the creatures around us. With each swing, he cleaved through demonic flesh and inhuman forms. His skill as a warrior was evident in every movement. And within no time, body parts began to pile up behind him. It created an obstacle for the others trying to get to us.

Despite our efforts, the creatures pressed on. Their numbers seemed endless. They remained fixed on us with a hunger for bloodshed. The noise of my magic battling Lyra's was deafening. It was clear why she'd lived this long performing forbidden magic. She was not going to be easy to beat. My defense faltered when the stench of sulfur filled the space. That had everyone looking around. Aidon had removed his Underworld charm and slammed it into the side of one of the demon-like creatures. One of the scaly things had snuck up behind him and sliced open his side.

"Aidon!" I shouted. He turned his gaze to me for a split second before he sliced the creature in two. I learned two things in that moment. One, his amulet hadn't sent it back to the Underworld, so these weren't demons. And two, he was fine and would be pissed if I let this distract me. "We need to take out that artifact!" I shouted above the din. My voice was barely audible over the chaos of battle.

Nana put her hand on my back and said, "I'll try to disrupt its power." She'd stayed behind me and Stella and had thrown her offensive spells from there.

The rest of us fought fiercely, buying Nana the time she needed. I could feel Nana's power building. It was like a roaring fire behind me. She unleashed a powerful wave of magic and directed it toward the artifact. The glyphs on its surface glowed fiercely for a moment, resisting her efforts. I couldn't help because I was still combating Lyra's spells. There was a pause in her next attack. Without thinking, I threw a magical arrow at her. It was slender and harder to detect. It was also harder to hit someone. I crowed when her eyes went wide, and blood started pouring from her shoulder. It was then that Nana finally managed to hit the artifact.

The sphere shattered into a thousand metal pieces, all covered with sigils.

Lyra and her creatures faltered. She recovered quickly and resumed throwing shit at me, but their movements were slowed. Their attacks became less coordinated. Lyra chanted something, and her creatures perked up. They fought with renewed vigor. I lost track of what the others were doing. It was enough to stay in front of Nana and keep Lyra's spells from hitting us.

I didn't know how long I could keep this up. Yes, the creatures were thinning and the sirens had either fled or been killed. Except for the leader. She was still there. In fact, she threw something at me from the side. I turned when the rock hit me in the side of the head. That distraction cost me. One of Lyra's spells hit my left breast. The babies managed to erect a protective barrier, but the force spun me around.

I heard Nana cry out and scrambled to right myself while continuing to stop Lyra's spells. I heaved a sigh of relief when she was reacting to Stella. She'd formed a faint, shimmering light between her palms. My eyes widened as the glow intensified. I tried to keep an eye on what was happening while also battling Lyra. Not that I was able to throw anything at her. I was going to need to practice and come up with something better than a magical bomb to beat her. I almost faltered when I saw Stella's hands move with a grace and power she had never had before. She was weaving intricate patterns in the air and tapping into something ancient and profound.

"Stella?" I whispered, awe creeping into my voice.

Aidon's keen eyes caught the subtleties of the magic at play and was the first to piece it together. "It's Stella," he grunted as he decapitated one of the creatures. "We were wrong about the prophecy. It's her."

Stella's eyes widened in shock, but she didn't stop

moving. The light from her hands cast a radiant aura that filled the chamber. "I don't understand," she said and yelped when a scaly beast lunged for her. Layla tackled it from the side. "How can it be me?" Stella asked as if she hadn't just almost been eaten.

"Because you're the best of us," I told her as the power emanating from her filled me with hope. "You can do this, Stella. You're stronger than you realize."

Nana grunted and tossed a spell toward the siren leader who was trying to reach us. "Trust the magic, Stella. It has chosen you for a reason."

Layla and Murtagh positioned themselves to guard Stella as she worked. Tseki had shifted back to human and was racing around the room, tackling creatures from all over. Stella took a deep breath and continued. She was more confident now. The glow around her intensified. The ancient magic of the oracle's prophecy swirled through the air.

Stella unleashed a series of powerful spells. The intricate patterns she wove in the air shimmered with energy, and each one resonated with a force that shook the foundations of the cave. The closest creatures summoned by the artifact shrieked and writhed as Stella's magic washed over them, banishing them back to whatever nasty realm they had come from.

Lyra growled, shifted gears, and began throwing spells all around the chamber. It shattered Stella's focus and rattled her. She continued what she was doing, but her power had more to combat. I saw some of Stella's power hit Lyra. Of course, that enraged the corrupt witch. Her siren friend joined her in the battle. The chamber trembled as Stella's new power clashed with the siren and Lyra's dark magic. The walls pulsed and rippled and the air was alive with the battle between light and darkness.

Lyra stopped and smirked. "It's been a pleasure, but I have

an important appointment to keep." With a salute, the Dark witch vanished into thin air.

"How the hell did she do that?" I blurted.

"We will figure this out later. We need to end this and free my mom," Stella snarled. She was right. The battle was not over. However, we had taken a significant step toward victory in making Lyra retreat.

CHAPTER 19

"*W*hy don't they tuck tail like their leader? Or change sides?" Nana asked from behind me. "I guess we can't all be blessed with intelligence."

My snort was lost in the cacophony of clashing steel, snarls, and the crackle of unleashed magic. There was no responding when my breath was coming in ragged gasps. Her question was rhetorical anyway. My forearm wiped the sweat dripping down my forehead and stinging my eyes. A sharp pain in my abdomen made me freeze in place. Was something wrong with my babies? They each rolled at the same time as if in response to my worries.

My arms shot up to protect myself from the claws coming at me. Distraction was not good in battle. Thankfully, Aidon's blade flashed through the gloom and sliced through the creature with deadly precision. His face was a mask of grim determination, and his muscles strained with every swing.

Stella stood beside me, her hands glowing as she fired bolts of magic. Each one struck true but was taking its toll on her already pale features. I'd bet anything she was still trying to wrap her mind around being the chosen one. The magic Nana sent forth illuminated the darkness the sirens thrived in, making it easier for Layla and Murtagh to stalk their prey. I'd thought all the sirens were gone before. This was why I was better with my family by my side. I grinned when the sleek, predatory wolves lunged and snapped with relentless ferocity.

Exhaustion gnawed at the edges of my resolve and I could see the others were getting just as tired. Aidon's swings became slower, and his breath more labored. Stella's energy bolts came less frequently, and her hands trembled with the effort. We had a chance to win this. Our enemies were just as tired. That was why the lead siren's skin was flickering with dark scales. She was losing her control over the shift. That happened when creatures capable of changing forms were fatigued.

"You should listen to Nana and give up!" Aidon's voice cut through the noise as he taunted the lead siren. He parried a swipe from the siren's sharp fingernails. He spun, but she evaded his blade. Unfortunately for one of her friends, Aidon delivered a devastating slash that sent the creature reeling. Its screech was a horrific sound. It was music to my ears when more filled its place.

I gritted my teeth, focusing my remaining energy on a shockwave that sent a group of sirens sprawling. Beside me, Stella fired another bolt. Her face was etched with exhaustion and determination. "We can't keep this up much longer," she panted as her eyes darted around the cavern in search of any reprieve.

"Just a little longer," Nana urged in a steady voice despite the weariness in her eyes. There was the strong woman who had helped raise me. I got my grit from her and my mom. Without them, I wouldn't have been deserving of Hattie's magic. And I hadn't realized precisely how astonishing they were until I was facing a divorce after a twenty-year marriage. Nana raised her hands and threw another spell. "We have to hold on," she told us.

Layla growled deep in her throat, her fur bristling as she tore into a creature that ventured too close to us. Murtagh was equally ferocious and held the line beside her. Their coordination was flawless and fierce.

In the midst of the chaos, the lead siren's gaze locked onto Nana. With a malicious grin, she lunged, her claws extended and aimed for Nana's throat. "Nana, look out!" I screamed. The words tore from my throat, but the warning was almost too late. The siren's claws were a breath away from slashing into her.

Tseki roared and shifted in a blur of motion. I expected him to crush us all in his reaction. Nana treated him like her grandson and gave him the family a Tainted witch named Myrna had stolen from him. Scales erupted along Tseki's skin as he transformed into his partial dragon form. His massive frame interposed between Nana and her attacker. With a powerful swipe of his claws, he sent the siren crashing back against the cave wall.

Nana looked up at Tseki eyes wide with shock and gratitude. "Thank you," she breathed, quickly regaining her composure and magic to defend him.

Tseki remained steadfast with his half-dragon form, making a formidable shield. "Stay behind me," he growled, his voice deeper and more resonant with his dragon strength.

The lead siren recovered and snarled with fury. Her eyes narrowed as she assessed her new opponent. She raised her hands, energy crackling menacingly between her fingers. "You cannot win," she hissed. Gone was the musical quality. Now, her voice was a grating sound that made my skin crawl. "This is our domain."

"Not for long," I shot back, summoning the last reserves of my strength. I directed a blast of energy at the lead siren, hitting her square in the chest. She staggered, and I summoned more power for another attack. Stella, Aidon, and Nana joined their magic with mine, creating a brilliant wave of light that pushed the sirens further back.

The lead siren screeched in rage. She wavered as our combined light engulfed her. The remaining creatures faltered as well. Their strength was tied to hers! It was like a lightbulb went off in my head. Hope flickered in my heart. The fight was far from over, but we weren't out of this yet.

"We end this now!" Aidon shouted as he obviously saw what I had. He raised his blade high. It became a rallying point for our battered spirits. We reassembled our remaining strength, gathering every ounce of power we had left. The cavern filled with the combined force of our magic and might. It was much easier to reach into the dregs of my reserves and pull out more energy when I was in my twenties. Sheer stubbornness was the only way I was able to muster anything more at that moment.

The lead siren's presence became more menacing and her power more palpable as she did the same. Several curses slipped from my mouth. She shouldn't have anything left, dammit. Her eyes glowed with an eerie light, and a cruel smile played on her lips. The cavern was a battlefield of chaos and desperation. Aidon's blade flashed as it sailed toward the lead siren. Somehow one of her people managed to throw herself in front of the assault. Aidon sliced through the newcomer with a swift practiced motion. He didn't let up as he continued trying to reach the lead siren.

The offensive spells I tossed at her came slower which enabled other creatures and sirens to intercept those as well. At least they were taking themselves out. Next to me, Stella's magic sparked erratically while Nana's fell short of any of the enemy. I was okay with that because it meant she was well out of harm's way. It took more courage than I ever thought I had for Nana to continue fighting regardless of the danger and how tired I knew she was. I prayed I was like her at ninety.

Layla and Murtagh's wolves were a blur of fur and fangs. Their growls and snarls were a constant background to the clash of steel and magic. Tseki was still partially shifted and tearing through our enemies with relentless fury. It helped that his scaled arms were able to deflect the worst of what the sirens and creatures could throw at him.

Panic threatened to swallow me whole when my magic dwindled, and that pain was back in my abdomen. I had to push myself, but every spell became a strain. Crap. All we had to do was take out the lead siren, and we could end this bullshit. Unfortunately, she seemed inexhaustible. Her movements were graceful yet deadly. She wielded Dark magic with a cruel precision as her laughter echoed through the cavern. Aidon's black wings flew out of his back. He parried a swipe from one of the remaining creatures standing between him and the siren. His sword sliced through it with a burst of dark ichor.

With a final, desperate surge of power, I directed my power toward the lead siren. Stella and Nana joined forces with me. Our combined magic formed a brilliant wave of energy that struck the siren with unyielding force. She screamed a sound of pure rage and pain. We'd torn a massive hole in her chest.

"We almost have her. Just a little more!" I yelled, feeling the strain in my voice and body. We poured every ounce of strength into the attack, our magic intertwining into a blinding beam of energy. Aidon's sword joined ours while Tseki, Layla, and Murtagh fought the other creatures.

The lead siren staggered as her screams filled the cavern.

Aidon ended things with a powerful swing of his sword. His blade struck true, cutting through her with a finality that echoed through the space. When pieces of her body fell to the floor, the remaining creatures faltered. Their strength was tied to her Dark magic, and we'd dealt them a blow. It didn't take long for my shifters to cut through them. One by one, they fell beneath Tseki, Layla, and Murtagh's assault. Silence fell over the cavern, the echoes of our battle lingering like ghosts.

We stood there, heaving and exhausted, surrounded by the aftermath of our desperate fight. The air was thick with the scent of sweat, blood, and magic. Stella's gaze turned toward the mysticall barrier that still held her mother captive.

"Mom," she whispered, her voice filled with longing and frustration. Rosemary's eyes filled with hope and fear.

Stella clenched her fists as a few tears escaped her eyes. "I had hoped," she said through gritted teeth, "that when the lead siren died, her spell would go with her." Her voice was heavy with disappointment and anger.

We stood amidst the wreckage of our battle and the heavy atmosphere left in the aftermath of our desperate fight. Stella's gaze remained fixed on the shimmering barrier that still held her mother captive. Nana stepped forward and placed a reassuring hand on Stella's shoulder. "Stella, you are the chosen one of the prophecy. You should be able to get past this barrier. You just need to keep trying," Nana encouraged her.

Stella snorted, rolling her eyes. "Being chosen is over-rated, Nana. I've got a magic hangover and a serious craving for a nap. Whoever selected me needs lessons in providing cheat sheets or instruction books. I can't do something I don't know how to do."

I chuckled and wrapped an arm around Stella's shoulders.

"We almost had it before the lead siren and Lyra showed up. We need to work together again. We can do this."

Stella nodded, her earlier frustration giving way to resolve. "Fine. Let's get Mom out of there."

We formed a circle around the barrier, our collective energy humming through the air. The familiar tingle of magic spread to my fingertips. "Alright, everyone. Channel your energy into me, and I'll focus it on the barrier. We've got enough weak spots along the outer edges that it should fall if we hit the middle with everything we've got."

Aidon, Layla, Murtah, and Tseki formed a protective perimeter. There was nothing left alive in the chamber, but they were taking no chances. Stella, Nana, and I closed our eyes, and the warmth of their power mingled with mine almost instantly.

"Focus on the barrier," I instructed. "Imagine our energy weaving together and striking it like a sledgehammer."

We concentrated, and our magic intertwined into a giant mass of power. When it was too big to hold, I pushed it toward the barrier. There was a resistance like a solid wall. We pushed harder. The barrier quivered, and cracks began to spread across its surface.

"We're almost through!" I urged.

We poured every ounce of strength into the attack. It didn't take as much as the first assault. It had to have been weakened by the siren's death. The barrier groaned under the assault, and the cracks widened. With a resounding crack, it shattered into shimmering fragments that dissolved into the air. We stumbled forward, the sudden release of energy leaving us breathless.

Stella rushed to her mother with tears streaming down her face. "Mom!" she cried, wrapping Rosemary in a tight embrace.

Rosemary's eyes filled with tears of relief and love. "Stella, my sweet girl," she whispered, holding her daughter close. "What is going on here? What was all that fighting about?"

Stella placated her mother, gauging her memory and how the stress of being kidnapped had impacted her. Unlike her children, Stella's mother didn't develop magic. It was a good thing with her Alzheimer's. We theorized that was why. Magic in her hands would be dangerous.

I watched the reunion, my heart swelling with emotion. It had been a long two days of hard fighting and trudging through Lyra's evil. Rosemary looked around at us, her gaze filled with confusion. "Can we go home now?"

I smiled, nodding. "Yes, Rosemary. Let's go home."

CHAPTER 20

*W*e had been home for a few days now, the surreal adventure behind us feeling almost like a distant dream. The kitchen was filled with the comforting aroma of freshly baked bread and the familiar hum of everyday life brought a sense of peace. Nana sat on her usual stool on the island. She had a cup of tea in her hands as she regaled Nina, Mom, Selene, and Mythia with the harrowing tale of our rescue mission.

"So there we were, surrounded by sirens and their demonic monsters," Nana said dramatically. Her eyes twinkled with mischief. "Phoebe's magic lit up the cavern like the Fourth of July while Stella and I broke apart the ranks like bowling pins."

Nina leaned forward with wide eyes. "Really? How were you not frightened and going out of your mind?"

Nana scowled at Nina. "I was scared shitless, but that doesn't mean I could sit there and suck my thumb. They would have all protected me, but they needed me. There will be situations where you have to set aside your fear and do the hard thing."

I chuckled, taking a sip of my own tea. "We had to use every bit of magic we possessed to break through the barrier. It was intense."

Mom looked from me to Stella and asked, "And what about Rosemary? Did Lyra do anything to her?" I knew what Mom was asking. She'd been turned into a tribred and was now part vampire and part shifter in addition to being a witch.

Stella paused in chopping vegetables nearby and turned to respond. "My mom seems to be fine. She was happy to be back in her room. So far, there is no indication Lyra did anything to her."

Aidon nodded in agreement. "We will keep an eye out just to be safe. But they've left out a key piece of information about how Stella tapped into some ancient magic because she's the chosen one of the prophecy."

"Chosen one? Ancient magic?" Mythia echoed as she fluttered near Stella's head. "Tell us more about that!"

Stella shrugged, trying to downplay her role. "It was... unexpected. I didn't know I had it in me. And when the time came, it just happened. I don't know how to use it. I hope I can call on it when we face Lyra again. I lost control, and she got away."

Nana nodded sagely. "That's the thing about prophecies. They reveal themselves in their own time. It will be there when you need it."

As they continued discussing the details, I leaned back and took it all in. The kitchen was filled with laughter and chatter. The normalcy of the moment was a stark contrast to the chaos we'd faced. My gaze drifted to Aidon, who was grabbing something out of the pastry bin. A swell of gratitude filled my chest. Despite the danger and fear, we had come through it stronger and more connected than ever. My eyes wandered to Stella, who caught my gaze and smiled. She had grown so much during our adventure, and I was endlessly proud of her.

My hands rested on my growing belly. The triplets I was expecting kicked and squirmed in response. They were eager to be part of things already. The pregnancy had been a joyful journey so far, but it was also one filled with moments of anxiety. As I stood there, listening to the familiar voices of my family, a sharp pain suddenly shot through my abdomen. I gasped, clutching at my stomach, and the room fell silent.

"Phoebe?" Aidon was at my side in an instant. There was worry etched into his beautiful features. Another wave of pain hit me before I could respond, and my legs buckled. Aidon caught me just in time and carried me to the living room.

"Pheebs, what's wrong?" Stella's voice trembled as she knelt beside the sofa where Aidon had laid me. Her hand went to my shoulder.

"I... don't know," I managed to whisper. My vision blurred with tears. The pain wasn't normal. I couldn't help the deep, instinctual fear for the lives growing inside me.

Aidon didn't waste a moment. He pulled out his phone and dialed a number with shaky hands. "Mom, it's Phoebe. Something's wrong with the babies. We need you and Dad here, now." This was bad if he was calling them. He knows Hades and Persephone are the last people I would want to see like this.

At the same time, my mother hurried to the other room to call Clio, the local healer. "Clio, we need you at the house immediately. It's Phoebe. She's in trouble."

I tried to speak, to tell them I would be alright, but the words wouldn't come. My breath hitched in my throat, and I felt a cold sweat break out across my forehead. Aidon held me tightly. He wasn't able to hide the slight tremble in his arms.

"Stay with me, Pheebs," he murmured, brushing my hair back from my face. "Help is on the way. Just hold on."

Nana knelt by my head and placed a hand on my cheek. Her usually calm demeanor was replaced with a look of deep concern. "You're strong, Phoebe. You've got this. Hold onto those babies and breathe."

I nodded weakly, focusing on the steady rise and fall of Aidon's chest as he held me. But beneath the surface, a terrifying thought gnawed at me. What if I lost our babies? Fear gripped me and tightened its hold with each passing second.

Clio arrived swiftly. Her presence brought a measure of relief. She was a gifted healer. I hoped she could find out what was going on and fix it. I hadn't done anything, so I wasn't so sure it was something in her wheelhouse. She knelt beside me, and her hands moved over me. Her warmth bled into me as she assessed the situation.

"She's bleeding internally," Clio said, her voice calm but urgent. "We need to stabilize her and the babies. Aidon, keep talking to her."

Aidon squeezed my hand, his voice gentle but firm. "Phoebe, you're going to be okay. We're right here with you. Just hold on."

I clung to his words, trying to steady my racing heart. But deep down, the fear persisted. A dark cloud overshadowed the love and support around me. I couldn't shake the worry that something might happen to our precious triplets. And that thought threatened to overwhelm me.

As Clio worked her healing magic, Aidon's parents appeared in a flash of light. The room was filled with a tense silence as Clio continued her work. Aidon's parents and the rest of our family gathered around the couch where I lay. Aidon's hand tightly gripped mine, offering silent support. Clio worked for several more seconds before she stopped and sat back on her heels. The fear and uncertainty from earlier still lingered. I had to steel myself for whatever she was about to say.

Clio's face was etched with concern, her brows knit tightly together as she began to speak. "Phoebe, I need to be straightforward with you," she started, her voice steady but tinged with worry. "During my examination, I discovered an injury to your spleen. It was the source of the bleeding. I was able to stop the worst of the bleeding, but not all. It appears to be a result of the Dark magic you were exposed to during the battle with Lyra."

A chill ran down my spine. My mind raced back to the fierce confrontation and the searing pain that had followed one of Lyra's spells. Clio's expression softened slightly as she continued. "Like I said, I've managed to heal the physical damage to your spleen. However, there's a lingering injury caused by Lyra's Dark magic that I can't completely mend. Her magic is deeply entwined with your tissues. And it's resisting all conventional healing methods."

Aidon's grip on my hand tightened. His concern was evident. "What does this mean for the babies?" I asked, trying to keep my voice steady despite the mounting fear.

Clio took a deep breath. Her eyes met mine with sympathy and understanding. "Carrying triplets is already a significant strain on your body. With this injury, it's even more critical that you make substantial changes to ensure you carry them to full term. You'll need to minimize stress, avoid any strenuous activities, and get plenty of rest. Any further complications could pose serious risks."

The gravity of her words weighed heavily on me. My mind was a whirl of thoughts. It took about a millisecond for a fierce resolve to emerge. "I'll do whatever it takes," I said firmly. "I will protect my children, no matter what."

Persephone, Aidon's mother, stepped forward. Her presence was calm yet commanding. "Phoebe, there might be something I can do," she said. "But I must warn you, it carries significant risk."

Download the next book in the Mystical Midlife in Maine subseries, POLTERGEISTS & CHANGE OF LIFE HERE! Then turn the page for a preview.

Download the next book in the Midlife Magic & Mysteries series, SWEATY NIGHTS & GATOR BITES HERE. Then turn the page for a preview.

"*W*hat?" I asked. My mind was a jumbled mess. I couldn't be sure that I heard her right or if it was wishful thinking. My gaze skipped around the room. All of my loved ones except for my son Jean-Marc were in the house.

Nana was sitting on the arm of the couch and watching with keen interest. Mom was wringing her hands. Nina, Stella, Aidon, Tseki, Layla, Selene, Mythia, and Murtagh formed a protective barrier at the other side of the room. The atmosphere was thick with anticipation and concern.

Persephone sat on the coffee table in front of me. Her ethereal presence was both calming and intense. She was the reason I was pregnant in the first place. She'd given me something to boost my fertility when I was in the Underworld. She and Hades had balked at me being with their son, but they knew we were Fated for one another and decided to take matters into their hands regarding grandchildren.

"Phoebe," Persephone began, "I said there is a way to counteract the Dark magic injury to your spleen, but it comes with great risks."

She snapped her fingers, and several papers appeared in her hand. They looked like they were old, which meant they were likely vellum. Aidon helped me sit up and I looked at what she laid on the table between her and Hades. There were ancient runes and diagrams on the sheet. Everyone leaned in, curious about what she had. "The potion required to neutralize the dark spell is incredibly complex," Persephone explained. Her finger traced the intricate symbols. "It needs the essence of a shadow orchid which is a rare ingredient found only in the Underworld."

A hushed silence fell over the room as her words sank in. I felt Aidon's hand tighten around mine. His support grounded me as the gravity of the situation became clear. "This potion," Persephone continued, "can neutralize the dark spell. But its effects are unpredictable. It might save you and the triplets. But it could also harm all or some of you."

Aidon shook his head. "We cannot risk my mate," he insisted. The torment in his eyes when he looked at me nearly killed me. My hand went to my stomach, where the babies rolled. He put his hand over mine.

"This is our only chance, son," Persephone said, getting our attention. I blanched when I looked over. Her gaze penetrated my soul. "They will all be lost if we do nothing."

I swallowed hard. My worry wasn't for myself. I was frightened for my unborn children. I might not have chosen to get pregnant. but they were mine. I would do anything to protect them. The thought of our triplets, so tiny and vulnerable, fueled my resolve. "We have to save them. What do we need to do?" I asked.

Persephone nodded, acknowledging my determination. "Aidon," she said, turning to my mate, "you must journey to the Underworld to retrieve the shadow orchid. Only you can retrieve this for your mate. And time is of the essence. The longer the dark magic remains, the more it endangers Phoebe and the babies."

Aidon cupped my cheek, making me look at him. I allowed everything I was feeling into my eyes for him to see. His face hardened with determination, and he inclined his head. "I'll go," he said as he held my gaze. "But Phoebe, you need to promise me you'll stay safe while I'm gone."

"I promise," I replied, squeezing his hand. "I won't leave the house until you get back."

"That is best, Phoebe." Persephone grabbed my hand, snagging my attention. "The process of extracting and combining the essence of the flower with other rare ingredients is delicate and fraught with peril. I will need to use your sanctum once Aidon returns with the ingredients."

"What else do I need to get?" Aidon asked his mother.

"I will make you a list. You can find most of it in my garden at the house." As Persephone spoke, Nana reached out and placed a comforting hand on my arm. "We're all here for you, Phoebe," Nana said softly. "You're not alone in this."

Mom nodded in agreement, her eyes shining with determination. "We'll do whatever it takes to keep you and the babies safe," she said, her voice firm.

Stella gave me a smile from where she was hugging Nina. "We've faced so much together, Phoebe. We'll get through this too." Her voice was filled with confidence and strength.

I nodded to them and listened as plans were made. It felt like I was in a nightmare and just needed to wake up. Unfortunately, this was my reality. Aidon would soon depart for the Underworld, and I would have to prepare for the risks of the potion. It was comforting to know I had my family and friends by my side. Knowing I was not in this alone made all the difference in the world.

The Underworld was a place of shadows and danger, even for the son of Hades. Aidon's eyes were usually so warm and reassuring. Now they reflected a steely resolve that made my heart ache. His brow furrowed as he met my gaze. "I'm worried about leaving you here, especially with Lyra still a threat," he admitted.

"She can't get past the wards," I reminded him. "We've boosted them many times, and we have pixies patrolling the entire perimeter. This is the safest place for me."

He took my hands in his. His grip was firm, grounding me amidst the swirling emotions. "I know. It's impossible for me not to worry, though. You need to stay safe, Phoebe. And protect our children. I'll return as quickly as I can."

The warmth of his touch was a stark contrast to the chill that had settled in my bones at the thought of him venturing into the Underworld alone. "I will," I whispered, my voice catching. "Just come back to us."

He kissed me gently, his lips soft against mine, but the kiss was filled with an intensity that conveyed everything he couldn't put into words. His eyes were filled with love and resolve when they locked onto mine for a moment longer before he turned away. Hades stood up and did something with his arms.

A swirling vortex of darkness materialized in the middle of the room. It was a portal to the Underworld. Aidon stood up and stepped toward it without looking back. When he crossed the threshold, the evil seemed to swallow him whole. My heart lurched when he disappeared. I had to bite back my sob. I was being ridiculous. Yes, it was dangerous, but he was the son of Hades, and he had a contingent of UIS agents who would be by his side protecting him.

The silence that followed was deafening. I lay there, staring at the spot where he had disappeared. Fear and hope churned in my chest. Remembering he went to save the babies, I helped to ease the ache in my heart so it was bearable.

With Aidon gone, a fierce determination welled up inside me. I placed my hands on my growing belly, feeling the life within me. "I won't let anything happen to you," I vowed quietly, sensing their faint movements in response. Despite the Dark magic threatening my life and the relentless danger posed by Lyra, I had to stay strong.

Nana moved closer and placed a comforting hand on my shoulder. "He'll be alright, Phoebe," she said softly. "He's strong, and he loves you more than anything."

I nodded, trying to muster a smile, but it felt hollow. "I know, Nana. I just hate that he has to do this alone."

Mom stepped forward and took Aidon's vacant spot on the couch. "Everything will work out, Phoebe. You need to think about you and the babies. They need your full attention right now."

The room seemed to come alive with the collective resolve of my family and friends. The unity and love that surrounded me bolstered my spirits. As my swirling emotions settled, I took a deep breath and straightened my shoulders. "You're right," I said, my voice stronger now. "Let's get ready. What can we do while he's gone?" I asked Persephone.

"Prepare the sanctum by cleansing it so the ambient magic doesn't fight against me when I get to work. Normally, a witch's energy won't bother me, but you're a Pleiades, as was the witch before you. Most importantly, I do not want to take any chances with this process. Too much is riding on my successful endeavor."

Hades placed a hand on Persephone's shoulder and interrupted before I could agree to ensure the sanctum was cleansed. "My wife is right. There is too much on the line. I want to go and explore every possible avenue to minimize the risks this potion poses to you and the babies. Persephone will help. Trust that we won't leave anything to chance," he assured me.

The temptation to ask for clarity was overridden by the desire to have Aidon's parents out of the house. They'd been frosty with me at the beginning, and I had a hard time getting past that. It would be good not to have them hovering over me, so I nodded in agreement. Hades opened another portal, and the couple left without delay.

The room buzzed with activity after that. Nana talked to Mom about brewing one of her many herbal concoctions. I lost sight of them when they went into the kitchen. Nina grabbed a pillow and put it behind my back, then grabbed my favorite fluffy blanket. "Lay back, Mom. Can I get you anything?" my daughter asked as she tucked the soft fabric around my legs.

Shaking my head, I smiled up at her. "No, thank you."

"This tea will help keep you calm, Phoebe," Nana said as she and Mom returned to the living room. "You need to stay relaxed for the babies."

Mom had a tablet and pen in hand and sat on the table where Persephone had been. "We'll make sure you have plenty of rest and minimal stress," Mom promised as she scribbled down a detailed schedule to help manage my days. "You need to let the rest of us help with anything you need and stay off of your feet."

"I can still do stuff, Mom," I objected. Making a sandwich isn't going to hurt me.

Mom scowled at me. "Clio recommended you remain off your feet as much as possible."

Sighing, I nodded in agreement. With luck, Aidon and his parents would return, and this wouldn't last long. Nina waved her phone at me. "And I've got a few people who can help with security outside the wards," she informed me. "They'll make sure no one gets close to the property."

Tseki, his eyes sharp and vigilant, spoke up from his place near the window. "I'll keep watch from the skies. Nothing will get past me."

Layla nodded in agreement. "Murtagh and I will increase our patrols. And I can have Clio here in under ten minutes if you need her."

Selene was always a calming presence. She approached with a gentle smile. "I'll fill in anywhere I'm needed. I'll handle any cases that come in. You just focus on taking care of yourself and those little ones." That was the kindest offer she could give me. The calls hadn't stopped coming in since the day I received Hattie's powers, and that wasn't going to change.

"Every call needs extra screening. If the case involves Lyra or if we even suspect it, no one will respond. I'm not taking any chances while I am down," I told Selene loud enough so everyone heard me. Knowing that Dark Witch, she planned this, and we will receive a rash of emergencies any second."

Mythia, the pixie who had become an integral part of our household, flitted over with a determined look on her tiny face. "I'll make sure there are no gaps in the border patrols," she said as her wings beat so fast behind her back they were a blur. "If anything unusual happens, you'll be the first to know."

I took a deep breath, feeling a sense of calm wash over me despite the turmoil. "Thank you, everyone," I told them honestly. "I couldn't imagine facing this without you all."

Over the next couple of days, we settled into a routine. Every decision I made was with my babies' safety in mind. I rested as much as possible and avoided anything that might cause undue stress. Mom's teas helped soothe my nerves. And her schedule ensured I wasn't overexerting myself.

Each morning, Nina updated me on the security measures in place. My daughter was seventeen going on thirty, but her reports gave me peace of mind. Stella and Selene were always nearby and ready to offer a comforting word or a helping hand. Tseki, Layla, and Murtagh took their patrols seriously. In fact, I only saw them through the window. Nana or Mom took meals out to them.

I was already going stir crazy on the second morning so I took my mid-morning tea on the back patio. I had just sat down and hadn't had a chance to begin enjoying the fresh air when Mythia flew to me. "I've been keeping watch with my clan, and so far, everything seems quiet," she said, landing lightly on the armrest of my chair.

I nodded, grateful for her vigilance. "Thank you, Mythia. I appreciate the update."

The connection to my babies was growing with each passing hour. Every flutter and kick reminded me of why I had to stay strong. The dark magic and the danger lurking outside our ward threatened to close in on us, but I was stronger than Lyra knew. She was not going to win this one.

On the second evening, I was sitting by the fire with Stella and had to confide my fears to her. "I'm so scared, Stella," I admitted, my voice trembling. "What if something happens to Aidon? What if I can't protect the babies?"

Stella wrapped her arm around me, pulling me close. "Your mate is an honest-to-goodness *god.* He can protect himself. And you're one of the strongest people I know. And you're not alone in this. We'll do whatever it takes to keep you and the babies safe."

I leaned into her embrace, feeling a surge of gratitude and love for the support I had received. I made a silent promise to my babies: *"We'll get through this."* I rested my hand on my belly. *I won't let anything harm you. We'll be a family, and we'll be strong together."*

Later that evening, we gathered around the kitchen island, the heart of our home. Mom made multitasking look easy. She was busy at the stove, preparing my favorite comfort food. The smell of freshly baked bread and simmering stew filled the kitchen and wrapped us all in a comforting embrace.

"Mom," I began, watching her deft movements, "how are the tribred victims of Lyra handling things at the halfway house?" She hadn't been able to get over there the last couple of days.

Mom paused with a ladle in hand and turned to face me. "They're doing as well as can be expected, given the circumstances," she explained and then grabbed some spices and added more to the pot. "It's been tough for them not seeing me in person the past couple of days. They miss the direct contact, but we're managing with calls and video chats."

Nina looked over from her makeshift command center on the kitchen table. She had set up the hotline at the desk built into the side of the kitchen, but she needed more room for this. Her laptop was open, and papers were spread around. "I've been coordinating with the halfway house staff," she added. "We've set up regular check-ins and support groups. They know we're all still here for them."

Layla was leaning against the counter when she asked, "Do they need the potion to help them remain in control of all their side effects? Or do they still have enough?" I prayed they were good. The last thing we needed was a bunch of tribreds out there hunting mundies when their vampire side took over.

Mom nodded thoughtfully. "There is enough for the next week. We've been working with Lilith to ensure everyone who needs the potion will always have it. It's not easy, but she thinks she can brew it if necessary."

"I can take some when I go home if she can't make it," Stella offered and then squeezed my hand. "How are they

BRENDA TRIM

handling the transition? They've relied on you a lot up to this point," she pointed out to Mom.

Mom sighed and placed a steaming bowl of soup in front of me. "It's been a mixed bag. Some are adjusting well, finding comfort in their routine and support. Others are struggling more with the changes and the loss of their former lives. It's not an ideal time to be away from them."

Tseki stood by the window, his eyes scanning the darkening horizon, and turned to add, "I'll check on them tonight. They've gotten to know me, and it will be a familiar face for them."

Selene dug into her bowl of stew. "Remind them that this won't be forever. Aidon will be back, and Phoebe will be healed soon."

Just as we settled into dinner, Mythia burst into the kitchen. Her tiny wings were a blur of iridescent colors. Her panicked voice cut through the air, filled with urgency and fear. "Phoebe! Something's happening in the woods!" she cried, fluttering around me in frantic circles. "I saw shadows moving and heard terrible noises. It's not natural."

My heart skipped a beat. The calm that had settled over our home shattered in an instant. I exchanged worried glances with Nana, Mom, Nina, Stella, Layla, and Selene. Something had gotten past our ward. It shouldn't have been possible, which meant whatever was out there was not to be taken lightly.

"We need to check it out," I said. I was relieved my voice was steadier than I felt inside. I stood up and hid my trembling hands behind my back. I placed one on my belly and felt the reassuring movement of my unborn children. They seemed to sense the tension and responded with tiny flutters.

Nana scowled at me. "You need to stay here."

I gaped at her and shook my head. "I'm fine. I have been sitting around for over two days now and I need to be there for this. Something got past our wards. You're going to need me." I didn't let anyone argue further as I stood. "We will take the golf cart. Grab some potions. I've got my daggers," I said, snatching them from the table where I'd left them.

Mom moved swiftly, gathering supplies. A flashlight, some herbs, and a protective talisman while Nina selected our best offensive potions. Stella walked beside me and took the keys from me. "You will stick to my side and stay away from danger. Add your magic from there. You will not go charging in there, or I will tie you to your bed right now."

I gave her a solemn look. "I promise not to do anything stupid. My babies are the most important thing. But I have to be there for the rest of you, too."

We squeezed onto the golf cart while Mythia fluttered ahead of us. She led the way to the disturbance. A chill wind whipped through the trees as Stella drove. It carried with it an ominous whisper. The woods were usually serene and welcoming. A shiver traveled down my spine when I took in the shrouded darkness and danger.

We moved cautiously, following Mythia's guidance deeper into the woods. The moonlight filtered through the canopy above and cast eerie shadows on the forest floor. Every rustle of leaves, every snap of a twig, set my nerves on edge. Stella veered into the brush when a piercing shriek echoed through the night. Layla raced up to the cart and was growling low in her throat. Nina clutched my hand and whispered, "There's something pissed out here."

Ahead, the trees parted, revealing a clearing bathed in an unnatural glow. Shadows danced and flickered, taking on grotesque shapes that seemed to writhe and twist with malevolent intent. We got out of the golf cart and headed to the spot. My magic burned beneath the surface of my skin, eager to combat the vile energy that was now thick and oppressive.

Nana stepped forward with her witch fire burning in her palms. "Stay at the back, Phoebe," she instructed. "We don't know what we're dealing with."

The sense of foreboding intensified as we cautiously approached the clearing. Mythia hovered nervously overhead, her wings fluttering erratically. "Be careful," she whispered, her voice barely audible over the cacophony surrounding us.

I took a deep breath, summoning every ounce of courage I had. With my family beside me, we walked into the clearing, and my heart stopped. "No fucking way," I muttered, unable to believe what I was seeing.

Download the next book in the Mystical Midlife in Maine series, POLTERGEISTS & CHANGE OF LIFE HERE!

EXCERPT FROM SWEATY NIGHTS & GATOR BITES MIDLIFE MYSTERIES & MAGIC BOOK #48

*D*ahlia

The morning light filtered through Willow-berry's lace curtains. I sat there lost in the delicate patterns it made on the worn wooden floors. Dani and I sat in our usual spots at the table, with the comforting aroma of freshly baked cinnamon rolls. They weren't homemade like they would have been if Kota were there or if Cami had done it, but the frozen kind were a good substitute.

I looked up and over when I heard the gentle hum of morning chatter. Dre and Kota were coming in the back door. A smile creased my face when I heard them talking about the smell of something delicious cooking. The insistent buzz of my phone interrupted me enjoying the calm before the storm of our day. I glanced down to see Britney's name flashing on the caller ID. She was a witch in the coven and had never called us before. What could she want? A party? Or was something wrong with Kaitlyn?

Accepting the call, I put it on speaker. "Hey, Britney. Is everything alright? Or did you need the party planning services of the Six Twisted Sisters?"

"Hello, Lia," Britney's voice crackled through the line. "I'm sorry to call you so early. I honestly didn't know who to call. The protocol says to call the supernaturals' leaders when we have an emergency. But there isn't one for this one and you guys are the expert private investigators of our world. You guys are the only ones we could think of to handle this."

I took a deep breath and interrupted her blabbering, "It's okay. Just get to the point." I hadn't had enough of my energy drink yet.

She squeaked and said, "Sorry. I'm nervous. We've got a situation. A Fae discovered a body near the swamps. They said it looks suspicious."

My heart lurched in my chest. "Suspicious how? And where did they find it exactly?"

"The caller indicated the wounds looked as if something supernatural was involved. When I questioned them more, they said it could have been a wild animal, but it seemed too controlled for that. They were near the old Oakwood trail. I'll send you the coordinates."

Adele came into the kitchen and rubbed her side against Kota's leg. *"That area isn't easily accessible for mundies. The call was warranted,"* she said into our heads.

Kota and Dre had walked in the door and had concerned looks on their faces that only increased my concern. There was no way we could ignore this. It made me think of the time my childhood friend was killed by one of Marie's minions.

"Is the dead a supernatural or mundie?" Dani interjected.

"That wasn't clear, and I didn't think to ask. I should have. That would be important to know. Should I have called Lucas in case this is a shifter?" I could hear the doubt in Britney's voice about calling us to deal with this matter.

"You could have called Lucas, but you did nothing wrong by calling us. This situation isn't clear-cut," Dre reassured

Britney. "We will create more guidelines to add to the manual for those answering the hotline. In a situation like this, always call us. We can do a cursory investigation and reach out to the appropriate leader if needed."

"Is the Fae still there?" I asked. It would be good to ask more questions.

"I have no idea. They sounded eager to get the hell out of there, but I can try and call them back," Britney offered.

Dre nodded her head and grabbed a to-go tumbler for her coffee. "Please do. We might have more questions for them after we go out to the scene."

"I'll do that right away," she replied. "Let me know if I can do anything else. I'm on shift for another three hours."

"Will do," I agreed. We thanked her and then hung up the phone.

"I suppose we should leave right away to check this out," Dani said, her voice tinged with a sense of frustration.

Kota took the rolls out of the oven and grabbed a plate. "The last thing we need is a mundie coming across a body. Let's go."

"Be sure to gather as much evidence as you can while there. You never know what you can use to track the killer," Adele told us.

I lifted an eyebrow and looked down at the kitten. "You assume this was a murder."

Adele's green eyes focused on me. *"Better to assume that and be prepared for anything than lose evidence and clues that might lead to solving the case."*

"If this is a case of a mundie who found themselves on the wrong side of a wild animal, we aren't going to do anything," Kota told her.

Adele inclined her head. *"Fair enough. I will be here if you need anything."*

Nodding, we gathered our belongings and hurried out into the warm morning, leaving Willowberry's cheerful ambiance behind. Kota grabbed some cinnamon rolls, and Dre snagged napkins.

I ate on the drive to the Oakwood trail. The atmosphere in the car was silent and tense. I was not looking forward to investigating a death. Dead bodies made me sick to my stomach. It got so bad I had to set my roll aside. Rather than churn up more bile, I focused on the drive. The cityscape gradually faded into a winding road flanked by ancient cypress trees, their gnarled roots clawing at the mist that hung like a spectral veil over the landscape. Along with the Spanish moss dripping from the limbs, it created a mystical ambiance.

I drove as close to the location as possible and parked the car on the side of the road. The heat and humidity pressed in on us, as did a sense of foreboding. "Ready for this?" Dre asked.

"Not really," Kota replied. "But we have to do this, so let's get it over with." She headed to the trail leading into the swampy wilderness.

Although nature was reclaiming the path, it beckoned us forward. It was shrouded in an eerie silence broken only by the distant calls of unseen creatures. After a few minutes of walking, the earth beneath our feet started squelching with each step, and dampness seeped through our shoes.

"Careful," I cautioned. "We don't want to step into the swamp."

Dani shook her head and scanned our surroundings. "We should look out for gators, too."

Mist swirled around us, veiling our surroundings in a ghostly haze. And shadows danced among the tangled branches, adding to the magical allure of the place. We followed the winding trail deeper into the heart of the swamp, our senses heightened by the unsettling ambiance. The air was thick with the mingled scents of decay and wet earth, creating a unique blend that hung heavy in our lungs.

I wondered if we were too late when we finally stumbled upon the body. It was a chilling scene that froze us in our tracks. A body lay half-buried in the muck, its form obscured by the murky waters. The sight sent a shiver down my spine, and I felt a knot tighten in my stomach.

I stood next to Dani, whose eyes narrowed as she examined the gruesome remains. Dre and Kota stood guard, their gazes sweeping the surroundings for any signs of danger lurking in the shadows.

"We need to gather more information," Dani said, her voice steady despite the grim discovery. "We need to get a better look at the body to see why this was called into the hotline."

Dre used her telekinesis to lift the victim out of the water. She moved it to a more stable section of the swamp. There were no missing limbs or anything else that you'd expect of a gator attack. The wounds were the only thing that made me think animals. They were wide furrows cut across the man's chest. But there was only one row of four that I could see. There were some puncture wounds, but I didn't get up close to see more details.

My hand went to my stomach as I focused on other details of our investigation. "We should also look into recent missing persons reports. Focusing first on supernaturals. There's definitely something sinister at play here." This wasn't a lost hiker who was attacked by a wild animal.

"Is this a mundie or supernatural?" Kota asked. "We might not need to do more investigation. This could be attributed to an animal."

Dre nodded her head and crouched close to the body. The back of my throat burned, and my stomach roiled. Not wanting to leave this to my sisters, I followed suit and was struck by how handsome the man was. Putting everything aside, I focused on wanting to know if he was a magical creature. I cast a spell that would give me that information a second after my sisters.

"He's a selkie," Dre blurted with a frown. "Did you know they lived out here?"

Kota stood and backed away. "I assumed they lived near the coast. You should call Lucas. I don't feel safe investigating this further here."

"Selkies rarely live outside the ocean. You should assume this one was visiting. Don't let your guard down," Adele interjected into our minds. *"I'm too far away to pick up on anything, so one of you should be vigilant while the others gather evidence."*

Pulling out my phone, I sent Lucas a message about the body. His reply was quick. "Lucas and Noah are on their way. We should take some pictures and look for clues like Adele suggested."

Dre moved away from the body and to the edge of the water. "There's something down there." She twitched her finger, and something silver floated out of the water. It was an amulet of some kind.

"That has some power in it," Adele said. *"I can feel it through our bond. It'd be best not to touch it in case it's cursed or something worse."*

I opened my crossbody bag and unzipped an inner pocket. "Put it in here," I told her.

Dre did as asked, and we snapped pictures of everything within a fifty-foot radius. Dani led the way, her footsteps deliberate and purposeful, navigating us through the labyrinthine maze of swampy undergrowth. "I assume we're searching for any signs of movement through the area. Tracks, clothing remnants, anything that might tie back to our culprit."

Picking up a small piece of cloth, I carried it to our growing pile. I texted Lucas and asked him to bring a bag to carry stuff in. "That's what I'm looking for. I tried using my magical senses to pick up anything with power, but there is so much around us, I didn't get anything specific."

"Same," Dre agreed.

As we delved deeper into the bayou's shadows, the canopy above thickened. The ancient cypress trees loomed like sentinels, their twisted roots clawing into the dark waters.

A few seconds later, Dre's voice broke the silence, like a whisper on the breeze: "Over there—do you see those markings on the tree trunk?"

We converged on the spot, examining the deep gouges etched into the weathered bark. I snapped several pictures. From what I could tell, the jagged patterns bore a striking resemblance to the teeth marks on the dead selkie.

"These marks are too large for a normal gator," Dani mused, her brow furrowing in concentration.

Kota's gaze swept the surroundings, her eyes flickering with heightened awareness. "If gator shifters are around, they won't be far. And we don't know shit about them to know if they'd be friend or foe."

"Stay vigilant," Dre warned.

I wiped sweat from my brow with the back of my hand. "Always."

Lucas and Noah arrived as we finished up. Lucas handed me an empty duffle bag. "Here you go, Flower. You're sure this is a selkie?"

Nodding, I took the bag from him and set it next to the random things we'd seen while taking pictures. We had no idea if they were clues or not but decided to take them anyway. "Yeah. Did you know there were some here?"

Lucas laid a tarp down next to the body. "No. They tend to stick to coastal areas. These injuries look like marks from a gator. Are you sure something nefarious is involved?"

I lifted a shoulder. "Fairly certain. We need to investigate this more."

"Okay, let's load up and get out of here," he replied.

We put everything in the duffel while he and Noah wrapped the body and carried it to their truck. With a sense of purpose driving us forward, we retreated from the harrowing scene, the weight of unanswered questions hanging over us like a heavy fog. Whatever malevolent force lurked within these murky depths needed to be unveiled. My nerves were strung taut. A thought passed through my mind as I headed home. We needed to unearth the truth before more lives were claimed by the darkness that haunted those ancient waters.

The oppressive Louisiana heat bore down upon us as we regrouped at Willowberry. The air was thick with the scent of magnolia blossoms and the distant murmur of tourists taking Cami's tour. Lucas and Noah drove right to the back portion of the plantation where mundies never went. They put the body in one of the old buildings, and we cast a spell creating a barrier no one could get through.

Sweat glistened on our brows as we gathered around our familiar table. I ran a hand over the surface that had been worn smooth by years of shared meals. Dani cradled her tall-boy, her eyes fixed on the notes spread out before her like a map of the unknown. Her expression was grave, the usual spark of mischief replaced by a solemn determination that mirrored the weight of our discovery in the swamps.

"I can't get past the victim's injuries," Dani finally spoke. Her voice carried the soft lilt of the bayou, each word was measured and deliberate. "The pattern of the teeth marks... they're too large and jagged to be from a normal alligator."

The implication hung heavy in the humid air. To us, gator shifters were more beings of myth and legend, said to haunt the remote reaches of the bayou. We'd never met one, and yet they were a haunting possibility in this case. I looked at Lucas and asked, "Could it be gator shifters? I don't know much about them. All I've heard are the stories that say they're protectors of the bayou and guardians of their domain."

"They're willing to defend their space with deadly force," Adele added.

Dre's brow furrowed in thought, her fingers absently moving around the rim of her mug. "If gator shifters are responsible for this death, we'll need to approach this with caution. They're unlike anything we've encountered before."

Kota nodded in agreement, her gaze fixed on the horizon beyond the windows, where the sun shone through the moss-draped canopy. "We should delve deeper into the local lore, consult our contacts, and uncover any hidden knowledge that might shed light on this mystery."

Lucas sighed and put a hand on the back of my chair. "Gator shifters are reclusive. They rarely interact with others. If they did this, the selkie had to have done something significant."

Dani nodded in acknowledgment. "We can examine the evidence to see what it can tell us, but first, we should reach out to the other council members and see what else we can learn about gator shifters."

"Adele," I began, addressing our familiar, "what's your take on this? Could gator shifters really be behind the death of the selkie in the swamp?"

Adele jumped onto a chair next to Dre. *"It's within the realm of possibility,"* she replied, her voice carrying a hint of caution. *"Gator shifters are known to roam these waters, and like I said, they can be quite protective of their territory. Although, I can't see a selkie doing something to cause them to kill him. Selkies are passive and peaceful creatures."*

Lucas ran his fingers over my shoulder. "Gator shifters don't take kindly to intruders, especially near their nesting grounds. The selkie might have run across a pregnant gator."

Noah nodded in agreement. "That would be seen as a threat to their unborn, and when provoked, they are as dangerous as the creatures they resemble."

Before we could delve further into the details of gator shifter behavior, Dani's phone buzzed, filling the room. My stomach twisted further when Dani's eyes widened.

She answered and put it on speakerphone. "Marie," Dani greeted cautiously, "what brings this unexpected call?"

Marie's voice, smooth and authoritative, resonated through the room. "I need your assistance in planning and hosting the Leveau family reunion," she declared.

Silence fell over us as we processed her request. Planning an event of this magnitude for Marie Leveau's descendants was no small feat. Especially given the family's complex history and the intricate dynamics among its members. Not to mention that she'd tried to kill us more times than I could count. It was only recently that she seemed to stop.

"We appreciate the request, Marie," I replied diplomatically, "but could you provide more details about your vision for this reunion?"

Marie's tone remained confident. "I want a grand gathering," she explained, her voice tinged with nostalgia. "A celebration of our shared heritage and a time for family to come together. The males of our line are largely forgotten, and I want to change that. It will be easier to envelop them into the fold if I begin with a celebration of our bond as a family. I want this to be an annual thing."

Dre raised an eyebrow, her skepticism palpable. "What prompted this reunion?" she inquired.

Marie's response was cryptic. "Let's just say it's long overdue, my dear sisters." Her voice carried a hint of mystery.

Kota leaned forward, her curiosity piqued. "And the venue?" she probed, her gaze fixed on Dani's phone. "You want us to host it here, at Willowberry?"

Marie's answer was decisive. "Of course. The power in your lands will add to the grandeur of the event."

The weight of Marie's request settled upon us, mingling with the new mystery of the selkie's death. Planning a family reunion for the descendants of Marie Leveau would undoubtedly test our abilities to navigate supernatural intrigues, intricate family ties, and possible betrayal. I still didn't trust her.

My sisters and I shared a look, and I shrugged. I had no idea if we should do this or not. On one hand, doing it would prove we didn't hold grudges and gave people second chances. On the other, it could bite us in the ass.

Dre inclined her head to Dani, who said, "When would you like to have this? If we are available, we would be happy to do it for you."

I held my breath as Kota pulled up the calendar on the tablet that was connected to Phi's. My heart twisted in my chest when we had an opening the day she wanted. After putting her in, we set up a time later to discuss ideas for the event.

"Well, that was unexpected," Dani mumbled as she stared at the blank cell phone screen.

"Do you think she's going to use this event to take us out?" I asked.

That got everyone's attention. Adele was the first to speak up. *"It's something to consider. However, none of her family will be able to step foot on your property if they have ulterior motives. When you recast the wards after Kezia's infiltration, we modified it, remember?"*

Dre's shoulders relaxed, and she smiled at our familiar. "I never thought I would be grateful for Kezia's evil plan. That makes me feel better about doing this. If Marie has plans of using her family against us, they won't be able to pull into the parking lot."

Dani's gaze snapped up and focused on Dre. "We should reach out to each descendant individually." Her eyes were alight with planning. "It is going to be important to understand their needs and their grievances. From the sounds of it many have been ostracized. Ultimately, I see this reunion as about more than a celebration. It's about healing old wounds."

"Given the Leveau family's history in our city, we should embrace the spirit of New Orleans with this one. Jazz music, Cajun food, and the paranormal community. We might not like her legacy, but we will create an event worthy of it."

Dre nodded in agreement, a glimmer of excitement in her eyes. "We can't forget to add a touch of voodoo. It should be subtle but not enough to give them power over our wards. Honoring that will be significant. We don't want to be known as event planners that ignore culture."

As we brainstormed ideas and divided tasks, the lace curtains billowed softly in the breeze. With each plan and proposal, the anticipation for the Leveau family reunion grew. I wanted it to be a manifestation of a beacon of hope amidst the tumultuous relationship we've had with the Queen of Voodoo. A history like the one we shared was impossible to ignore, so it remained a glimmer.

Regardless, we were taking on the ambitious endeavor and determined to unite the descendants of Marie Leveau. It wasn't going to be easy to navigate their intricate histories and create a memorable event that would honor our shared legacy and heal old wounds. But we would try.

. . .

Download the next book in the Midlife Magic & Mysteries series, SWEATY NIGHTS & GATOR BITES HERE.

AUTHOR'S NOTE

Reviews are like hugs. Sometimes awkward. Always welcome! It would mean the world to me if you can take five minutes and let others know how much you enjoyed my work.

Don't forget to visit my website: www.brendatrim.com, and sign up for my newsletter, which is jam-packed with exciting news and monthly giveaways. Also, be sure to visit and like my Facebook page, https://www.facebook.com/AuthorBrendaTrim to see my daily posts.

Never allow waiting to become a habit. Live your dreams and take risks. Life is happening now.

DREAM BIG!

XOXO,

Brenda

CLICK THE SITE BELOW TO STALK BRENDA:

Amazon

BookBub

Facebook

Brenda's Book Warriors FB Group
BooksproutGoodreads
Instagram
Twitter
Website

ALSO BY BRENDA TRIM

CLICK HERE FOR A COMPLETE LIST OF THE HUNDRED PLUS OTHER TITLES I HAVE AVAILABLE IN PARANORMAL WOMEN'S FICTION & PARANORMAL ROMANCE!

Made in the USA
Las Vegas, NV
09 October 2024